Big Fish

By the same author

METZGER'S DOG
THE BUTCHER'S BOY

Big Fish

Thomas Perry

CHARLES SCRIBNER'S SONS
NEW YORK

230224

Copyright © 1985 Thomas Perry

Library of Congress Cataloging in Publication Data
Perry, Thomas.
   Big fish.

   I. Title.
PS3566.E718B5   1985   813'.54   84–29813
ISBN 0–684–18367–6

This book published simultaneously in the
United States of America and in Canada—
Copyright under the Berne Convention.

1 3 5 7 9 11 13 15 17 19   F/C   20 18 16 14 12 10 8 6 4 2

Printed in the United States of America.

For Jo

OREGON

IS THERE LIFE AFTER DEATH?
TRESPASS AND FIND OUT.

The poster on the fence rail was commercially printed in vermillion ink with a veneer that made it look wet. As Altmeyer glanced beyond it into the shadowy woods, he could see several more nailed to the gray bark of tree trunks, each protected from the weather by a sheet of clear plastic that puckered a bit at the edges. Raymond was a man who took everything into account.

Altmeyer turned off the van's engine and lit a cigarette, then cocked his head. "Wait where you are. I hear the Hope of Mankind's truck." Rachel watched him step down from the van and walk across the gravel, his cowboy boots leaving the only tracks, then lean against the fence post.

Flights of tiny brown sparrows retreated with nervous flutters to higher branches of the surrounding trees as the sound of the engine came nearer. Then the black pickup truck bounced around the dog-leg turn, its oversized knob-treaded tires kicking particles of gravel into the weeds beside the road. When the driver saw Altmeyer he stopped fifty feet away, backed the truck over a patch of wild strawberries to turn it around, and waited, the covered spotlights on the truck's roof brushing the low-hanging leaves of an oak tree. Altmeyer slowly walked up the road to the driver's side of the truck and looked into the cab.

Raymond's head was resting against the rear window of the cab. Under the green baseball cap his curly hair stuck out like a frayed wool lining. His eyes squinted at the rearview mirror. "Is that your daughter?"

"She's nobody. I have a heavy load of guns and a lot to keep track of this trip. She doesn't know what state she's in."

"Heavy load?" Ray's clear blue eyes swept to Altmeyer's face, suddenly alert. "Somebody around here?"

Altmeyer blew a cloud of smoke out and watched it move slowly down the road, rising into the calm air, then disperse among the leaves. "I've got your order."

Raymond reached to the seat beside him and handed Altmeyer an envelope.

Altmeyer walked back to the van, tossed the envelope in the window, and returned with a canvas bundle tied with twine. He laid the bundle down on the bed of the pickup truck and waited while Raymond walked around to the tailgate before untying the twine and unrolling the canvas. Inside were three short black AR-15 carbines, their barrels and receivers gleaming with a thin coating of oil. Raymond brought one to his shoulder and sighted it into the trees. "Looks all right." He studied the left side of the receiver and flicked the selector with his thumb. "Is it?"

"It's all there. Genuine M-16 bolt carrier, hammer, trigger, disconnector, and selector. The auto sear was machined privately and it's better than anything out of the factory. All put together like the cat's ass. You want to break it down and take a look? Or you can spend the next couple of hours blasting your livestock into piles of hamburger—they say it's the sport of kings—and I can swing back through here tonight and pick up your written endorsement."

"No," said Raymond. "They'll do."

"I'm having a special today on forty-round magazines for

those. You interested? I can give you six for a hundred and fifty. They're top of the line."

"Regular army issue?"

"The army doesn't issue forty-round clips—must figure if you shoot somebody twenty times you've done enough for him. I told you they were top of the line."

Raymond stared into the distance, then shook his head. "Next time you're around, give me a call."

Rachel watched Altmeyer walk slowly back to the van, then climb in and start the engine. She said, "There's exactly three thousand. Is that right?"

He lit another cigarette, smiling. "I forgot to tell you. It's different with these people. They never shortchange you. They're not in the business, they're addicts. That one probably counted the money fifty times while he was saving it up. Perfect customers."

"What do you mean? That isn't much profit, is it? We've always done better than that."

"They're steady and predictable. That one just got himself three fully operational automatic military assault rifles. Just possessing a rifle like that is worth five years in Leavenworth, but he's got to have them, and whatever else he can save up the cash for."

"Why did he want three?"

Altmeyer shrugged and stepped on the gas. "Because he couldn't come up with the cash for four? It's hard to say. Probably wants a couple stashed in bunkers around his place in case he's too far from the house when the Russians sail up the Rogue River in submarines or waves of Chinese stream through Grant's Pass to gang-rape his pickup truck. You've got to admit the truck's a little beauty, isn't it? I could hardly control my own lust."

"Stop leering, Altmeyer. Be serious for a minute. If you want me to learn this business, you've got to tell me what the business is."

"By themselves none of these survivalist types amounts to much. The year before last Raymond bought a few things.

5

Last year I guess he probably spent what he had on dried food or something. Maybe next year somebody will talk him into building a bomb-proof shelter for his outhouse or an electric generator that runs on nuclear fallout, but in the long run I'll get my share of his money. These people wake up in the morning and read the papers and something happens to them."

Rachel shook her head. "It doesn't seem like a good idea to do this kind of business with people you think are stupid and crazy. When I signed on we were shipping arms to the Afghans, not delivering automatic weapons in twos and threes to a bunch of maniacs."

Altmeyer sighed. "This isn't much different from what we've always done. You meet a man on a dirt road, take his money, put what was in your truck into his, and get out."

"The trouble with you is that you try to be worse than you already are, which is about as bad as anyone can be."

"You're wrong. It's a good time to get out of the war business. We've been lucky to last this long, and gun nuts are a safe, easy way to keep all our suppliers happy. For the next year, we'll sell lots of small arms to solid citizens who can pay idiotic prices for things they don't need. Then we'll quit."

"We're used to dealing with people who know what they're doing."

"These people are even better. It's a cash business, because they're more scared than you are of the government figuring out what they spent it on. Tonight Raymond will fire off a burst from each of those AR-15s just to see if I cheated him, then put them away somewhere he thinks nobody will ever find them. He'll never touch them again, except to clean and oil them, until he sees the first Russian in his henhouse."

"Did you cheat him?" said Rachel.

Altmeyer laughed, and put his cigarette in the ashtray. "That's one part of the business that never changes. You have to understand your customers, but you have to resist the temptation to sell them shit. Otherwise, one of them is going to come looking for you with a machine gun that only works medium-well. The damned things never jam when they're pointed at you."

"But you're overcharging, aren't you?"

"They know what they're getting, and they know the price. Ray Minor lives out here in the first place because he's positive that pretty soon something's going to happen that makes money obsolete."

"Everything about this feels like trouble."

"Is this the girl who showed no fear when the Russian helicopters in Afghanistan were firing rockets at her?"

"I thought they were aiming at you."

SAN FRANCISCO

Rachel's eyes were focused on the candle flame, and she seemed about to let herself smile.

Altmeyer whispered, "If you're going to slip into an erotic trance, I hope it's anticipation and not just memory."

Rachel looked up at him. "If we ever have a baby, I'd like to have it be a time like last night. Every few years we could all drive by that little hotel up north, just to see if it's still there."

"What's wrong with this hotel?" asked Altmeyer. "We can be pretty confident that the Prince Andrei de San Francisco will make it to the next earthquake." He considered. "In any case, we can count on it for tonight."

"Altmeyer," she said. "I'm being romantic, and you're just being dirty. I don't think I want to look forward to taking any child to this place."

"It's the height of elegance. The food is astounding. You can't complain about the clientele—that woman's sable coat would buy that little hotel in Oregon six or seven times over."

"What she did for it would buy her an even littler place in Leavenworth six or seven times over. If you really liked the Prince Andrei, we'd come here more than just once a year for the annual smugglers' convention."

" 'Importers' Trade Conference' is the term."

"If the authorities had any sense they'd throw a net over this place. Can you see even one person in this restaurant who isn't here to make a deal that's illegal?"

"I don't know this waiter very well." He lifted his hand in a little wave, and the waiter stepped toward them. "My wife would like to know . . . if we could have two more of these brandies."

As the waiter swept away from the table, Rachel smiled. "I love you."

Altmeyer touched her hand. "I love you, too. We'll be on our way early in the morning so you won't miss Bucky's party, if that's what's worrying you. I just figured that since we were in the area, I'd see who's got what this year."

Rachel's green eyes were veiled by her long, brown hair. "Maybe we should stop scrambling around like door-to-door salesmen collecting money for Altmeyer's Last Deal and face our future."

"Retirement?"

"Maybe. What will you do, Altmeyer? Get fat and pickle yourself in alcohol?" Rachel tried to pinch his side just above his belt, but couldn't find any spare flesh.

"I thought I'd keep in training by entering sexual marathons."

"Marathons?"

"You know, this isn't something a man my age should just leap into without training for it. I happen to know there's another nice little hotel about a hundred miles from here that—"

She leaned over and kissed him on the cheek. "That's very interesting. You old-timers certainly do know the terrain, don't you? And your mind is still clear, even at your age."

"A simple yes would have warmed my old bones, and perhaps guarded against future heart problems."

A blond man suddenly appeared beside their table, pulled out a chair, and sat down. "I've got a gun you can see." He

12

was wearing a charcoal suit, and had one hand in his coat pocket. He was in his thirties, and his chest and shoulders strained against the fabric of his coat as though he were compressed to an unnatural density.

"No, thank you," said Rachel. "I'm sure that lady over there would be titillated by anything you care to show her." She pointed to the woman carefully moving her white shoulder into more attractive proximity to the black sable draped on the back of her chair.

"I'm serious," said the man.

The waiter returned with the two glasses of brandy on a small silver tray, and placed them on the table. As Rachel took hers, the waiter asked the blond man, "Can I get you anything, sir?"

"No, thank you," he said. "We're about ready for the check."

Altmeyer said quietly, "You were telling us you're serious. That's a good quality. Get up now and go to a table where people will appreciate it."

"You don't understand. I know you're here for the convention."

Rachel lit a cigarette, and shifted closer to the man. "We're not here to look at guns this year. We're just passing through, and we'd like to be alone."

The man's broad face seemed to brighten with confidence. "Oh, this won't take long. You've got either lots of merchandise or lots of money somewhere, probably in your car. You take me to it, and then I go away."

Very slowly, Altmeyer smiled. He turned to Rachel and said, "I get it, Sandra. This man knows we're selling stolen perfume, and would like to rob us. That's the purpose of the gun."

Rachel was still leaning close to the man, and didn't pull back.

The man nodded and said, "I take what you've got, and we all go away. You won't make trouble or call the police

13

even after I'm gone, because they'd like to have you more than me."

As the man was speaking, Rachel seemed to move even closer. Her glass of brandy had disappeared under the tablecloth. Finally, she set the empty glass on the table and stubbed her cigarette out in the ashtray with impatience. She said to the man, "You know, dear, you really should have picked someone else. Any table in this room would have been better for you."

The man said, "Here's the check." The waiter misunderstood and set it down in front of him, then retired.

Altmeyer tossed some money on the tiny tray and looked at the man almost sympathetically. "Sandra's right. You're really not ready for us."

Rachel picked up the lighter and lit another cigarette in a smooth motion that brought the lighter down beside the man's coat.

The man began to speak calmly. "I'm . . ." Then there was a soft *poof* as his brandy-soaked coat ignited. He jumped to his feet and shrieked, "I'm perfectly happy." The coat tails and left side glowed with a bluish aura of burning brandy, and bright yellow flames flickered up toward the man's face. He was flapping both arms now, frantically trying to put out the fire, but in his right hand was a Smith and Wesson police special with a thick, checkered grip.

People at surrounding tables stood up, their mouths open in little circles, and a murmur of voices filled the room. The crystal chandelier over the center table began to tinkle softly with the vibration. Altmeyer yanked the man's coat downward as though he were trying to get it off him, but the sleeves held the man's arms down at his sides and wouldn't go over the gun in his hand, which was now entangled in the burning coat.

Altmeyer shouted in an officious tone, "Don't be alarmed about the gun. This man is a police officer."

Four waiters threw the man to the floor and wrapped him in tablecloths as Rachel and Altmeyer slipped into the throng of diners who were making their way to the door. A man in a cashmere suit held a menu up as though to shield his face from the photographers that commotion seemed always to summon from nowhere.

Rachel stopped in the doorway and said, "It's all right. He says he's perfectly happy."

LOS ANGELES

"Altmeyer!" The fat man's stiff little legs jerked him forward across the circular mosaic set into the lawn. "And the lovely Rachel." He shielded his eyes with the hand that held his glass, spilling a few drops of liquid onto the shoulder of his dark blue blazer. "That is the lovely Rachel, isn't it?"

"You know it is, Bucky," said Rachel. "I keep telling you that Altmeyer just plays hard. He doesn't cheat."

"Good. Hate to begin the evening with another classic humiliation." He stood on tiptoes to kiss her cheek. "You look better, if possible." He turned to Altmeyer. "Better than I remembered. I'll give you forty thousand for her, as is."

"No thanks. I'd have to give her a percentage."

"Stop trying to jack up the price. God, I hate businessmen," Bucky sighed. Then he grasped Rachel's arm with his chubby hand and leaned toward her. "Seriously, I'll bet I could get you a commercial in two weeks. Just today I placed a girl who looks exactly like a beagle. Dump this loser now. You've been discovered by Bucky Carmichael, more than a mere agent––a way of life."

"Not until his youth and beauty are gone."

"Suit yourself. But always remember that Bucky lusts after you and that he gives good parties. Come on. Let's get

19

you both drinks and then launch into the introductions. You can think of them as a memory test."

Across the swimming pool they could see the crowds of people on the patio, some sitting at round tables and others milling about in small groups. At the bar, a tall, thin, white-haired man in a black velvet coat leaned on his elbows and watched the bartender pouring ingredients into a cocktail shaker.

Bucky tapped the man on the shoulder and he moved only his head, turning it slowly and with little interest. When he spoke, his voice was deep and resonant. "Bucky, get out of here. This gentleman is trying to demonstrate how to make a decent martini, and if I have to order many more—"

Bucky ignored him. "Arthur, these are my neighbors, the Altmeyers." He turned to Altmeyer and Rachel. "And this is The Great Arthur Paston."

"Pleased to meet you," said Altmeyer.

"Yes," said Paston. "How many martinis would you like?" He didn't wait for an answer, but said to the bartender, "Give those to these nice Altmeyers here, and start over again, slowly. These old eyes aren't what they were when I got here tonight."

The bartender, shrugging his shoulders, handed Altmeyer and Rachel a pair of sixteen-ounce tumblers, then started to mix another round under Arthur Paston's squinting gaze.

"Who is the great Arthur Paston?" whispered Rachel.

Bucky smirked. "One of the biggest directors ever. *The Killers. Cellblock Nineteen.* He did musicals when there were musicals, westerns when there were westerns. He's older than he looks—probably helped Benjamin Franklin with his home-work. I know for sure he directed Garbo, and that's about the same thing."

"And now he's directing the bartender," said Altmeyer. "An industry giant at play."

"Don't laugh," said Bucky. "That man is the secret of my success as an agent. Actors come and go so fast I hardly have time to learn their names, but Arthur Paston is forever. I have offers lined up for him that he wouldn't finish if he were his own great-grandson." Bucky's alert little eyes focused on a distant point. "Hey, can you two be trusted to mingle for a few minutes?"

"We'll manage," said Rachel.

"Thanks. I see my good friend and fellow agent Billy Bittmeister arriving, and if I don't shepherd him around he'll talk to somebody." He started to jog off, but held his drink in the air, spilling some more on his coat. "Don't get lost, though. I want to see you."

A YOUNG MAN with blond hair curled in tight ringlets sauntered up to them. "Good evening," he said. "I'm Bob Scranton. I heard Bucky call you the Altmeyers?"

"That's right. We live down the road from here. I guess Bucky thought if he had a noisy party it'd be smart to invite the neighbors."

"Oh, Bucky's smart, all right," said Scranton. "Being smart is what he does. What do you do?"

"The answer is pretty dull in this crowd, I'm afraid," said Rachel. "We're in business. You know, buy low and sell high."

Scranton's handsome face slackened. "Oh. I thought I'd seen you at Warner's."

"No," said Altmeyer. "Rachel's not one of Bucky's clients." He took a guess. "But didn't I see you on television the other night? What was that movie, honey?"

Scranton beamed, and held his face steady, and waited.

"No," said Rachel. "Was that you?"

"I'm really flattered. I'm amazed you even saw me. You really have a great eye, Mr. Altmeyer. It was called 'They're Here.' The part was better before they edited it. There was supposed to be a whole scene before I get run over by the truck. But when they got it home they discovered that a ray of sunlight was on Angela's nose through most of the shots. She looked like she was wearing a joke nose, so they cut it."

"Sorry that happened," said Altmeyer, taking Rachel's

21

glass. "Excuse me, I'll be right back." He walked to the bar. The bartender was gone, and Arthur Paston had taken his place. He was happily mixing martinis, and when he noticed Altmeyer he quickly refilled the glasses.

"Where's the bartender?" asked Altmeyer.

"Him? Oh, he's wandering around with a tray trying to unload our martinis on the unsuspecting public. Let me know if those aren't perfect, will you?"

As Altmeyer turned, he felt a light pressure on his arm. It was a young woman with chestnut hair, and she was smiling. "Excuse me," he said. He wondered if she was the one who looked like a beagle.

"Not at all. Bucky tells me you're an importer."

"Not exclusively," he said. "My name is Altmeyer."

"I'm Ronnie. Pleased to meet you."

Altmeyer looked past her shoulder. He could see that Bob Scranton was talking to Rachel with animation, probably telling her about other parts he hadn't had. "Nice to meet you," he said. "Are you an actress?"

"No. I'm in production. As soon as I heard you were coming I decided to meet you."

"That was very kind," said Altmeyer. "Very neighborly." He started to move toward Rachel and Bob Scranton, but she touched his arm.

"Here is my office number." She stuck a business card into his breast pocket. "When you come by a nice shipment of coke, please give me a call. I'll pay more than Bucky does, since he seems to be a friend of yours."

Altmeyer looked down at her. "I'm afraid there's a misunderstanding. I'm not that kind of importer."

She stared at him, her face suddenly empty of expression. It looked broad and round, like a pastry. "What kind are you?"

"Electrical parts from Japan, minerals from Africa and South America. You know, the boring kind of importer."

"Oh," she said. "Oh."

"Sorry."

"My mistake." Her hand shot to his breast pocket and

retrieved her business card. She whirled and walked to the other side of the swimming pool, where she hovered on the fringes of a group until they noticed her and stepped back to let her slip into the circle.

As Altmeyer made his way through the crowd, he saw Bucky approach Rachel and Bob Scranton, pulling with him another short, fat man with a black moustache and thick, bushy hair that looked in the dim light like a woolen cap. He could see Bucky gesturing at each of them in turn, then leaning back to send a hearty laugh up into the night sky. It would have been difficult for any of them to see that Bucky's eyes were on Altmeyer. He gave Bob Scranton a pat on the stomach with the back of his hand that made Scranton appear to bow.

Then Bucky sidestepped sharply and reappeared beside Altmeyer as he was handing Rachel her drink. "This rodent is The Immortal Billy Bittmeister," he said. "And this gentleman is The Grand Duke Altmeyer, Prince Consort to Queen Rachel, whom you've already ogled with such embarrassing relish."

The short man grinned and extended his hand. "Pleased to meet you, Mr. Altmeyer. Rachel was just saying she's not one of Bucky's clients. How did you get to know The Poster Boy for Greed? Surely Bucky doesn't have any actual friends?"

"Altmeyer owns a fat farm near Big Bear. Runs forty head of fatties each season, but don't bother to ask him about it. You couldn't afford the fees for the intensive care unit. Rachel, can you keep Billy's hand out of my pocket for a few minutes? You know, don't let him talk to anyone who isn't carrying a tray?"

Bittmeister smiled. "That leaves the field clear." He turned to Rachel. "All of Bucky's clients get lots of experience as waiters. I don't have to lure anybody away from him. If I yelled for a menu right now I'd be trampled to death by Bucky's talent."

"Come on, Altmeyer. There's somebody I want you to meet," said Bucky, tugging Altmeyer's arm. Bucky made a steady, inexorable progress through the crowd, his belly clearing the way before him. Altmeyer followed. A tall Latin American waiter carrying a large tray that seemed to contain bowls of guacamole and thin pink strips of sashimi cut across his path. The tray whisked over Bucky's head like a scythe as he stopped to glance up at the underside, and then moved on in the direction of the tables.

At the edge of the patio, Bucky turned right and made his way up the path to the house. The door opened into a small study lined with shelves of leather-bound books. Each shelf contained a single size and color, and it was a moment before Altmeyer realized that each row consisted of dozens of copies of a single volume. "I see you buy books by the yard," he said. "Fifty copies of *Moby Dick*?"

Bucky waved his arm in disgust. "Yeah. Save the whales. I was once married to a decorating moron. It was a nightmare. I have enough *Uncle Tom's Cabins* for a housing project, because there was a pretty decoration on the spine."

"I'm sorry. You wanted me to meet someone?"

"That was a polite fiction. I wanted to get out of the noise for a minute to see if you could help me with something." He sat down on the edge of a leather chair, lit a cigarette, and sighed. "I don't know a whole lot about importing. I know you must be good at it, because every time I read a newspaper there's another company going broke, and every time I see you, you're adding a koi pond to your backyard."

"If it's a loan, Rachel's got the checkbook in her purse. If Billy hasn't made her into a movie star already, we'd be happy to—"

Bucky jumped to his feet and took three quick strides across the room. "No. Not that. It's not that at all." Then he seemed to remember something. "Thanks, though." He walked back to his chair and dropped his body onto it, both feet kicking forward off the ground. "No, what I think I need is a contact. You must have all kinds of contacts everywhere—the people you play Monopoly with, or whatever it is." He smiled, but his brow was knitted. "If you can get me in touch with the

24

right one, I swear on my twenty copies of the Oxford Annotated Bible that nobody will ever know. Besides, this is simple."

"I'm sorry, Bucky. The drug trade isn't my line. You're the second one to ask tonight, and I just don't carry—"

"You're wrong again. It's harder than that. Look, you met Arthur Paston out there. He's my problem." He shook his head and stared at the carpet. "Where do I begin? Arthur Paston is not only my best and most dependable client. He's immensely powerful in ways that are hard to explain to a normal person."

"So?"

"Wait. You have to understand. In this business the big test is whether you can last more than a year or two. Arthur Paston has made something like sixty motion pictures, and financed the last dozen himself. I think he deposited a dime in a savings account to celebrate the ground-breaking for the Parthenon, and the interest bought him thousands of acres of land in a ring around what is now San Diego, and nobody knows what else. He was probably around in 1776 to buy the screen rights to the history of the United States. When he decides on a project he doesn't screw around with getting treatments and having story conferences and negotiating with agents and lawyers and backers. He tells me what he's going to do, who he wants to work with, and what he's willing to pay them. Most of the time he gets what he wants. But more important, I get what I want. He's about to make another movie. If it goes the way he wants it, three-quarters of the people out there gobbling up the sushi by the pool are going to find themselves employed."

"And you get ten percent from each of them?"

"At least. Arthur knows that it sometimes costs to find exactly the right people. He's a perfectionist. That's what got him where he is, and that's what got me where I am—in a jam. If he doesn't get what he needs, the project is off."

"What does he want?"

Bucky's shoulders shook as he chuckled. "Jesus, that's

the question. It doesn't sound like much. It sounds like a joke. This is a man who made World War Two movies that sent combat veterans home with shell shock. I mean, the man has used aircraft carriers. Do you know what it takes to borrow an aircraft carrier?"

"Never thought much about it."

Bucky stood up again and resumed his pacing. "For *Spitfire* he assembled the seventh largest air force in the world. And now what's stopping him?" He shook his head in disbelief. "A couple of lousy machine guns, and maybe a portable rocket launcher."

"Maybe?"

"Yeah. He thinks he needs that. He can show a couple of guys with a cardboard tube and a shot of a truck being blown up with dynamite, and nobody will know the difference."

"So what's the problem? Don't the studios have what he needs in their property departments?"

"Look, the history of Arthur Paston's relations with the major studios is about as complicated as the Peloponnesian Wars, and probably started the same day. Most of them won't let him in the gate."

Altmeyer sipped his giant martini and studied Bucky. "This could use a pound of olives. What exactly is he looking for?"

"He needs two or three small submachine guns. Those little Uzis, or maybe Ingram MAC-10s, and a couple thousand rounds of live ammunition."

"Not blanks?"

"I told you, Arthur's a perfectionist. He wants to churn up the landscape a little bit, the way they used to in the old days when they had cameras that cranked and brains to match."

"You must have your clients insured," Altmeyer said. "But I guess there shouldn't be much of a problem for a man like him. Give a call to the Federal Building downtown, explain what you want, and they'll fix him up with a special license or something. The ammunition you can buy at any gun shop."

"It's not that simple. I looked into it already. The first problem is getting a federal license. You know what they want? An application signed by the police saying it's not against any local law. There are thirty-five states where it isn't, but California isn't one of them. There is a special provision for the movie industry, but the red tape is amazing. Just to get around to looking at the application takes them three months."

"That's the only way to go, Bucky. I don't know much about these things, but you can't go around breaking federal laws and then show films of it in theaters."

"It'd take six months. That's why I need help. I've got to have the damned things in hand as soon as possible. Paston has already decided to do the movie, put people on salary, rented equipment, the works. The clock is already running, and old Bucky's got the ball. Look, you must know somebody who can help me. I'll apply for the license tomorrow. When it comes through I'll go through the motions and buy some guns legally. Meanwhile, Arthur will have finished shooting on schedule and under budget, and nobody will ever know what was filmed when."

Altmeyer sat in silence, sipping his drink. Suddenly there was the sound of something beating against the door. It seemed to be coming from a spot only a few inches above the ground. Bucky stood up and opened the door to reveal Rachel standing on the threshold carrying three drinks.

"Here, take one," she said. "You may need it. I'm afraid Billy eluded me, and is now trying to cut several prime head of beef away from your herd. The man's a rustler." She turned to Altmeyer. "You could help me too, you know. Kicking down doors in high heels isn't that easy."

"We were just talking about business," said Bucky, "but I guess we're finished now. Will you at least think about it?" He stared at Altmeyer.

Altmeyer nodded.

27

Rachel smiled. "Whenever men go off in secret to talk business, women wonder which kind it is. Are they selling our heirlooms and mortgaging the roofs over our heads, or just talking dirty?"

Altmeyer's face was expressionless. He stood up and walked to the door, took one of the drinks from Rachel's hands, and then slipped the dead bolt on the door. "Sit down for a minute, and I'll fill you in."

Bucky tried to laugh, but his voice came out in a shrill cackle. "No need to go through the whole thing a second time now. All I ask is that you keep me in mind. Hell, people will start wondering what happened to us."

"This won't take long, Bucky. Rachel's picked up my business quickly, and her brain carries more voltage than mine does anyway."

"That's okay. Let's not make Bucky more uncomfortable than he is. Let's just concentrate on resting my aching feet for a minute and then we can all go save Bucky's livelihood from Billy Bittmeister."

"In a minute," said Altmeyer, leaning against the door. "Bucky just told me he needs two or three automatic weapons because old Arthur Paston is a stickler for authenticity. The thing is, Paston doesn't seem to give a shit if the guns are Uzis or Ingrams. He'd also like a rocket launcher, but doesn't care what kind, and can fake it with a cardboard tube if he doesn't get the real thing. On the other hand, he does insist on using live ammunition. The big problem is, he can't get a license for all this stuff because it takes too long and production costs are mounting up already. Most of the people outside are on the payroll, and Bucky is getting ten percent of their salaries, but he doesn't seem to feel good about that for some reason. Paston is a big power in this business, so Bucky and everybody else all have to do what he wants, but Paston can't get this problem solved in any way except to have his agent dig up the props for him. And of course Bucky, whose job it is to know everybody in the movie business, naturally thought of the most direct and logical way of solving the problem. He

28

remembered that his neighbor was in the importing business, and would undoubtedly know somebody with submachine guns to sell. What do you think?"

Rachel frowned. "There's no point in picking on him, Altmeyer. Bucky's gotten himself into trouble." She turned to look at Bucky, who had collapsed in his leather chair and was staring at the ceiling. "What is it, Bucky?"

Bucky closed his eyes and sighed. "I'm a fool. I'm sorry."

Rachel walked to his side and said, "Who are you afraid of?"

Bucky rolled his head from side to side on the chair back. "Who am I afraid of? Who have you got? Arthur Paston? I'm afraid of him. Billy Bittmeister? Sure. If this party goes on long enough, he can lower my income by thirty percent. As of ten minutes ago, you can add Altmeyer to the list. Please, just leave me. Forget I said anything."

Altmeyer turned to Rachel. "What do you think?"

"I like Bucky. Nobody flatters a girl the way Bucky does. He doesn't care what lies he tells. Besides, he did lend us his food processor once."

Altmeyer stared at the fat little man slouching in his oversized chair. "Tell us the truth and maybe we can do something to help."

Bucky leaned forward. "You mean you'll get me—get Arthur and me the—"

Altmeyer held up his hand. "Wait. The truth doesn't have anything to do with movies. And the solution isn't to turn you loose with an automatic weapon you've never fired and would probably use to blow your own ass off the planet. Just tell us."

Bucky pursed his lips and squinted. "It involves drugs." His little eyes shifted to Rachel, as though he expected a reaction. When he didn't see one, he sighed. "In order to do the kind of business I do, I have to spend time on maintenance."

"Did you say maintenance?" Rachel moved to a chair three steps closer.

"Yeah. I have to be sure every client thinks I stay up nights working out ways of making him rich. When I meet somebody powerful I have to do things to be sure he remembers me so when I call him he isn't out of town. I have to keep up a network of people who aren't clients or customers but might tell me something I can use. I have to know who does what, who's on his way up, and who's out. All that takes maintenance."

"So?" said Altmeyer.

"Maintenance isn't making a list of people and calling them up on the phone once a week to say we've got to have lunch sometime. It's keeping all these people convinced that you're somebody. If they don't hear your name mentioned for two months they think you're dead. If they don't hear of something you're doing for two years you are dead. You have to be big right now, not two years ago. Big people dispense things— favors, introductions, a mention in the right place, a job, a chance."

"Bucky," said Rachel softly. "This is taking a long time."

Bucky nodded. "I should get out there and make sure they're all getting their weekly dose of old Bucky. You know what this evening cost me?"

Altmeyer shrugged. "How much?"

"Don't ask." He paused. "Anyway, this is part of it. You have parties, you make them all glad to be around you any way you can. While you're at it you make sure you look like you're the guy who invented prosperity. Give them everything they think they want. Right now they're out there eating caviar and truffles like they were peanut butter and jelly. In a little while, a few of them will nose-dive into the last of my cocaine."

Rachel said to Altmeyer, "I think the old Buckaroo has just approached the point."

"You could be right. Press on, old Buccaneer. And cheer up."

"Buck up," she corrected.

"It's not a cheerful story. When you deal with people who sell Russian caviar and French truffles you just *think* you're dealing with criminals. When you buy cocaine you *are* dealing

30

with criminals. I made a deal to buy some—actually, a lot—from a man named Kubitz."

"A lot, Buckskin?"

Bucky said the words slowly, as though he were surprised to hear them himself. "Two hundred thousand dollars. A half pound."

"You really do think big, Buckingham."

"Hell, you're a businessman. If you don't buy in quantity you'll get screwed on the mark-up by the middlemen."

"How did you get screwed?"

"The stuff was supposed to be available two weeks ago. I was supposed to meet Kubitz in a car in a parking garage at the Beverly Center—I give him the money, he gives me the coke, we shake hands, et cetera. But it doesn't arrive. Kubitz comes into my office that day, and says there's a problem. The problem is that the people who brought it from Colombia had to be paid in cash when they got to Miami. Then the people who were supposed to bring it here decided to close Kubitz's line of credit. If he wants it, he's got to pay for all of it on the spot. The deal is just too big. They're out so much money already that they're holding on to it until they see the cash. It's a real pain in the ass, he says, because now he has to scurry around to all his customers and collect something like five million dollars. But—"

"He'll give you a big discount if you'll pay in advance."

Bucky closed his eyes and nodded. "And the worst thing was that it was believable. I mean, this guy Kubitz is—he's hard to describe, but criminal doesn't cover it. He's something out of a nightmare. I remember sitting there thinking it had to be true, because this guy is, well, somebody you wouldn't give a whole bunch of cocaine to unless you already had the money in the bank."

"Great logic, Buckminster. When did you find out the shipment was hijacked by creatures from Venus?"

Rachel said, "Altmeyer, you could be more sympathetic with old Buckeye."

31

Bucky sat up and waved his hand at her as though his chair were about to move him off into the distance. "I deserve it. No excuses. Anyway, I hear nothing at all from Kubitz for about a week. I'm starting to get a little suspicious, so I start calling him. First he's out of town, then he's in town but they don't know when he'll be in. Finally he answers the phone, but he's not eager to talk money, and keeps acting like his phone is tapped. He won't even set up a meeting. He says he's too busy, that he'll get in touch with me. He says it like he's talking in code because he's got seventeen FBI agents in the room with him."

"Of course," said Altmeyer. "Go on."

"Well, you can imagine what I'm thinking by now. If he really is that worried, maybe he should be and so I should stay the hell away from him. But that's just what he'd want me to think if he were trying to rob me. Either way, what am I going to do about it? This guy goes around all the time with two bodyguards that are indescribable—they'd get turned away at a tattoo parlor. They both carry guns, and Kubitz does too, in shoulder holsters, like cops."

"It doesn't sound promising, does it?" said Rachel. "I take it you decided to write it off. So why do you want all the guns, old Buckshot?"

"What could I do but write it off? I spent the next few days in mourning. In a way, I sort of got over it, like you get over losing a leg. On a chilly night you can still feel your toes get cold until you remember you don't have any, and that's a real consolation."

"Why the contemplated violence, Bucking Bronco?" Altmeyer strolled over to Rachel's chair and took one of her drinks.

"Because last night Kubitz called me here. He said that now everything's set and he's ready to deliver the cocaine. He wants me to meet him tomorrow night. I put it off."

"Why? Maybe he just doesn't want to get kicked out of the Chamber of Commerce."

"I think he's planning to kill me. He doesn't want to meet

at the Beverly Center this time. He wants me to go eat at Du-Par's on Ventura and then walk down Radford to the big parking lot beyond CBS carrying a briefcase."

"Maybe they'll pick up the series if the pilot sells."

"The way I had it figured is, I show up and pull out one of those nasty-looking little machine guns. I wouldn't have to do anything. It would scare the shit out of him."

"That's probably true." Rachel looked at Altmeyer. "Do you think it would be a good idea to frighten a man like Mr. Kubitz?"

Altmeyer walked to the bookcase. "Not if he's got time to blow your head off." He looked at his new drink. "This one's a little better. Arthur is learning." He walked back to the door. "What do you think about Bucky? Is he learning?"

Rachel gave Bucky a sympathetic look. "I don't think so, poor thing. It sounds like he made some of that up."

"Whole cloth, Buckram?"

"That would be childish, Buckwheat," Rachel said. "How can we help you if you don't trust us? You weren't just buying, were you?" She reached out and placed a hand on his shoulder.

Bucky slumped forward, his elbows on his knees. "I'm sorry. I can't help it. It's all true but that part. I was going to try to turn a profit on some of the cocaine. But that doesn't change anything. Kubitz wants to meet me alone in a dark place, and he owes me enough to make it worth killing me about fifty times over at current rates. I need some kind of edge."

Altmeyer turned to Rachel. "What do you think now?"

Rachel smiled. "I think that's all of it, or enough of it, anyway. Please, Altmeyer. I know what you're thinking, but let's do it. He's our friend, and look at him. All alone, so sad and frightened he can't even keep his lies straight. And what if they did kill him? Wouldn't you be ashamed?"

Altmeyer set his glass on the desk. "Step over to our house tomorrow at ten, Buck-and-Wing."

.   .   .

BUCKY CARMICHAEL WALKED CAUTIOUSLY, facing oncoming traffic and trying to stay as close as he could to the mortared flagstone retaining wall that kept the hillside from shifting to bury the road. He heard a whine from somewhere around the bend and higher up the canyon as somebody down-shifted into one of the curves. He stopped and leaned against the jagged surface of the wall to peer up the next stretch of road. It was empty at the moment, so he ventured around the bend, now brushing his left calf against the weeds and dwarf foliage at the edge of the pavement as though he were navigating by touch. The engine sound sharpened and the black Porsche's trajectory swung it into view in an arc that seemed certain to pass through a point occupied by Bucky's right kneecap. He turned sideways, and the Porsche flashed by him along the canyon, accelerating again to hold to the inside of the curve.

He passed the crumbling concrete steps that led up through the weeds on the embankment to terminate abruptly at the trunk of a scrub oak tree. People had told him that this had once been Houdini's house, long ago burned down in one of the canyon fires. Either they were right or they weren't, but Bucky always told people he knew it was true because he'd seen the records.

A few yards beyond stood the brick pedestal with the statue of a swan perched on top that marked Altmeyer's driveway. He started the climb up the steep, winding path, pausing at times to keep the chirping of the invisible birds louder than the sound of his heart, then moving on. At last he reached a level stretch and caught his breath as he followed it through the trees to the beginning of the lawn.

He started across the grass toward the front door when he heard Rachel's voice call, "Hello, Bucky. Right on time, almost." He turned to see Rachel kneeling beside a circular pool in blue jeans and a sweat shirt, her hair tied in a tight ponytail behind her head. Beyond her was Altmeyer sitting in a lawn chair at a metal table, drinking coffee out of a mug.

"Sorry. I forgot how far it is from the swan down there to the house."

34

"Goose," said Rachel.

"Goose?"

She nodded, looking down into the shallow pond, where several large speckled fish glided slowly in and out of little forests of plants.

"Sit down, old Buckboard," said Altmeyer. "If you get a stroke and fall into Rachel's new pond, the carp will gum you to death and she won't save you."

"A nasty way to go," Bucky said, and sat beside him at the table. He stared over his shoulder at the fish. "The koi must have set you back a bit. Arthur's got one that's supposed to be over a hundred, and it cost him ten thousand."

"I got a deal on the fish from a guy I do business with," Altmeyer said. "We dug the hole ourselves."

Rachel stood up. "All right, time to get to work, you two. I'll catch up with you after I've taken care of the goats."

"Goats?" said Bucky.

Altmeyer nodded. "Ideal goat country up here."

"What do you do with them?"

"I'm teaching them computer programming. Come on, let's head for the house. I'm out of coffee, and you didn't get any."

Bucky followed him across the dichondra in silence. As they skirted the swimming pool he said, "What do they—what does she feed them?"

"Goat food."

They went in the side entrance and into a large, white kitchen, where Bucky sat at the butcherblock table while Altmeyer released coffee and steamed milk from a brass espresso machine into a mug for him.

Bucky sipped his coffee and tried to formulate the question that would make Altmeyer explain the goats. Somewhere outside he could hear nasal voices making a sound like *na-ah-ah* as Rachel showed up to do whatever she did with them.

Altmeyer returned to the table and set a telephone in front of Bucky. "Call Kubitz and tell him tonight is okay after all. Make sure the place hasn't changed. You're going to be

35

out all day where he can't reach you, so you've got to know now."

Bucky said, "But what's the plan?"

"That depends on what he says. Call him."

Bucky dialed the number and heard a voice that could only be Kubitz. It was deep and flat, with no inflection or accent. "Yes."

"This is Bucky. I'm calling because I got an appointment cancelled. Is tonight still free?"

"Sure. Same place. Eleven."

"I'll be there." Bucky hung up, but he could hear the receiver go dead before his hand reached the telephone cradle. He could feel his heart beating again, and he noticed he'd been breathing hard through his mouth. He felt it all clearly: this was wrong. He'd let it happen too quickly. Maybe if he'd left Kubitz alone for a few weeks he'd have just taken the money and gone away. Maybe the moment wasn't really gone, and he could call Kubitz back and tell him he'd changed his mind. But every second he thought about it, the farther the distance to go back.

"VERY GOOD," said Altmeyer. "You can stop worrying." He cocked his head, listening. "Rachel's goats are fed."

Bucky stared at him and felt the panic take the form of a pounding in the center of his forehead. He studied Altmeyer's thin, tanned face with its strange almond eyes, empty of any feeling Bucky could identify, except some kind of watchfulness. Suddenly Altmeyer seemed to be the problem. Who the hell was he, after all? He said he was an importer, and what did that mean? All the questions that Bucky had never asked himself seemed to matter now. You couldn't even tell how old he was, or if he and Rachel were married, or where they came from or—

"Okay," said Altmeyer. "I guess we'd better get downstairs. Bring your coffee."

Bucky felt something that could have been nausea. As

36

he followed Altmeyer out of the kitchen, he detected a horror at leaving the telephone behind. If he couldn't call Kubitz again now, that still didn't mean he had to show up tonight.

Altmeyer opened a door and started walking down a stairway to the basement. Bucky accomplished a few steps behind him, then stopped, his legs feeling weak. Altmeyer was already at the bottom. He called, "Come on, Bucky. Rachel will be with us in a minute."

The panic seemed to take on an urgency. "Wait," Bucky heard himself say. "I'm scared."

Altmeyer returned to the foot of the stairway and stared up at him, his strange, empty eyes alert and unblinking. "Of course you are. You're an intelligent man. Come on." He disappeared into the dim space below.

Bucky stood gripping the railing hard. Then he noticed that his other hand was holding the coffee cup steadily, without spilling it. He looked at it for a second, took a sip, then walked down the stairs to the cool, damp basement.

Altmeyer was waiting for him a few feet away, leaning on a high wooden table that blocked the entrance to a narrow corridor. On the table were several sets of earphones that weren't connected to anything.

Bucky said, "What's this?"

"It's a firing range."

Bucky's coffee cup began to shake slightly. "Why do you have goats?"

"Rachel likes them. They're clean and affectionate and pretty." Altmeyer's voice was quiet, and the watchful eyes seemed tired.

For no reason he could understand, Bucky said, "Okay, what now?" He heard Rachel coming down the stairs, her footsteps lighter on the boards than his or Altmeyer's.

"How are we doing, Buck Private?" she called.

"Fine," Bucky lied.

Altmeyer said, "We have to get you set for your part of this. The strategy you figured out wasn't bad, but it was a little ambitious for you, and it had a couple of flaws."

Rachel walked up behind them and said cheerfully, "It would have gotten you killed."

Altmeyer reached over the counter and pulled up a short, heavy shotgun, then pumped it five times rapidly. "This is a little more realistic. It's a Remington Eleven Hundred, just like the police use. It's reliable, quick, and simple. Have you ever fired a shotgun?"

"Once," Bucky answered cautiously, "but it looked different."

"Fine. You never forget. Did you hit anything?"

"I wasn't too good at it."

"No problem. That's why we're here: to give you a little practice. The main thing is not to imagine you can bang away and the pattern will take care of your lousy aim. It won't. But a shotgun has advantages."

"What?"

"If Kubitz is a pro, this will scare him as much as anything that isn't dropped from an airplane. In the unlikely event that you have to use it, you may be able to hit something. The load will be double zero buckshot, so there won't be any question of repairs at the emergency room. That's twelve steel pellets, each the size of a .38 bullet. At twenty feet they'll blow a five-inch hole in him. Take it."

Bucky accepted the shotgun. It felt heavy and alien and cold.

Altmeyer handed Rachel a set of earphones and said to Bucky, "Now you're going to fire it. Keep it pressed hard against your shoulder to cushion the recoil. The barrel is sawed off, so use the ramp sight on the muzzle or your shots will go high of the target. We've got hours and hours. I want you to get comfortable with it."

Bucky frowned. "I can't walk down Radford carrying this. I can't do this."

Altmeyer said, "Last night we parked a car on Radford. Inside is one of these, all loaded and lying on the backseat under a dirty blanket. We've got all day to talk about the rest of it."

"I can't do this," Bucky repeated.

Rachel put her arm on his shoulder. "Altmeyer and I talked about it, and there's no way out. The chances are about ten to one that Kubitz will come through with the delivery and nothing will happen. Anyway, if he really is trying to kill you, he won't succeed. We'll be there." She smiled.

Altmeyer took the shotgun and pushed five shells into the slot at the side. "Just press the safety, pump it, and fire. If you're going to make any mistakes, make them now."

BUCKY WAITED, peering down into the lighted glass case at the cherry cheesecake that sat in vulnerable perfection surrounded by a cordon of chocolate-covered doughnuts. He heard the cash register buzz and stutter, so he moved along the case past a regiment of brownies and let the lady's pastry-white fingers flick the bill away. When the hand swooped out a second time to take his money, he felt an impulse to touch it.

You could stay in here forever, Bucky thought, watching the daily changing of the pies and cakes. You could just keep eating and letting the plump, comfortable ladies float past and fill your coffee cup. All you had to do was give them a little money now and then. All you had to do to keep them happy was keep eating.

He took a deep breath and felt the constriction again. Altmeyer's bulletproof vest was too small. It was thin and light, but he felt as though someone had wrapped a rope around and around him so he could hardly breathe.

Bucky walked down Ventura Boulevard toward the crossing. What kind of man had a bulletproof vest he could lend you? He glanced at his watch as he reached the crosswalk. It was four minutes to eleven. Kubitz was probably watching him already from a car in the plaza, or maybe down the block.

The light changed and the cars drifted to the right edge of the crosswalk, creeping a few inches over the line to remind him that they were stopped by the color of the light and hadn't even seen him.

As Bucky stepped up onto the curb he heard the engines race again behind him. The first few yards took him past the milk-white facade of an office building, and for a second he saw his own shadow projected and swept across it by the headlights of a turning car. Then there was a stretch of spiked iron fence, and behind it a couple of long, low buildings at the edge of the CBS property. There were lights in two of the windows, and he decided to believe that somebody was doing some late-night editing, or the music copyists were finishing a score. He didn't want them to be night watchmen in uniforms.

He stared down the street as he walked, trying to see if any of the parked cars looked different from the others. When he looked at the horizon, he became aware that his body was swaying in short little steps, like a man walking on the deck of a ship.

He imagined someone, maybe a police captain, but anyway someone in authority, saying, "He was staggering down Radford carrying an empty briefcase," and then, "He was wearing a bulletproof vest."

He passed the lighted cubicle where a parking guard sat facing the other way, and then the long, white concrete side of the office building, and then the entrances to three sound stages. When he'd thought about this it had been different, all dark alleys and bushes where somebody would be hiding. It seemed strange that he'd forgotten what it really looked like—he'd been here a hundred times, but it hadn't been this way. It was like walking the cleared ground at the perimeter of a high walled fort. There was probably some old-fashioned name for it, from the days before no man's land.

Bucky felt better when he passed the third gate and moved into the shadows where the road passed over the dry concrete canal—was it the Los Angeles River or the Tujunga Wash? He glanced at his watch again. It had been only two minutes, and he was almost to the car now.

He could hear his footsteps as he approached the dark green Ford sedan. He slowed his pace, trying to control his breathing in the tight vest. He strolled slowly up to it, and then past it a few steps. In his peripheral vision he could see the button was up on the right rear door. He stopped. Altmeyer had said not to hover around the car or Kubitz would do something to draw him into the open. What kind of— He stopped himself. He was the one who was in trouble, and scared, and he didn't wonder about Altmeyer anymore. "Altmeyer, God loves you," he thought. "Bucky loves you too. Don't lose track of poor old Bucky. Not now. Please, God."

A car's headlights appeared at the end of the street, and Bucky's breath caught in his throat. He walked a few paces unsteadily as the car glided past. He sighed and started to walk back in the direction of the studio again, but then he heard the car backing up behind him. He pretended he didn't hear it, just strolled back toward Altmeyer's Ford sedan. The car passed him, then jerked to a stop.

The side door opened, the dome light flashing on to reveal Kubitz, smiling. "Hey Bucky!" There were two other men in the car.

Bucky waved. "Hello."

"Come here," said Kubitz. "Get in."

Bucky could feel himself sweating, and it made him feel cold. "I don't want to. You come here."

He heard Kubitz and one of the other men laugh. He couldn't tell which one gave the high-pitched cackle, but it made him feel suddenly angry. He said, trying to make his voice sound even, "Just drop it on the ground and drive on. I've got things to do."

There was a pause while Bucky counted five, then the dome light flashed on again and Kubitz was standing in the street, holding a leather jacket crumpled into a bundle. The car coasted a few feet forward away from him, and its brake lights glowed again.

"Okay, Bucky. Let's put this in the briefcase."

Bucky set the case down on the sidewalk and backed away from it. On his left he could feel the Ford sedan without looking at it, and he sidestepped toward it.

Kubitz walked to the briefcase, snatched it up with his free hand, and then dropped it. He pulled the jacket away, and Bucky saw the barrel of the pistol, and saw a flash, or maybe only decided he must have seen it, because he was on his back, the wind punched out of him. Some reflex made him gasp and try to sit up, but there was another flash and a spitting sound that kicked him back down.

He could see the sky, with the dark upper foliage of the eucalyptus trees on the right side, and what he thought of as he lay there as the usual number of stars. He found himself changing the position of his head to see them better. Moving made him think about the present. He could move, and he was breathing, and it didn't hurt much, and he heard the sound of feet. He rolled over on his side and squinted. There was his briefcase on the ground, and Kubitz was walking away. It puzzled Bucky that nothing else had happened in all this time. He reached up to the side of the car, swung open the door, and groped under the blanket on the floor. The shotgun felt light and familiar in his hands. He stood up.

The car was still in the street, and the side door was open. As he watched, he heard a sound like a buzz, and the rear window seemed to explode into a million chunks of sparkling glass. Then the sound of the rifle reached him, a muffled crack from somewhere far away. He remembered Altmeyer holding the long rifle, all blond wood with a telescopic sight the size of a man's forearm, and saying, "Don't worry. All she's got to do is hit the car. Rachel can hit a car, for Christ's sake."

Bucky leveled the shotgun on Kubitz, who was running toward the car. Just as he reached the open door, the car jolted forward a few feet. Bucky fired, the recoil slapping the muzzle into the air. He pumped it and leveled the barrel again and saw Kubitz was still standing. There was something happening to the car, though he couldn't see exactly what it was. As he aimed, Kubitz crouched and fired at something on the other side of the street. This time Bucky could see the sparks spitting out of the muzzle of Kubitz's pistol, but he didn't have time to watch it. From across the street something big and horrible happened. There was a loud *wooooow-ow* sound, and a long thin flame like a blowtorch swept sideways; Kubitz seemed to jump backward into the air, and then the side windows of the car blew out in the same direction, as though a strong wind had passed through. Then he could see Altmeyer step out of the bushes holding something in his arms.

Bucky had his finger on the trigger and there was nothing where Kubitz had been, so he started to run toward the car. There were no heads visible, and the car had begun to drift. As he ran it picked up speed, and he knew he couldn't catch it. His chest hurt, and he could hardly breathe, but he ran, his chest straining against the tight bulletproof vest. Finally he stopped and shouldered the shotgun.

"Hold it," said Altmeyer's voice. "They're all dead."

Bucky aimed at the slow drifting car, but as he stared down the barrel at it, the car crashed into the rear end of a parked Mercedes. There was a bang like the sound of a hammer, and then a tinkling of glass, and the car stopped. Bucky lowered the shotgun. The only sound was the idling engine of the car.

"Come on, Old Buck Rogers," said Altmeyer. "We've only got a few minutes unless everybody around here is deaf."

"Let's go," said Bucky.

"No curiosity?" said Altmeyer. He was already opening the door of Kubitz's car. He leaned in and Bucky could see him flinging things around. There seemed to be a piece of cloth, and then some papers, and then Altmeyer returned. Bucky could see now he was carrying a short, stubby weapon with a long magazine jutting down from the pistol grip and a leather sling that dangled as he walked. In his other hand he was carrying a brown paper bag.

"Home again, Home again, Jiggity-Jig," Altmeyer said, opening the door of the old Ford sedan. "The main thing is, make sure you've got the safety on on that shotgun, Mister Bucks."

Bucky nodded and laid the shotgun on the floor of the backseat, then covered it with the blanket again. He climbed

43

in beside Altmeyer, and stared at the dashboard. When Altmeyer turned on the headlights, he could see the spray of broken glass shining in the street, and the twisted body of Kubitz sprawled beyond it, the clothes and flesh all in tatters and a stream of blood that seemed to run from beneath it into a black pool by the curb.

Altmeyer prudently steered around the glass and turned left onto Valleyheart. "Well, Bucko, how does it feel to be alive?"

"I can't remember."

They drove on, Altmeyer turning again onto Laurel Canyon and making his way across Ventura Boulevard and up the winding road into the hills. He drove up Bucky's driveway and stopped next to the kitchen door.

Bucky turned to Altmeyer. "I forgot to thank you, didn't I?"

"Some other time."

"No. And I've got to give back this vest. Is tomorrow okay?"

"No hurry. I've got to talk to you in a day or so anyway. There wasn't any cocaine in the car that I could see, but this whole bag seems to be full of money. Looks like it was a lot more than you gave him."

Bucky shrugged. "I just want to remember right now to thank you. If I forget now, then later on it won't mean anything. He killed me." Bucky tried again. "I mean he shot me. He was planning to kill me. I'd be dead now."

Altmeyer said, "Don't mention it. Rachel will be home by now, and I don't want her to worry."

"COME ON BUCKY, open your shirt," said Rachel. "Let's get a look at that manly torso."

"All right, but no disparaging remarks. The embalmer I have works cheap, and I don't want him insulted." Slowly and carefully, Bucky unbuttoned his shirt.

Rachel stared at his chest. "You certainly do bruise nicely.

44

Just like a big peach." She gently touched one of the two dark purple blotches on the white skin, and he winced. "But isn't he a lucky boy, Altmeyer?"

Altmeyer glanced up from his newspaper. "Yes. I've always said he was a lucky boy." His eyes returned to the newspaper.

"In a few days I hope to feel lucky. Right now I feel like I've been trampled."

"Just bruises," said Altmeyer. "We were afraid you might have a broken rib or two, but there's nothing under those bruises to break. It's all guts."

"Thank you," said Bucky. He thought for a moment. "I guess I mean that."

"You'll be romping on the playground with the other moguls and mogulettes in no time," Rachel said. "And besides, we've got a nice rebirthday surprise for you." She poured him a cup of coffee.

Bucky eased himself onto a chair at the kitchen table and picked up his cup. "This will be fine, thank you. In the last couple of weeks I've had more surprises than I need."

"You don't have any choice," Rachel said. "Does he, Altmeyer?"

Altmeyer shook his head, folded the newspaper, and set it on the counter. "You originally gave Kubitz two hundred thousand. Last night he didn't have any cocaine to give you in return, but he did have a hell of a lot of money in the car. Do you know anything about him you forgot to tell us?"

Bucky tried to shrug, but gasped instead.

"I think that means no," said Rachel.

"Then I guess we have to assume he was either on his way to buy something or had just sold something."

"A shrewd business deduction," said Bucky. "He sure as hell wasn't giving refunds."

"We counted it last night, and it comes to exactly three hundred and fifty thousand, all in hundreds. A round number in identical bills always means wholesale," Rachel said, "not a lot of little sales."

45

"What are you going to do with it?"

"We talked about that," said Altmeyer. "We're going to split it up into two parts, capital expense and profit. The capital expense is your two hundred thousand. You get all of that back. That leaves a hundred and fifty thousand in profit. We have decided that part should be shared with us on an equitable basis."

"Keep it. Twenty-four hours ago I was dead. You don't have to give me any money at all."

"No. We agreed to get you your money back as a favor, so that part is settled," said Rachel. "I've got it all wrapped up for you in this bag." She held up a grocery bag. "The profit is business. Without really thinking about it we became part-ners, and now we're ready to liquidate the partnership and—"

"Don't put it that way," said Bucky.

"What she's saying is this. In any corporation there are shares. Each of us holds one share for going out there last night. You get an extra share for being the decoy, the one who had to get shot. That makes four shares. Each share is worth thirty-seven thousand five hundred. So you get seventy-five thousand, we get the same."

"And you're happy with that?" Bucky's eyes were wide.

"It doesn't matter," said Rachel. "It's fair. Altmeyer is always fair. Besides, it's all a bonus. All we thought we'd get is a chance to borrow appliances from you whenever ours break down. Now we have an appliance replacement fund."

"It's not fair." Bucky set his cup down and shook his head.

"Don't say that," Rachel said. "Altmeyer is the ultimate capitalist. If he thought it was fair to screw you out of your last cent he'd be just as happy with that. Oh, listen." There was the plaintive sound of the distant goats calling *na-ah-ah*. "Aren't they sweet? They're afraid I forgot about them. I'll be back in a minute."

Bucky turned to Altmeyer. "Listen, please. I don't want all this."

"Yes you do."

"Of course I do. I got into trouble in the first place for money. This is different." He waited, but Altmeyer said nothing. Bucky could hear the goats again, but now the cries were excited, and they seemed to be coming from right outside the window. He turned his head to listen. "Do they just run around loose?"

"Since we got the yard fenced. Sometimes they come looking for her."

Bucky stared at his cup. "You're both crazy." His head jerked toward Altmeyer. "I'm sorry I said that. I don't mean you're crazy, either of you. I just don't understand. I like you. I'm grateful to you. But I'm afraid of you—both of you." He seemed to lose his ability to speak. He stared at his coffee cup again, then rubbed his eyes. "People don't keep goats in Los Angeles. You're supposed to be a businessman, but you're some kind of criminal. I know that, and I don't care. I'm not surprised that I don't care. I wanted you to be one, because I knew if you couldn't help me I was dead. I want to give you as much of the money as I can because I'm afraid of being involved with you now that I know. I need money as much as I ever did in my life, and I'll probably do something stupid again to get it, but right now I'm scared. What the hell are you?" He shook his head. "No, please don't tell me."

Rachel walked in, leaving the kitchen door open. A black-and-white goat stepped to the threshold, stuck its face into the doorway, and sniffed, its upper lip quivering. "Go away, silly. You can't come in," said Rachel, but the goat stayed, staring at Bucky suspiciously.

Altmeyer leaned back in his chair. "Bucky," he said quietly, "you're going to take the money. If you need more, I've got an investment you might be interested in."

"I hope this doesn't mean I'm going to find out what you do for a living."

Rachel laughed. "Bucky, you already know. Altmeyer does importing and exporting. He really does, and it's too boring to talk about. He just figures out what's hard to get or too expensive in one place, then buys it in another place and ships it to the first place."

"Look, I really do need some way of investing this cash. It's what you might call my life savings. But is this—"

"Don't worry, Bucky. Altmeyer has been running around for weeks clearing his inventory to put together capital for this. It's not some midnight meeting with drug dealers. It's just business. If you want to invest, we just make it a bigger transaction."

"And who is the other party?"

"Some nice Japanese businessmen. What could be better than that?"

VICTORIA

Altmeyer and Rachel walked along the gray limestone wall on the quay, under antiquated iron lamp posts hung with baskets of red and yellow nasturtiums. Below the railing, the green harbor water seemed to rise and fall tamely in its stone enclosure. Across the street were the sprawling, ornate buildings of the British Columbia Provincial Parliament, all cut stone and spires and greenish domes, set far back in the center of a vast green lawn.

"I like Victoria," said Rachel. "It's what people wanted the world to be like in the nineteenth century, only they couldn't change it all fast enough."

"That's probably why there are so many old people." Altmeyer lit another cigarette and stared ahead at the tall mansard roofs of the Empress Hotel. "Some of them probably checked in before the first world war."

Rachel stopped. "Okay, Mister Fun. Let's hear what I have to know. This isn't going to be as easy as we told Bucky, is it?"

Altmeyer exhaled some blue smoke from his cigarette and watched it float out over the water. "Nothing special. We can get something they want. If the price is right, we deal. Either way, we all go home. It's not dangerous at this stage."

"So why do we need these guns? My purse feels like it's got a bowling ball in it."

"They're samples."

"Come on. What am I supposed to expect? Who are these Japanese businessmen? What do I say?"

Altmeyer smiled. "Okay. I'll tell you what I know. There will be four of them, and only one of them supposedly speaks English. He calls himself Nagata, but it's probably not his real name. He may not be the only one who speaks English. We'll know he's not if he ever leaves us alone with the others."

"That's enlightening. All I got out of that was that we can't talk to each other."

"More than that, I'm afraid," said Altmeyer. "There are various ways of dividing countries for business purposes. There are the ones where you only use your right hand in public, and others where you use both. The Japanese aren't interested in hands. There are countries where you can't burp, and others where you must. The Japanese are nonburpers."

"I see. You're working around to telling me they don't do business with women present."

"No, Japan has moved over to the other side. It's one of the countries where women work. The thing is, we've both got to be watchful all the way through this. See what you can figure out."

"What do you mean?"

Altmeyer smiled. "In a Noh play there is an eight-man chorus. You know how you can tell who the leader is?"

Rachel shook her head.

"He's the second one from the right in the back row."

THEY STROLLED into the cavernous hotel lobby, their heels clicking on the marble floor and echoing among the carved wooden beams far above them. They approached the registration area, a massive structure of dark, polished wood that must have incorporated whole trees planed and beveled and laid in place with the same incomprehensible expenditure of labor that built Stonehenge.

A white-haired man with a long nose so thin it appeared to have no nostrils presided at the counter in an Edwardian morning coat.

"I'm Mr. Altmeyer, room four thirty."

"Yes, sir. Mr. Nagata asked that you meet him in the conservatory."

"Thank you," said Altmeyer, and they moved away from the counter.

"That's another one," Rachel whispered.

"Another what?"

"Another oddity for Altmeyer's Travels. He didn't have it written down."

Both sides of the long hallway were lined with small shops. There were jewelry stores, and display cases filled with Eskimo soapstone carvings, and finally a whole row of furriers. The windows were all festooned with urgent-looking signs in red or blue Japanese characters.

"It's all Japanese. None of it's English," Rachel said.

"That's who buys it," Altmeyer said. "Canadians don't come to a hotel to buy fur, and Americans can't take it home with them."

"Oh no. Baby seals?"

"I suppose, and whatever else is endangered these days. That's what makes this a good place to meet. It's neutral ground, and it's full of Japanese tourists with a lot of money who are on their way to someplace else in squads and bunches."

At the end of the hall there was a broad, rounded portal that led into the glass dome of the conservatory. The light was filtered through ferns and potted palms and climbing vines that leaned outward toward the panes of glass that formed the walls, and the air seemed to bear some damp, pungent trace of humus and decay.

A middle-aged Japanese man in an immaculate gray suit sat in a wicker chair beside a miniature tree of orange and pink roses. When he saw Altmeyer, he stood up and took three steps forward, extending his hand to Altmeyer, but looking at Rachel. "I'm very pleased to meet you," he said. "They're waiting." He walked out of the conservatory and down a long, narrow corridor past dozens of broad, wooden doors with smoked-glass transoms, then stopped at one and entered without knocking.

Inside, three Japanese men stood in a row before a canopied bed. Mr. Nagata said, "Mr. Bridges, Mr. Walker, and Mr. Bone." The three nodded, then went to chairs in different parts of the room.

Altmeyer repeated, "Bridges, Walker, and Bone," his face expressionless. Then he seemed to remember something. "Allow me to introduce my associate. Her name is Ralph Waldo Emerson."

Nagata spoke to the others in Japanese as he conducted Altmeyer and Rachel to two armchairs that flanked the window, then closed the heavy blue velvet drapes.

The man who sat in the chair nearest to the door spoke, and Nagata nodded. "Mr. Bridges has asked if you've considered our proposal."

"Yes," said Altmeyer. "There are several ways I can fill a large order." He reached for Rachel's purse on the floor beside her chair, and peered inside. "You specified nine millimeter, didn't you?"

"Yes," said Mr. Nagata. "The ammunition problem, you see."

"Very good," said Altmeyer. He pulled a blunt, heavy automatic pistol out of Rachel's purse. The four men's eyes widened with pleasure as though he'd revealed something miraculous. "This is the top of the line. It's a Browning P-35 Hi-Power." He handed it to Nagata, who carried it first to the man beside the door, who ignored it, then to the man beyond the bed, who took it in his hand, examined it closely, worked the slide back and forth, carefully tested the hammer spring, and smiled.

Altmeyer continued. "The retail price in the United States is about five hundred dollars."

"We're familiar with that," said Nagata. "Everyone knows this weapon. In Japan it would bring five thousand. But you're not here to sell us Browning pistols. They're all numbered and counted and registered. Nobody can get a thousand of them without coming to the attention of the authorities. Show us what you came here to sell."

Altmeyer smiled. "You're right. I agreed to sell you an imitation. I wanted to show you how good an imitation it is."

"Where is it? We'll have to see it."

"You already have." He pointed toward the man beside the bed, who was still aiming the pistol at the pillow and making little puffing sounds with his lips. "That's it."

Mr. Nagata translated, and all four men laughed in appreciation. Then he said, "Excellent, Mr. Altmeyer. You're a talented salesman."

"I can deliver a thousand, all rolled with the Browning trademark and false numbers. They'll cost you eighteen hundred each, with delivery in Japan in under thirty days."

RACHEL AND ALTMEYER walked down the quiet, carpeted corridor to their room and locked the door behind them.

"Very good," said Altmeyer. "I should be able to make the shipment in a couple of weeks without any trouble, and we'll have our money out of it a couple of weeks after that. It's been a long time coming."

Rachel sat down beside him on the bed. "I suppose that means no more scrambling around trying to collect cash for a while?"

"Probably better than that. It took a lot of care, a major investment, and a lot of patience, but from here on it's going to be easy. It won't last forever, of course. But before the idea gets worn out we're going to be very much in demand."

"Selling guns to Mister Bones and Mister Interlocutor?"

"Hell no. If this works out they may want to talk to us again sometime, but they're only one outlet. I've got something nobody has. I've got an acceptable counterfeit of one of the most salable pieces of merchandise on earth, and I can get it cheap. I don't have to worry about anybody tracing it, because it's easy to trace—right to the Browning company in Arnold, Missouri. Only when they trace it there they won't find a record of the serial numbers or any lost guns."

"How did you manage to do all this?"

"I'm a partner in a gun factory. Well, not a partner, exactly. You might say I'm the full owner of the night shift."

LOS ANGELES

Altmeyer backed the van to the edge of the loading dock and turned off the engine, but Rachel couldn't hear the difference. The raindrops pattering on the metal roof seemed to grow louder. She stared through the windshield, her view distorted by rivulets of water streaming downward. "What a rotten night to go sneaking around."

Altmeyer lit a cigarette. In the glow of the flame she could see that his eyes were looking beyond, darting from side to side as though he were searching for something. "It's a great night for sneaking around. It's sneaking around that's a pain in the ass."

"I hope the goats are warm enough in their shed."

He shrugged, not looking at her. "They'll be fine. They're waterproof."

"And their Daddy's getting rich."

"I'm not their Daddy."

Rachel was quiet for a moment. "You're getting rich, though, aren't you?" She didn't wait for an answer. "Tell me that you were once just an ordinary guy running an importing business, and then you saw a chance to make some profits. Maybe you had trouble—foreclosure, or something?"

"Did I tell you that?" He looked amazed.

"No. Sometime I wish you would." After a few seconds she laughed. "You know. Just something the goats can tell their friends."

"I'll try to think of something that'll hold up." Altmeyer studied her. "Maybe I was the hereditary ruler of a small and remote country that was overrun by the Communists in the early fifties. I don't remember much about it because I was only a child at the time. But I was clever for my age, and before my nanny put me on the plane I sewed the national treasury inside my three hundred and seventeen teddy bears."

"Bright lad."

"Smart as a whip. That's what *Look* magazine said at the time."

Rachel sighed. "The goats will like the part about the nanny, but I don't think they'll buy the rest of it." Through the blurred window she saw a man trotting in the rain, hunched over holding his jacket collar tight around his neck. "Here comes the man with the teddy bears."

Altmeyer stared past her. "That's the one. He used to be Secretary of the Interior." Altmeyer jumped down from the van and vaulted to the loading dock, where he stood under the overhanging roof holding a briefcase.

Rachel picked a cigarette from Altmeyer's pack on the dashboard, pushed in the lighter, and then slipped the cigarette back into the pack and stared through the rain at the dirty red brick wall of the little factory.

The man climbed onto the loading dock and Altmeyer said, "Hello, Sterne. Ready to go?"

"Sure I am. Are you?" Sterne frowned down at the van. "They weigh two pounds apiece. That's a ton."

"It has special shocks and springs and rear axle."

They walked to a metal door and Sterne opened it with a key that had been clipped to his belt. Inside, he flicked a wall switch and a single bank of overhead lamps cast dim circles of light on the concrete floor. There was a forklift holding a wooden pallet packed with cloth bags, and beyond it Altmeyer could see gleaming machines and wooden bins filled with metal parts.

Altmeyer said, "Want to count the money before we load?"

"No," said Sterne. "No thanks." He took the briefcase and set it on the floor beside a workbench. "I haven't got time to count a hundred and fifty thousand now. I've got the rest of my life."

"I'd rather you didn't take that long," said Altmeyer. "I want you to get started making another batch."

Sterne glanced back at the briefcase. "Not now. I've got to let the inventory settle down a little. It takes a long time to put aside that many parts. I've been writing them off as defective. It takes months to build up the parts for anything like a thousand. It means we've got to make ten times that many, so we can pretend to scrap a few and bring in the night shift. We don't do that kind of business."

"What if the price went up? What if you could get two-fifty for the next batch?" Altmeyer leaned against the forklift.

Sterne stared into the dark factory, moving his lips silently, as though adding figures. "Well, we could invent a couple of short count shipments, write a few more off as defective, even say we broke a few here. It's no problem with the parts we machine ourselves. But the inspectors are on my neck all day long. This isn't easy."

"Then I guess you'd better get started."

ALTMEYER CLIMBED INTO THE VAN carrying the last of the cloth bags from the pallet. He loosened the drawstring, reached in, and pulled out one of the dozen paper packages. Carefully, he pulled the tape off, opened the package, and examined the pistol inside. He held it close to his face in the darkness, then moved it down somewhere near his knees. Rachel could hear a series of rapid clicks and the sound of oiled metal sliding back and forth. Then she could see him wrapping the pistol in the paper again.

61

"Is something wrong?"

"Nothing serious. I just had an ugly thought. Sterne didn't want to count the money."

"It's an awful lot of counting."

"He wasn't too lazy to do the rest of the work. The one I checked looked perfect. I'll have to test-fire a couple to be sure, but it looks like he came through."

"Then what are you worried about?"

Altmeyer started the van and drove toward the gate. "Ron Sterne is pretty much the guy you were talking about before. He's a legitimate businessman who needed a fast profit this year or he wasn't going to make it to tax time. He'd inherited this old gun factory from his grandfather. It was an antique. They made special-order commemorative six-shooters for stupid collectors, engraved a few shotguns too expensive to carry in the field, modified and customized and refurbished rare pieces you could hardly get ammunition for. When he took over, he started looking for ways to break even. The first thing he did was to start gearing up to go after the mass market with a couple of variations on old favorites—a police special .38 and a couple of automatics. The second thing he did was realize he was going to be bankrupt before his plant was ready for production."

"So you corrupted him," said Rachel. "No wonder he's too depressed to look at his ill-gotten gains. I think I like your teddy-bear story better."

Altmeyer chuckled. "I do too. The problem with corrupting people is that it takes a lot of what Bucky calls maintenance. You have to keep thinking of ways to keep them corrupt after they've got as much money as they thought they needed. Otherwise they stop doing business."

Rachel watched him as he drove through the rain, slowing down to plow through a stream of water that flooded the intersection. "Are you afraid that this is some kind of trap? That he told the police?"

Altmeyer shook his head. "He hasn't gone to the police. If he had he'd have been all smiles and false confidence, and he wasn't. He didn't want to hang around and look at his money because he's nervous. Since these guns seem to be as good as the first ones, he's not nervous about me. Something about this doesn't feel right to him."

Rachel sighed. "Maybe he's finding it hard to look his goats in the face."

"People who make weapons don't have that problem. I think he's got an instinct that something's going wrong. It's as though he sensed that somebody's been watching him."

"What are we going to do about it?"

"I think that sometimes people who don't know a lot about the specific facts see and feel little changes, things that aren't exactly the way they were yesterday. Maybe Sterne saw the same car parked near his factory a couple of times."

"Maybe he didn't feel good when he woke up this morning."

"I could live with that. His digestive system isn't going to show up at our door with a warrant." He lit another cigarette as he drove onto the freeway entrance ramp, and held the pack toward Rachel.

"No thanks."

"Quitting?"

"I don't know yet."

ENSENADA

"I suppose it's necessary to drive across the border with a ton of pistols packed under the rug," said Bucky. "It only seems crazy to drive through the most closely watched border crossing in the Western Hemisphere in a van full of guns. Right?"

Altmeyer shrugged. "Nice to have you along. See the sign? Tijuana welcomes you."

Bucky shifted in his seat to stare at the long line of cars slowly creeping toward the row of toll booths ahead. They seemed to shake in the heat waves rising from the chalky white pavement. As a small pickup truck with a camper shell coasted forward a few feet, a ray of sunlight from its back window printed a blinding flash on Bucky's retina. He closed his eyes and studied the after-image, like a small crimson object exploding in slow motion into a blue-green cloud. "I wish Rachel were here. Even better, I wish I were with her. No offense, Altmeyer, but you're not exactly a normal person."

"Somebody's got to be ready to bail us out," said Altmeyer, reaching for his cigarettes. "You'd screw it up, Rachel wouldn't." He smiled. "She's not a normal person either."

Altmeyer let the van move forward a few feet, lighting his cigarette and squinting past the flame at the car ahead. "Beautiful day, isn't it? Nothing like a little rain to clean the air and make you want to spend a weekend in Mexico. It seems to have brought everybody out." He surveyed the hundreds of cars slowly converging on the row of booths. "A fine day for smuggling."

"For Christ's sake," said Bucky. "Somebody'll hear you." He eyed the driver of the car beside him, who seemed to float backward as Altmeyer stepped on the gas.

When Bucky turned back to face Altmeyer, a dark-haired man in what looked like an army uniform was staring in at him. "Good morning," the man shouted over the traffic noise. "Anything to declare today?"

"No," said Altmeyer. "Just down for the weekend."

The man nodded and stared at Bucky. "And you, sir?"

"Me too," said Bucky. "I'm with him."

But the man had already stepped back out of earshot, and was waving them on and looking to his right at the next car in line.

Altmeyer took a winding road marked with a shield and a big 1. After a few hundred yards it straightened and grew into a divided highway. "Very well done, Bucky. Only about an hour and a half to Ensenada."

"Then what?"

"The usual tourist things: meet Rachel at the hotel, have a drink, bale some cotton, maybe go for a swim, then dinner, then—"

Bucky gazed to his right at the vast blue ocean. He said, "Have a drink, bale some cotton?"

ALTMEYER DROVE ALONG AN EMPTY STREET scarred and pitted by heavy trucks. On both sides were high chain-link fences surrounding sheet-metal and cinderblock buildings. After several unmarked intersections there was a battered, diamond-shaped traffic sign that said PELIGRO. CAMINO EN REPARACIÓN in faded letters.

"There he is," said Altmeyer.

A young man in a bright white T-shirt sat on the loading

dock behind one of the buildings, smoking a cigarette and swinging his feet. As Altmeyer drove up to the dock, the man pulled his legs up and crossed them.

Altmeyer got out of the van and spoke with the man, then returned. "He's all ready to go. The cotton's been here since yesterday morning, and they ship it out late tonight. Let's get unloaded." He pulled back the rug and then lifted the plywood platform off the floor to reveal the layer of guns, still wrapped in paper and arranged neatly on a layer of cloth sacks.

Bucky and Rachel gathered the pistols, beginning at the front of the van and moving backward, and then Altmeyer carried each load into the building. Within a few minutes the van was empty, and Bucky helped Altmeyer replace the plywood and the rug.

Inside the building Bucky could see a large empty space with electric hoists and chains and pulleys dangling overhead from steel beams. There were long tracks with metal rollers stretching in all directions. Along the far wall, piled in three tiers, were hundreds of rounded, five-foot brownish cubes wrapped in tightly stretched burlap and clamped with metal bands.

Altmeyer and the man were already busy at a workbench. They were wrapping sacks of guns in plastic packing material with air bubbles in it, then placing the bundles in cartons.

"What's this?" asked Bucky.

Rachel stepped forward. "Here, grab a box. The cotton is packed tight, but it's still not as heavy as steel, so we need to do some adjusting. Fifty guns weigh a hundred pounds. A hundred pounds of compressed cotton is about twelve and a half cubic feet. You get the idea—a cube about two feet four on each side. So we've got twenty boxes."

"I get it. These go inside the bales of cotton?"

"Right," said Altmeyer. "A ship was loaded two days ago at Mazatlán. Every bale on it was weighed and measured and certified by the customs people and officially sealed so they won't have to fool around with that when they reach port to unload. The ship stops here tonight to pick up a shipment of tuna. The thing is, by the time it gets here, twenty bales of the cotton will be missing. But when they load the tuna, they'll also load twenty bales of cotton, so the bill of lading will agree with what's on the ship."

"Is all this necessary? What does it all cost?"

"You buy cotton in fifty-thousand-pound lots, and the going price is about seventy cents a pound."

"Don't worry about Altmeyer," said Rachel. "He gets to sell the cotton, too." She pushed a box toward him. "Come on, now, Bucky. Stuff it."

THE SWIMMING POOL was a mosaic of small ceramic tiles hand made and decorated with the crest of the Playa del Mar Hotel, the tiles of the sloping floor a blue like lapis lazuli, and the walls coral and white. The mind that designed the pool must have called swimming "bathing," Rachel thought. Any fool whose eccentricity required strenuously flailing his arms and legs against inert and reluctant water had only to look through the ten-foot-high glass wall that protected the pool from the cool western breezes to see the deep blue ocean stretching across the world.

The waiter was standing over them, pulling his pad from somewhere in the breast of his scarlet dinner jacket. "I'll have a margarita," said Bucky. "In fact, we'll all have margaritas. Bring us a pitcher to start."

"I'll have a glass of orange juice," Rachel said to the waiter.

Bucky turned toward her on his chaise longue, his belly lurching to the side to rest on the surface of the chair. He raised his sunglasses and squinted at her. "Are you serious?"

Rachel smiled. "Perfectly. I'm in the mood for orange juice. I can celebrate with orange juice."

The waiter gave a rapid half-bow and turned on his heel.

Rachel faced the garden across the pool, her eyes half closed. She felt a little like sleeping now in the sunshine, but somehow looking across the water at the bright flame-colored fuschias and the dark juniper trees with their clinging red bougainvillea vines was enough like sleeping. Lying back in the chair she could see the distant blur of flowers between her feet, and her knees and thighs, and even a small smooth stretch of her stomach, the gleaming skin warmed already by the afternoon sun. Her eyes shifted to the left toward Bucky and Altmeyer, the two of them so different from each other and from her that they might have been different species. Altmeyer seemed all edges and corners, the muscles in his arms and legs now as always taut and working as though he were on the verge of doing something unexpected. She stared down her body again, and acknowledged that she was a particular kind of creature at a special moment in its existence. Things were going to change. She didn't know exactly what the changes would mean, although she could have made a list of them if she hadn't been so sleepy. Gradually things seemed to lose their sharpness, as though the flowers, the white facade of the hotel, and the sunshine were far away, like a memory or a dream.

"Altmeyer," she said quietly. "Do you love me?"

"Sure."

"I mean, do you really?"

He turned to face her. "I get embarrassed out there on the dance floor alone, and I like to have somebody hear me laugh at my own jokes."

Rachel stood up and walked toward the pool. Altmeyer watched her from his chair. "Where to?"

"To go and get ready for dinner, to try and look good enough so you'll still want to dance with me after."

Bucky was still lying on his back with his eyes closed. He spoke up into the sky. "She forgot her orange juice. Interesting."

THEIR TABLE was beside a large window looking out into the blackness that stretched beyond the shadowed beach. The window reflected the flames of the candles and the gleams of

71

the wineglasses. Rachel watched the images of the three waiters floating toward her out of the darkness, and turned her head.

"It's the crimper," Altmeyer was saying. "When we tightened the bands on the bales we used a thing that looks like a big pair of pliers to secure the clamps, remember?"

"It looked more like the tool a dentist pulls teeth with," said Bucky. "Everything you invite me to seems to involve sweat and pain." He watched the three waiters placing plates of food on the table with exaggerated precision. "Except this, of course. This place is more like it."

The waiters backed away and Bucky said, "So what about the crimper?"

"I welded a ridge onto it, so it makes a special dent on the clamps."

"So when does it all get to the stage where we transcend crimpers and heavy lifting and move into the abstract realm of assets and profits? As much as I've enjoyed the exercise and the sunshine, I'm really more the mogul type. We moguls prefer mental activity, like counting."

Altmeyer nodded toward the window. "See that? Right on time."

Rachel and Bucky peered out into the darkness to see a ship's running lights far out at sea.

"You mean that ship?" asked Bucky. "That was there a while ago."

"No, the other lights, off to the right. That's the barge going out with the tuna. They'll be gone in an hour or two, and the ship will be loaded with the tuna and the full fifty bales of cotton. They'll hit Yokohama harbor in about twelve days."

"And then?"

"Another day or so before you get to do your counting. Thirteen days from now you can return permanently to your life of sloth."

"My lucky number," said Bucky.

Rachel stared out at the tiny lights on the ocean. The two sets had moved imperceptibly during the past few minutes, and now they seemed much closer together. The barge lights looked as though they were about to pass into the reflection of the candle flame.

RACHEL WALKED between Bucky and Altmeyer down the cobblestone path through the garden toward the bungalow. Behind them was the flickering yellowish light of the antique wrought-iron lamp that hung above the portico of the main hotel building. The tinny music of the mariachi band seemed to fade into the calm, regular hissing of the waves on the beach below them.

"Is that the fourth or fifth time they played that?" said Rachel.

"I can't tell," said Bucky. "Just because it sounds exactly the same, that doesn't mean it is."

"Here's ours," said Rachel. "Do you want to come in for a nightcap? I noticed there's a bar. It's smaller than the television, but it should do."

"No thanks," Bucky said. "It'll just be harder to find Casa Bucky later on. See you at eight."

"Good night," Altmeyer said as he bent down to fit the key into the lock.

They heard Bucky's uncertain footsteps diminishing as Altmeyer turned on the light. Rachel closed the door, kicked off her shoes, and walked toward the bed, but Altmeyer said, "Listen."

Rachel stood still and waited. After a few seconds she heard it, too. Above her head there was a quiet sliding sound, and then silence again.

Altmeyer was standing beside the door staring up at the beamed wooden ceiling, as though he were trying to see through it.

Rachel whispered, "A tree limb moving?"

Altmeyer shook his head at the rafters as the sound came again; he walked two steps closer, frowning slightly now.

"Maybe an animal," she said.

Altmeyer stepped backward toward the doorway. "Big one," he said, then eased the door open and slipped outside.

Rachel heard the noise again, this time a sound that was softer, but seemed to come from a wider area, and then the silence returned. She tried to hear it again in her mind. It was a man, but what was he doing? He'd been moving along the roof slowly, a step at a time. But then he'd done something different. What was it? She stared up at the arch above her where the sound had come from, and she knew. He was lying on his stomach near the peak of the roof. His head was right at the peak where the center beam crossed above the bed.

Where was the gun? Altmeyer always had a gun somewhere. She rushed to the dresser where he'd laid his coat, but when she lifted the coat there was only cloth. She dropped it and ran her hands through the clothes in his suitcase as quickly as she could, lifting armloads of clothes and dropping them on the floor. The seconds were passing, and now in her imagination she could see the man. He was lying flat on the sloping roof, and maybe now he was staring down at Altmeyer. Maybe he was lining up the sights of a rifle, and Altmeyer was— Damn. Where was Altmeyer's gun?

She had to do something. She snatched up the heavy wooden hairbrush at the bottom of Altmeyer's suitcase. Then she ran to the bed, stood in the middle of the mattress, her legs flexing as she struggled for balance, and hurled the brush with violence at the spot on the ceiling where she knew the man's head would be. It caromed off the board with a sound like a shot, and she lost sight of it as she tried to keep from falling.

From above, there was a series of thumps and clatters, as though the man were sliding down the slope of the roof. Rachel remembered the heavy glass ashtray on the table near the door, and jumped off the bed toward it.

ALTMEYER STOOD with his back pressed against the wall at the end of the building. He knew that if the man had heard the door open, he'd think Altmeyer would go to the side of the building, where the overhanging eaves protected him from above and the bushes would complicate his silhouette. The man would be waiting for Altmeyer to step out far enough to see the roof.

Suddenly there was a sharp crack, and then a scrambling noise from the side of the roof toward the rear of the bungalow. As Altmeyer silently stepped toward the corner of the building, his mind stored things to think about later. There was no gun, so Rachel wasn't firing through the ceiling. It couldn't be a shot, because it didn't come from outside. But the man was sliding down the roof as though he'd lost his grip on the shingles.

He peered around the corner and saw a foot at the edge of the roof, the toe pointing downward. Then the other foot appeared. Altmeyer sprang forward and sprinted toward the spot directly below the feet. He concentrated on the timing, calculating the exact instant of vulnerability, when the man would be on his stomach, unable to turn his head to see below him, and the legs would be too far over the edge to pull back quickly. As Altmeyer dashed toward the place, his fingers flexed for the grip on the ankles, but in that second he saw that it was going to be too late. The man's legs were over the edge of the roof, and his body was bent at the hips, and Altmeyer was still four steps away. Even in the darkness he could see that a diving snatch at the legs would fall short, so he kept running.

As he reached the spot, the man's torso came down before his eyes. The man hung with his arms from the edge of the roof for the second it took to look at the ground he would hit when he dropped.

Altmeyer saw the head turn toward him and the body start to fall as he collided with the unprotected torso. Altmeyer took the shock of the collision on his shoulder and forearm, and focused his energy to keep his legs pumping hard. The man was carried along for a few steps, then seemed to go limp and drag as his feet touched the ground, and then both men went down.

Altmeyer used his momentum to roll clear of the man, then whirled to face him, crouching low to set his feet for the next spring. The man was on his back, and he rolled over to right himself before Altmeyer could attack, but the way he did it was wrong. It was a swift movement away from Altmeyer instead of toward him, his hand at his belt. Then he was on his knees.

The man looked off balance, his left forearm up to fend off a blow and the right hand behind his thigh, as though to keep himself from toppling over.

Altmeyer didn't need to see the knife. He dashed toward the kneeling man, then cut to his right and ran past. As the man lunged toward the place where Altmeyer should have been, he committed himself and had to use both hands to keep his balance. Altmeyer's kick caught the side of his head and jerked his body backward. Then Altmeyer had a grip on the right forearm, and brought it down across his knee.

To Altmeyer's disappointment, there was enough resistance from the muscles in the arm to keep it from breaking, but the knife was on the ground. It was a single piece of flat steel, the six-inch double-edged blade not ending at a handle, just more flat steel with four holes in it. When he snatched up the knife, his hand brought with it a few strands of grass. A moment later he noticed them on the front of the dead man's shirt and remembered where they came from, and that the bare metal hilt of the knife had felt warm.

ALTMEYER TURNED THE KEY in the lock and opened the door just as Rachel completed her windup and hurled a small brass table lamp shaped like a candlestick at the ceiling. When it hit, the base separated from the shaft and the two parts, still joined by the cord, flopped onto the bed. The floor was littered with shoes and broken glass and clothes from the overturned suitcases. When Rachel saw him she gasped, then exhaled in a long sigh, her shoulders drooping as she sat on the bed.

"Altmeyer, where did you hide your gun?"

"I have one in the van," he said. "Sorry I didn't bring it in. You could have pitched it at the ceiling."

Rachel watched him. "Are you okay?"

"Sort of, thanks to you. He panicked when you started making noise. He must have thought you were shooting at him through the roof."

"Good. So we scared him off. In spite of the way this place looks, he didn't steal anything. We can clean it up, and—"

There was a knock on the door, and Altmeyer opened it a crack, then reached out and pulled Bucky in by the arm.

Bucky was already talking. "You won't believe this. I heard a noise outside my bungalow, and so I went out to take a look." He held up a flashlight. "You won't believe what I found."

"I know," said Altmeyer. "Was it that loud?"

"You did that?" said Bucky, his eyes bulging. "Jesus, Altmeyer." He looked around the disordered room and slumped against the door. In an unconscious gesture he turned on the flashlight and shined it on the piles of clothes, the broken glass, the bed. Then he seemed to realize what he was doing, and hid the flashlight behind his back. "Did he rob you?"

"We scared him off," said Rachel.

Bucky turned to Altmeyer. "You scared him? Well, he's cured of that now. Doesn't she know?"

Altmeyer said, "Rachel, I didn't have a chance to tell you, but we've got a problem."

"Oh no."

"I thought I saw a chance to take him down and talk to him, but it was a stupid idea. He had a knife under his belt. I hit him pretty hard when he was coming off the roof, but not hard enough to make him forget where the knife was."

"It's self-defense," said Rachel. "It's not your fault."

"Wait a minute," said Bucky. "This guy tried to rob you by going up on the roof with a knife?"

"It does sound odd, I know, but what else?" said Rachel.

"Something else," Altmeyer said. "If he'd wanted to rob

us he'd have been in the room. I guess we'd better take a closer look now." He stepped toward the door. "Come on, Bucky. Rachel, keep an eye on us through the window. If you see us getting arrested, phone the front desk and have them call the police."

"What?" Bucky looked amazed.

"Don't think about it," said Rachel. "I'm the only one who needs to understand. If they come, this mess should help. A Mexican man with a knife broke in."

"He doesn't look Mexican," said Altmeyer. "Better just say a man in the darkness."

Bucky opened the door. "He looks like a Viking, actually. Big and blond with a lantern jaw and a little nose like a pig."

Altmeyer pushed past him and walked down the dark path, staring up at the eaves of the bungalow.

Bucky whispered, "Where are you going? He's over here."

"We'll get to him in a minute. I want to see what he was doing on the roof. He must have found an easy way up." Altmeyer kept walking until he came to a trellis where bushy plants with white flowers climbed and spilled over onto the roof in a small thicket. He shook the trellis tentatively, then climbed to the roof.

The device wasn't hidden. It had just been placed inside the knapsack and then the hooks on the straps had been secured to the peak of the roof so it didn't slide down the slope. Altmeyer carefully opened it and peered inside to be sure, then examined the shingles in the surrounding area to be sure there wasn't a protective trip wire before he moved it. Slowly and gently he freed the straps and made his way back to the trellis with the knapsack.

He handed it down to Bucky before he descended.

"What's this?" Bucky whispered.

"Don't set it down. It's a bomb." He stepped off the trellis, took the pack, and returned to the room.

Rachel gave a weary smile. "For me? Girls love presents."

Bucky stayed by the door. "This time he shouldn't have."

"What's in it?"

"A little of this, a little of that," Altmeyer said, reaching gingerly into the knapsack and then opening it wider to look at something. "There, that's good enough for now." He stood up and glanced at his watch. "It wasn't going to blow us up for two hours, anyway."

Rachel walked to the knapsack and bent over to look inside without touching it. "You mean you brought a bomb in here to defuse it? How sweet of you to include me." She bent farther to look more closely. "What's this in the jars? It looks like rock salt."

Altmeyer shrugged. "Could be a lot of things, but it's probably ammonium nitrate. Don't throw it at anything while we're gone."

"I'll try to remember."

ALTMEYER KNELT beside the body and ran his hands along the sides, patted the pantlegs, chest, and stomach, then rolled it over, but there was no wallet. Then he whispered, "Stay here," and returned to the bungalow.

Bucky stood beside the dead man in the darkness, hearing only the sound of the ocean waves rolling onto the broad beach below the garden. Even the music from the hotel was too far away to hear now. He moved back into the trees beside the path and waited.

Altmeyer returned wearing the knapsack on his back.

"Are you crazy?" Bucky whispered.

"Should I have left it in the room or brought it home with us?" said Altmeyer. "Come on. You can take his legs. When he gets heavy, say so and we'll rest. Don't just drop him, because I don't want to get jostled while I'm wearing this."

They lifted the body and carried it down to the beach. Bucky's feet seemed to sink deep into the sand at each step and then to slip backward as he pushed off, so the harder his legs worked, the more slowly he seemed to move. At last he said, "Let's put him down for a second. My arms are killing me."

79

They set the body on the sand and Bucky gasped for breath.

Altmeyer said, "Rest for a few minutes while I'm gone. And lie down next to him. If anybody sees you you're two drunks looking up at the stars and telling your life stories. If you're standing up and he's not, it looks wrong." He set the knapsack on the sand.

Bucky sat down, his legs feeling light. "Where are you going?"

"I saw a few boats they rent down there by the main building." He started down the beach.

Bucky stood up and staggered two steps after him. "Wait. I'll go too."

Altmeyer chuckled. "He can't hurt you." He went back and placed the knapsack like a pillow under the dead man's head, then set off for the hotel.

"This could be a little tough," said Altmeyer. "The only tools I've got are that moron's knife and the crimper we used for the cotton bales."

Bucky was silent, following Altmeyer along the beach below the hotel. When they approached the building, Altmeyer kept to the shadows under the high concrete foundation that stretched up to the ground level where white stucco walls began and the brightly lighted windows faced the ocean. Only an hour ago they'd been on the other side of those windows, Bucky thought. He tried to remember how much of the beach he'd been able to see. He remembered the dark ocean and a straight white ribbon of surf, but he hadn't really been looking. He'd been thinking about the food, and about all the money that was going to come when the ship reached Yokohama, because at that moment all the work, and all the risk, would be over.

Altmeyer was already standing over a row of small boats pulled up on the sand beneath the wall. Bucky could see a heavy chain attached with a padlock to a metal ring embedded in the concrete. Altmeyer examined it closely, then followed the chain with his hands as it ran through another metal ring at the bow of each boat.

Bucky stood behind him, wondering what to do, feeling time passing. Beyond the row of closed windows above him the mariachi band was playing the same monotonous song. It was muffled, as though it were coming from a distance. Altmeyer was lying on his back inside one of the boats now, peering up under the small wooden foredeck. Bucky saw him reach into his pocket for the crimper, then watched his body stiffen in some kind of exertion, then relax again. After a time Altmeyer eased himself back and sat up on the seat, holding a nut in his hand, then putting it in his pocket. He moved to the boat beside it and repeated the process, this time more quickly. Altmeyer stood up and walked to the bow of the first boat and slowly pulled the long ring bolt out of the prow, keeping the chain from clanking, and freed the second boat.

He whispered to Bucky, "Okay, the oars are under the seats. Push it over there along the wall before you head for the water so you're not under the windows."

Bucky pushed the boat a few yards, Altmeyer behind him pushing the other in his tracks. When they reached the end of the wall, Bucky stopped and sat on the boat's transom to rest. Altmeyer joined him and leaned on the bow of his boat.

"This isn't too bad if you can hold out," Altmeyer whispered. "A few more yards and we can load up and go down to the water."

"I wish you'd picked the aluminum boats," Bucky said. "This thing feels like it's full of rocks."

"Aluminum won't do," said Altmeyer. "Let's get going."

Bucky pushed the boat down the beach, aware only of the gritty, hissing sound it made as it moved over the sand. It reminded him of something he couldn't quite place. He closed his eyes, thinking how little difference it made in the dark, and the sound came back to him. It was pushing his sled in the snow when he was a child. His hands were on the shoulders of someone—maybe his brother Walter—and he was leaning forward slightly as he pushed. He opened his eyes and saw there was something ahead of the boat. It was on the ground, horizontal. With alarm he stopped pushing and stepped aside. "Wait," he said. "That's him."

Altmeyer caught up. He walked over and retrieved the knapsack, then grasped the body by the arms and dragged it to the boat. "Give me a hand." They hoisted the body over the gunwale and then stood facing one another. For the first time, Bucky realized Altmeyer was breathing heavily and slouching too.

Bucky said, "I still like aluminum boats better."

Altmeyer shook his head. "Come on. It's nearly one thirty. I'll take the passenger ship, you take the other one. Row straight out to sea. Keep your eyes on the hotel lights, and make sure you don't get more than ten feet ahead of me. If we lose sight of each other out there we're in trouble."

Bucky pushed his boat to the edge of the surf, then straight into a wave that lifted it free of the sand, and sprawled over the transom as the stern rose under him. The wave's backwash drew the boat outward as he crawled toward the center seat, bumping his knee on an invisible strut. He struggled to fit the first oar into the oarlock, and the next wave wrenched it backward out of his hands. Then he remembered to set the flat of the oar inside the boat before he worked on the other. When both oars were set he was already drifting broadside, and the next wave washed over onto his lap, the cold water causing a spasm in his lungs like a sob. But with the first pull of the oars he was heading seaward, and he sailed into the next wave without difficulty. He pulled three times, and then he was out of the surf in water that rolled gently in long, slow swells. As he rowed he could feel the boat surge forward and glide, and beyond the transom the black water eddied and bubbled in his wake. He looked around and saw Altmeyer rowing easily beside him.

They rowed for a time, and then Bucky looked at his watch. It was two o'clock. He glanced to the side and saw

82

Altmeyer rowing steadily and methodically, and Bucky rowed harder to remain abreast of him.

The next time Bucky looked at his watch it was because he was having difficulty seeing the lights of the hotel. It was dark enough now so the radium dial of his watch was brighter than he remembered seeing it. The air was different, too. He was shivering with cold, and there was a strong breeze that seemed to come from the land beyond the hotel, but had none of the warmth of the places where people lived. It was harsh and alien, and he thought of it as the wind outside the window of an airplane.

He said, "Altmeyer," but his voice seemed so quiet he could hardly hear it. "Altmeyer!" he shouted, putting up his oars.

Altmeyer rowed up beside him, their oars nearly touching as they rose and dipped on the slow, rolling swells. "Well?" said Altmeyer. "You still okay?"

"It's damned near two thirty, and I can hardly see the lights on shore. Isn't it deep enough here?"

"Sure," said Altmeyer. "I was thinking something like that myself. Give me a minute and I'll take care of our friend." He stepped aft in his boat, tinkering with something, then called, "Okay, come alongside so I can get aboard."

Altmeyer climbed in beside Bucky and took the starboard oar. "Let's see if we can get back in time to get some sleep," he said.

Bucky rowed for several minutes, then said, "Won't they find him?"

"No. Feel the wind? It's going to push him out to sea for the next couple of hours."

"Then what?"

"Hell, you gave me the idea. You said he looked like a Viking. At four thirty when nobody can see the smoke and he's out to sea, his firebomb goes off and gives him a Viking funeral. Whoever he was, he's getting a first-rate send-off."

.   .   .

83

THEY ROWED TOGETHER, matching the rhythm of their long, methodical strokes. The offshore wind made a low whistle now as it streamed down from the mountains and skimmed the surface of the ocean flat on its way out of the bay.

"It's going to be hot tomorrow," Altmeyer said. "The wind is right out of the desert, even if it doesn't feel that way now."

Bucky rowed quietly for awhile, then said, "This whole thing feels awful. It's like when I was a kid and the other kids were doing something, so I did it too. Like stealing things from stores. As soon as I was in the door I couldn't remember how I got into it, and I felt like I was going to throw up, and I wished I hadn't agreed to it. I've felt like that since you came to my party. It keeps getting worse. I'm not cut out for it."

He heard Altmeyer chuckle in the darkness. "You might go years without this kind of thing happening, if you were careful. Most of the time it's like any other business."

"I'm scared. Really scared. You're never scared. I don't know why, but it doesn't matter. There's us and them, and you're them. I'm the only us."

Altmeyer said, "What happens is that you get scared enough times to get tired of yourself. The first few times, you find yourself pleading with God. 'If I can just get through this I promise I'll never get myself in trouble again. Just this once.' "

"That's how I feel right now."

"Sure. The thing is, after a few times it starts to sound stupid. You know you're full of shit. Not later, after it's over and you're home in bed, but while you're saying it, your voice sounds like it doesn't even belong to you."

Suddenly Bucky heard the waves breaking on the beach. He looked over his shoulder at the hotel. It wasn't just a few lights in the distance now, but a dark, sprawling shape above the surf. Bucky and Altmeyer rowed hard to keep the boat before the waves until the keel plowed the sand, then they both climbed out and quickly hauled the boat onto the beach. Neither spoke as they pushed the boat back into its place

84

among the others. Altmeyer fitted the ring bolt back into the bow and replaced the nut while Bucky carefully slipped the oars under the seats.

They walked together in a meandering course along the track their boat had left on the beach, letting their feet dig deep and kick sprays of sand across the grooves from the keel and boards. At first they moved slowly and purposefully, but as they neared the water's edge they began to trot, to kick the sand into piles. Bucky ran back and forth across the trail, then tripped and rolled a few feet, pushing the cool sand at the surface aside to feel the warmth beneath, and below that, the damp, close-packed frigid layer, like a foundation.

He lay still for a moment, feeling the muscles of his back and shoulders aching from the exertion. Altmeyer passed him, and Bucky sat up and pushed himself to his feet, then followed. The breeze was warmer and gentler here, with a smell of plants. He walked behind Altmeyer across the lawn to the bungalow, brushing the sand off his clothes.

Altmeyer whispered, "Come in for a minute," as he swung the door open.

Rachel was sitting on the bed, still dressed for dinner, her back straight and her arms folded. The room was dimly lit, but Bucky could see that it had been carefully cleaned and the suitcases were packed.

Rachel said, "Okay?"

Altmeyer said, "Fine." He glanced at his watch and went into the bathroom. "The old Buccaneer came through for me."

Rachel walked to the sideboard and poured Bucky a glass of something that looked to him like Scotch. "Drink this, old Buckwheat. You're soaked to the skin. It'll help."

Bucky took the glass with both hands and swallowed some, feeling the warmth move down his throat into his belly.

Rachel was already filling two more glasses. Bucky glanced at the bed, the bedspread still smooth and tight. She hadn't even lain down, he thought. The only sign that anyone had even been in the room was the pillow tossed carelessly

85

beside the place where Rachel had been sitting. He looked more closely, and he could see the butt of a pistol like the ones they'd shipped today, the knurled black handgrip just visible beneath the pillow. It looked too big for her hand.

He said, "You're both over it, aren't you?"

"What?" said Rachel.

"Being afraid."

"Oh," she said. "You're never over it. Even Altmeyer is scared. What you get over is being surprised. It's not much. It's no comfort or anything, but it gives you a little edge. You don't spend a lot of time recovering from being startled, thinking about how you got into trouble, whether there's something you should do or some way you can avoid doing it."

"That's all?" Bucky gulped more Scotch.

Rachel nodded. "When he comes in here he's going to want to be hugged and fawned over, because it's over and he's alive and I'm alive. That's what he gets out of it, and it's what I get out of it too. We get to be scared together after it's over."

Altmeyer opened the door and entered the room wearing a bathrobe. He walked slowly, and rolled his right shoulder a few times as though he were trying to detect a stiffness in the joint. Then he picked up the glass Rachel had left on the sideboard and lifted it toward each of them before he drank.

ALTMEYER STOOD at the rear door of the van and watched the customs man scan the flat, empty floor, then nod once. "Got anything to declare in the suitcase?"

"Not today."

"Okay," said the customs man, and gave a wave of his hand that meant both close the door and go away, and stepped back to judge the next vehicle's potential for carrying contraband.

Altmeyer climbed back into the driver's seat and started the engine, then joined the traffic that streamed away from the border onto the highway. "Too bad about this, Bucky," he said. "Business isn't usually this strenuous."

"I can hardly lift my arms. I also managed to get exactly twelve minutes of sleep, one at a time."

Altmeyer drove on in silence, over a set of railroad tracks and past a row of whitewashed shops, then turned a corner marked with a freeway sign. "Well, you've done your part, and when I get back we'll all forget the worst of it."

"I always wanted something not to tell my grandchildren about," Bucky said. After a moment he added, "Get back from where?"

"Japan," Altmeyer answered. "The ship can't make Yokohama in less than eleven days, so I've got a few days to rest up, and still be there long enough to get used to the time zone before I have to do anything."

"Can't your men there take care of things?"

"Men?" Altmeyer grinned. "I don't have any men. What do you think I am, Robin Hood?"

"You had people in Ensenada, people on the ship. You don't have anybody in Japan?"

Rachel sighed. "Altmeyer doesn't employ people, he just corrupts them on a per diem basis. These people aren't his loyal minions, just independent entrepreneurs he knows."

Altmeyer said, "The guy in Ensenada owns the warehouse, or his brother does, anyway. The captain of the ship just doesn't mind picking up a few extra bucks by loading things in a different order from what it says on the manifest. He still ends up with fifty bales of cotton when he lands."

Bucky tried to shrug, but winced from the pain. "I suppose it keeps your payroll down."

"Why are we going to Japan, by the way?" asked Rachel. "That wasn't the original deal."

Altmeyer didn't move his eyes from the road, but now his voice was apologetic. "I'm sorry, baby, but I'm the only one who's going this time. It wasn't the original deal, but I'd say we have to see what we can salvage out of the new deal."

"I'm going," said Rachel. "You know I am, so it would be foolish to spend a lot of time arguing."

"No."

"Then it's all settled. We'll get a suite in the Imperial Hotel, right above the Emperor's Palace."

"This is very charming," said Bucky. "It makes you both seem—'youthful' is probably the term. But what are you talking about?"

"It's just Altmeyer being himself, The Self-Made Baby. His voice even gets deeper when he's in this mood, did you notice?"

"No," Altmeyer said distinctly.

"Don't interrupt." Rachel turned to face Bucky. "He's going to need my help, and so he's going to have to take it. But he won't do it unless he's satisfied that he didn't ask for it and that I convinced him. He also will spend some time trying to scare me to death at what's going to happen."

"What is going to happen?"

Altmeyer said, "I'm not sure, to tell you the truth. That guy last night wasn't a burglar. He was just plain trying to kill us in the easiest way, without having to take any chances."

"I don't know anything about your business, but you must have made a lot of enemies over the years. Everybody has competitors, even ones he doesn't know about."

Altmeyer shook his head. "The first rule of this trade is that you don't make any enemies. Any competitor would have hit us at another time, when we had the money or the guns. If he knew we were in the trade he'd know that sooner or later we'd have either cash or merchandise. Besides, nobody followed us there. I was careful about that."

"It doesn't sound conclusive," said Bucky. "Obviously they found us, whether you saw them or not."

"No, Bucky," said Rachel. "What he's saying is that it had to be somebody who knew in advance where we were going, and that means they knew about this deal. He's right."

"Why?"

"Because they knew where we were, and what they were going to do about it, but they couldn't have followed us— couldn't even have seen us."

"How can you tell?"

"Because they didn't try to kill you," said Altmeyer.

"Oh." Bucky stared out the window. For several minutes he said nothing. Finally he said, "I see. We're not going to get paid."

"It's nearly two million dollars," said Rachel. "It's probably worth going over to ask."

LOS ANGELES

"They X-ray everything from the side, like this," said Altmeyer, moving the edge of his hand along an imaginary conveyor. "It comes in from the plane on a luggage carrier and they scan it as it goes through. Some things you can arrange so they throw a silhouette on the machine that doesn't look familiar, but then you still have the chance that they'll take your suitcase apart looking for drugs or absurd amounts of money or whatever. And at Narita they keep moving the metal detectors."

"So you gave up," said Bucky. "A wise choice." He fondled his empty glass. "I prefer to live off the land, myself."

"Altmeyer doesn't like to do that," said Rachel. "He's too stubborn."

"I was afraid of that."

"It's simple enough," Altmeyer continued. "Everything has been tried, so you pick a way that's a little less obvious than the others, and maybe they'll be too busy with people who are being more flagrant."

"They're starting to soften," Rachel called, staring down at the pot on the stove.

"Good. When the whole mess comes to a boil, turn it down a little so it simmers. It has to stay hot."

Bucky smiled. "You're full of surprises. I had Rachel figured as the gourmet chef. What is it?"

"Lead fishing sinkers." Altmeyer sipped his coffee as he walked over and looked into the pot. "They'll be ready in a minute."

"I can wait," said Bucky. "I'm on a diet."

"You can help me," Altmeyer said. "The idea is to pour a little liquid into the can, slosh it around so it forms a very thin, even film over the whole inside, then pour the extra lead back into the pot."

"Without spilling any of it on the floor or stove," Rachel added.

"Without spilling any of it, or burning yourself," Altmeyer went on. "When you've done one, set it upside down on the dish rack so there won't be any drips or uneven places when it dries."

Bucky stood up and joined Altmeyer. "What exactly are we doing?"

"We're putting on aprons and gloves, for one thing," Rachel said. "I can spot a spiller at a glance."

"It's really pretty simple," said Altmeyer. "We line the cans with a little lead, so the machines in the airport can't see through them. Japan is a great place for this because half the people in the airport will be bringing in American food for homesick friends. Last New Year's the department stores in Tokyo were getting thirty bucks for a sixpack of Campbell's soup."

Bucky held his gloved hands in the air as Rachel tied a pink apron behind his back. "How do you know things like that?"

"Don't be silly, old Buck," said Rachel. "We're importers. Right now in Tokyo a side of beef would make a nice gift. Anything they don't raise in quantity makes a nice gift."

Altmeyer poured a dipper of molten lead into a shiny fifteen-ounce can and turned it quickly between his gloves, then poured out the excess. "I thought of this a few years ago when there was a brief surge in the arms market in Bolivia. I bought the canning machine in Seattle. The outfits that take sport fishermen out after salmon all have them so the customers can mail home the fish. After the pictures are developed it's about all you can do."

"What were you sending to Bolivia?"

"Ammunition. I was fitting ten ounces of 7.62-millimeter rounds in each can, sixty cans a case. Whenever there's a revolution going on, anything that looks like food gets in. By the time the market closed, one case was worth—"

"What closed the market?"

Altmeyer stirred the pot of lead as he talked. "It's like any other business. When the big chains decide to move in, the small businessman has to get out. That time the United States government picked the same side I'd picked, and about a week later ammunition was free."

Bucky picked up a can and stared warily at the lead bubbling in the pot. "When we've done this, what goes into the can?"

"Three little pistols I picked out. They're called 'Auto Nine' because they have an eight-round magazine and hold one in the chamber. They only weigh eight-and-a-quarter ounces, and if you take off the slide and the barrel you can fit the parts in a can."

"I see. Canned heaters. But you must have three dozen cans here."

"Four are for silencers and extra clips. That reminds me. They fire .22 Long Rifle ammunition, so if you have to use yours, remember what you're doing. You have to fire at close range and hit somewhere important. Once it's in there it'll rattle around a little and tumble, so it'll do a lot of damage, but don't expect to stop a charging sumo wrestler unless you see a couple of holes in his forehead. When in doubt, keep firing."

"Very appetizing. Last time I was in Japan I estimated that the chances of being charged by a sumo wrestler were about the same as my chances at home of being beaned by a relief pitcher for the Dodgers, and I decided I could live with that. What are the other cans for?"

"We'll have a few extras, to raise the odds," said Altmeyer. "If somebody decides to open one, we may as well have something with us that won't ruin his day."

"Like what?"

"Canned soup, beef stew, that kind of thing," said Rachel.

TOKYO

As they passed through the pneumatic doors to the sidewalk in front of the airline terminal, Bucky set his suitcase on the ground and held up his hand. "Taxi!"

"Not that one," said Rachel as the black car accelerated past them. "We want a yellow one."

"Why?"

"They only go to railroad stations." She peered up the drive, where scores of cars and buses maneuvered for positions near the curb. "That one," she said, and Altmeyer moved toward the drive. She turned to Bucky. "It's tricky during rush hour."

A Japanese man saw the cab and held up two fingers. The driver veered in toward him, slowing. Altmeyer stepped behind the man, just out of his peripheral vision, and held up three fingers. The cab rolled past the man and jerked to a stop beside Altmeyer, its rear door popping open automatically.

Altmeyer handed the driver a card with something written on it in Japanese characters. The driver nodded and handed it back.

Rachel said to Bucky, "You have to be ruthless, which is Altmeyer's only authenticated virtue."

"So now we're going to a railroad station?"

99

"The Imperial Hotel is about two blocks from Tokyo Station, which puts it close enough. At three times the meter price, two blocks will go by without his noticing them, especially after driving an hour or more."

"Then what?" asked Bucky.

Rachel studied her watch. "It's now five on Monday afternoon here, which means it's midnight Sunday in Los Angeles. So your only choices are sleeping or eating. You don't get to choose which day it is."

"How about you, Altmeyer?" Bucky said. "I read something that said you don't get jet lag if you force yourself to stay up until the locals go to bed. I'd say that means at least five hours of eating would help us brave the culture shock."

Altmeyer watched the heavy traffic around them. "Let's get settled in the hotel and pop open a couple of soup cans first. A few ounces under my belt will make all the difference."

Bucky turned to Rachel. "Does he have an itinerary, or does he just navigate by waiting for something to move in the water, like a shark?"

Altmeyer spoke without looking away from the window. "It's five thirteen. We'll be in our hotel rooms by six forty-five. It will take me until seven to open the cans and reconstitute the delights to be found therein. You will arrive at our room at exactly eight wearing a dark suit appropriate to dining in one of the better establishments to be found in the vicinity. They're called *ryoriya*. After dinner we'll go back to the hotel and sleep until nine in the morning. At nine thirty you'll join us again, this time for breakfast in the hotel. After that we go to Yokohama to watch the ships come in. The Shonan Express leaves Tokyo Station every half hour, and it takes only a half hour to get to Yokohama."

"Amazing," said Bucky. "Such premeditation. How long will we be in Yokohama?"

"That depends. The ship we want to watch isn't due until day after tomorrow. I expect it'll make a pretty sight steaming into the harbor tomorrow around sunset. At Yokohama you can watch it without getting the sun in your eyes."

100

"How do you know these things?"

Rachel sighed. "I'm afraid something moved in the water."

"You should remember," Altmeyer said. "It was the gentleman we took boating a few evenings ago."

ALTMEYER STOPPED WALKING and cupped his hands to shield the flame of his lighter from the breeze that swirled between the warehouses and out into the harbor, setting up complicated patterns of shallow waves. He squinted past the flame at the group of Japanese men in green coveralls who were sitting along the base of a dark blue cargo container on the next pier. "That makes twelve," he said, and glanced at his watch as he walked on.

"Is twelve a quorum?" said Bucky. "It'll be dark soon."

Altmeyer shrugged. "It might not be enough to unload a ship, but it's enough to convince me one's coming before tomorrow. Only it's supposed to be this pier, not that one."

"So it's true," said Rachel. She walked beside him, picking her way along the crumbling concrete of the pier.

Altmeyer flicked his cigarette into the water, then reached into his shirt pocket, extracted the pack, and studied it.

"What are you doing?" said Rachel.

"Memorizing the brand. 'Geobugson, Fine Korean Cigarettes.' " He tossed the full pack into the water.

They walked in silence along the weathered jetty toward the distant hillside above the water. Altmeyer stared ahead, his hands in his pockets.

Bucky muttered to Rachel, "I hope he's not planning on walking all the way up there to commune with nature before he gives up and goes home."

Altmeyer heard him, and quickened his strides unconsciously as he spoke. "We've got a little problem about that. They sent that guy—Leif the Unlucky—to Mexico after us. By now they must know he's not coming back, which means that we are. So home might be a lousy idea right now."

101

"So what do we do?" asked Bucky. He glanced at Rachel.

Altmeyer walked on. "It would help if I knew what they think they're doing. I can't figure out why they didn't just pay us off. Their profit is already enormous."

"I know studio executives who would kill to cut their overhead by two million," said Bucky. "Expenses are real money, and profits have a way of showing up after somebody else is sitting at your desk."

"It's not the same," said Altmeyer. "These people know of one thing I can deliver, but they don't know of anything I can't deliver. They might be tossing away a chance of making ten times as much."

"Maybe they don't appreciate you."

"It must have something to do with the guns," said Altmeyer. "They must be doing something special with them that they don't want me to find out about. It can't be just the money. I guess the only thing we can do that might help is find out what they're going to do with the guns. It's not very promising."

Bucky said, "I suppose we could show up for the unloading. I'm not suggesting that. In fact, I'm suggesting we don't. But we could."

"Too risky," said Altmeyer. "The cargo container is supposed to be sealed and safe, but until it's been signed off by a Japanese inspector we'd better stay away from it."

Rachel smiled. "Thank you."

"You're welcome."

"Not for being sensible, for giving me an idea. I'd almost forgotten about the authorities. They're our leverage. Pay up or we tattle. Isn't that what they're so worried about? It beats bursting into the warehouse and threatening those longshoremen."

"It'd be a waste of time anyway. It's pretty unlikely any of them would know what we were saying."

"What about the anonymous tip to the police?"

"One problem with it is that it's hard to give an anonymous tip if you have to bring along a translator. Besides, it's not enough of a threat to make them give us the money, just enough to make them a little more eager to kill us off."

"I was afraid you'd say that," said Rachel. "If you had more time you'd think of more reasons. But you don't."

"I don't?"

"No, you don't. Look down there."

ALTMEYER STOPPED and looked down the long, sloping street, past the warehouses and docks to the darkening slate-blue water. As he watched, a pair of tugboats gently nudged their bows against the black hull of a small freighter, easing it slowly up to the pier.

"There's no hurry," said Altmeyer. "It'll take a couple of hours of work with the crane to get the cargo containers off the deck. The people we want to talk to won't be any more anxious to be there for the customs inspection than we are."

"I'm tired," Rachel said. "I'm going someplace where I can sit down."

"Tired?" Altmeyer laughed. "I'd never have believed it. You're never tired. Even Bucky isn't, and he's a walking display of all the vices."

Rachel ignored him. "I'm also going to get some dinner. It's going to be very good and very expensive, and I'm going to linger over it for some time."

"Then we'd better go up on the bluff. That's where the foreign section used to be, and that's still probably the best place to look for a restaurant that'll serve Americans." Altmeyer stepped out into the street and waved his arm at a taxi that was whining up the long incline toward them.

As Rachel sauntered after him she said, "It's going to be a restaurant where I can get a steak from one of those steers that they raise on hot food and give massages to every day. I don't care if it comes from Kobe or Kansas, just so it's big."

Altmeyer stepped aside as the door of the taxi popped

open, then leaned down to brush his lips against Rachel's cheek as she entered the cab. "You're full of surprises."

"Not if you keep your eyes open."

As THEY WALKED out of the restaurant at the top of the bluff and approached the waiting taxi, Altmeyer stopped to stare down at the harbor, his head cocked as though he were trying to line up the lights below with a space between two manicured shrubs across the road.

Bucky and Rachel sat in the cab watching as he stepped quickly across the street to join them. He sat beside the driver and pointed his finger down at the harbor, smiling and nodding.

"Nice view from up here at night," said Bucky. "Lots of lights on the water." Then he added, "That doesn't mean I want to go rowing."

"They moved it," said Altmeyer.

"Moved what?" Rachel asked.

"The ship." Altmeyer sat tapping his fingers on his knees, as though impatient to get down the hill. "While we were eating they moved the ship to the next pier."

"Are you sure?"

They could see Altmeyer's head nodding in the dim light.

As the cab reached the bottom of the slope and bounced upward across the first intersection, Altmeyer waved his hand and pointed toward the brightly lighted window of a bar in the next block, where a crowd of men in suits seemed to be collecting.

The driver stopped and said something in Japanese, but Altmeyer nodded and smiled in a pantomime of dumb incomprehension until he gave up. Altmeyer handed him a few bills, and said, "I know, pal. No foreigners allowed, private club and all that." As he stepped into the street, he said, "Happy trails."

After the taxi turned the corner and slipped out of sight, Altmeyer ushered Bucky and Rachel along the street toward the harbor, walking quickly. He glanced at his watch, and seemed to walk faster. Rachel could feel the flat of his hand exerting a firm, gentle pressure between her shoulder blades.

As they turned the next corner they could see the short, black ship moored at the pier where they had stood that afternoon. The concrete platform was bathed in the bright yellow light of sodium flood lamps mounted along the eaves of the low hangarlike building on the pier. Already there were four stacks of cargo containers three deep on the wharf, and above them, another container dangling from the cable.

"What now?" said Bucky. "Can you recognize the container with the cotton in it?"

"They all have cotton," Altmeyer said. "The hold is full of fish in freezer compartments. What we want won't be here. Take a look at those guys unloading."

Rachel said, "They're not the same ones who were here before. The others were wearing green jump suits."

"What we want will be at the next pier. I should have figured it out before." They walked along the jetty, staying away from the glare of the lights.

When they were still a hundred yards from the rear of the warehouse that dominated the next pier, Altmeyer stopped and pulled them back into the shadow of a huge coil of steel cable that sat among some large, empty crates. Altmeyer whispered, "Do you see the car?"

Bucky peered down the road, where a black car sat behind the warehouse. He nodded.

Altmeyer said quietly, "It's got to be one of Nagata's bosses, Bridges, Walker, or Bone."

Bucky turned to Rachel. "Is he serious?"

"It's what they called themselves," said Rachel. "Nagata seems to be their interpreter."

Altmeyer spoke quickly. "That car can't carry a ton of metal, so there will be a truck inside for the guns. Rachel, you're in charge of the truck. When it comes by here, get anything you can: a license number, anything you can read, but stay invisible."

"Okay."

"Bucky, you're in charge of the area around the car. That includes the door of the warehouse. If the first head to pop out isn't mine, put a bullet into it, come back for Rachel, and try to make your way back to the train station. The last Tokyo train pulls out at twelve thirty. If you miss it or can't get to it, wait them out. They won't look very hard for you, because they can't hang around here with the guns." Without waiting for an answer, Altmeyer moved off in the darkness.

Bucky whispered, "Wait," but Altmeyer was already too far away. Bucky said, "I hate this. It's a lousy plan, and I don't even know what it is, except that I'm supposed to shoot people."

"Quiet," Rachel whispered. "Let's go."

"But he said you had to stay here."

"He meant 'here' in the larger sense. Come on."

The two followed in the direction Altmeyer had taken, moving quietly toward the warehouse in the darkness. Ahead of them there was a sudden splash of light as a door opened and a man's silhouette appeared in the doorway, and then the light vanished.

ALTMEYER CLOSED THE DOOR GENTLY, sidestepped behind a row of plywood boxes on wooden pallets, and stopped to listen. There were voices in the warehouse speaking rapidly in Japanese—were they angry, alarmed? He waited for two minutes, but the tone didn't seem to change, and the speakers were still a distance from him. But there was another sound in the background, like a small engine. Could it be a forklift for moving these boxes?

He felt reluctant to move from the door, but if there were a forklift, he couldn't wait for it. Slowly he worked his way down a row of boxes, stepping on the surfaces of the wooden pallets so his feet couldn't be seen under them.

As he reached the end of the row, Altmeyer stopped. There was the hollow, metallic slamming of a door. The forklift vanished from his mind and was replaced by a small truck.

106

He heard another door slam, and then a scraping sound, as though a bolt were being pushed into place in a metal track. He had to look now, he knew.

He looked through the crack between the last two boxes just as the electric motor lifted a wide garage door and three men in green coveralls climbed into the bed of a truck and then pulled the sliding door shut behind them. As they hauled it down, he saw another pair of feet step from the dark recesses near the front to help them. A man on the outside waved a hand, and the truck moved out into the night. Altmeyer squinted to see the truck more clearly, but all he could make out was the corrugated steel cargo door, and a black bumper, and then it was gone. He pulled back and waited, resting against the box. There had been a dozen men that afternoon on the dock. Both doors of the cab had slammed, so at least six had gone in the truck.

Altmeyer listened as the electric motor closed the warehouse door. The talking began again, and moved closer to him. Now he could hear footsteps, two or three sets of soft, muffled steps that could be work boots. Next there was a tapping step, louder than the others, and sharper, like the leather soles of street shoes. Altmeyer heard the steps veer toward the seaward end of the warehouse. He knew it was time to look again, while their backs were turned, so he crawled back to the end of the row of boxes and moved his head out far enough at floor level to give his left eye a clear view.

He pulled back. They were moving to a cargo container, and he could see it was open. He extracted his little pistol from his coat, checked the clip, and screwed the silencer onto the barrel. Beneath the broad wall of the cargo container, the floor was littered with scraps of brown burlap, gleaming metal bands, and mounds of bright white cotton. He studied the image with his eyes closed. There had been five of them, walking toward the container. He hadn't seen any of the guns. Nobody would do physical work with a two-pound pistol stuck in his belt. One of them, dressed in a suit, wasn't doing much, so he was the one to watch. Altmeyer could hear them talking

107

again. He stood up slowly, clutched his pistol in his armpit so that the coat concealed it, and stepped onto the floor.

Altmeyer walked seven steps, watching them stuff cotton into brown industrial drums, before one of the men in green seemed to catch the movement in his peripheral vision. The man was bent over and both arms were full of cotton, and his head jerked to the side no more than an inch. He stood up, pretending he had seen nothing, staring at one of his companions as though waiting for him to see. The second man seemed to sense his agitation, and looked up at Altmeyer. He spoke, and then all of them turned.

"Good evening, Mr. Nagata," Altmeyer called, still walking toward them. It had to be close, he thought. At more than fifteen feet the .22 bullet might not do much, and a Browning nine-millimeter would take him apart. "I was hoping it would be you so we could talk."

"Altmeyer." Nagata spoke more loudly than usual, but without apparent surprise.

"I just thought I'd drop by to see that you got everything on schedule. But I guess you got it a day early, didn't you?"

"And where is your associate, Miss Ralph Waldo Emerson?" asked Nagata. Altmeyer listened to the voice. Maybe Nagata was startled, maybe he was just used to shouting orders in a big empty warehouse, but probably not. Altmeyer dropped to one knee and rolled as the shot roared behind him.

He snatched the pistol from under his arm and fired at the only shape he could see, a man in a gray suit. The little automatic made a harsh, spitting sound and the man crumpled, but Altmeyer fired twice more into the body as he scrambled to his feet and ran. He dashed as fast as he could directly toward the five men. He knew it was the only move that could give him any advantage. As one reached inside his coveralls, Altmeyer fired into his chest. Another ran around toward the rear of the cargo container, but Altmeyer was directly behind him, the silencer nearly touching the back of his head when Altmeyer fired. As the man sprawled in front of him, Altmeyer saw another appear at the far end of the cargo container and stop. The man had time to raise a pistol a little above his belt before Altmeyer fired again.

Altmeyer kept running, firing once into the man's head as he passed him. At the corner of the container he stopped and replaced the clip in his pistol. He breathed as quietly as he could, but the gasps seemed to grow louder. There was a ringing in his ears, and he strained to hear any sound. He glanced down at the body at his feet, then kicked at the dead man's pistol. To some part of his mind the pistol was a surprise, but he decided to think about it later.

Then he heard the door on the other side of the warehouse swing open, and there were five or six spitting sounds, a shout, and then silence.

Bucky sat on the ground behind the trunk of the black car and slipped another clip into the pistol, but the weight of the old clip in his shaking hand told him it wasn't empty. Then he remembered he'd squeezed the trigger only three or four times when the door had opened. Everything had surprised him. The noise of the shots was loud, seeming to come from the breech, not the barrel, with the little gun spitting orange sparks that lit the shining surface of the car for an instant and seemed to stop the two men in motion and hold them as though it had been the pop of a photographer's flashbulb.

He struggled to get his legs under him, then pushed himself to his feet, using the car to steady him. Then he remembered that he was still holding the ammunition clip, so he slipped it into his coat pocket.

As he turned, he saw a dark shape appear beside him, and Rachel's voice whispered, "Oh God, hurry up. They shouldn't have been the ones. It should have been him."

She ran toward the open doorway, and Bucky followed. As he came around the car he could see that the door was held open by one of the bodies, a man in a dark suit who appeared to have stopped in the act of crawling out of the warehouse on his belly.

109

Rachel pushed the door a foot farther and moved in past the body as though she hadn't seen it. Bucky hesitated in the doorway, looking down at the shape on the ground. It was like a barrier that he couldn't step over. It looked as though it might move if he tried, the outstretched arms reaching up suddenly to grab his ankle. He blew out a breath and sidestepped past it into the lighted space of the warehouse, his eyes flitting from side to side, desperately trying to see it all at once.

There were big wooden boxes, and bright lights hanging on long cords from the beams of the roof, a few barely visible wisps of gray smoke drifting beneath the nearest one, but there didn't seem to be anyone standing up.

Bucky moved to the left to slip behind a row of boxes, but the space was too narrow. He moved to the right, and his eye caught a man in a gray suit lying on the floor. Bucky raised his pistol in a reflex and aimed at the man, but as his arm came up he saw that the man was lying on his back in a pool of blood.

Bucky scanned the room quickly, his pistol raised, his knees bent because that was the only way they seemed to work, his legs flexed to run or jump. He saw more bodies, shapes in green suits sprawled on the floor at odd angles as though they'd been thrown there.

Near them was a big, blue cargo container like the ones he'd seen at the other pier. He came forward a few steps, moving toward it along the wall, and then he spotted Rachel. She was moving parallel with him along the opposite wall, behind the long row of boxes. Of course, he thought. She's small. He moved forward more quickly to bring himself even with her, trying to keep from making noise.

It was then that he heard the voice. It came from behind the blue cargo container, and it seemed to increase its volume at each word. "Seventeen. Eighteen. Nineteen. Twenty. Damn."

Then Rachel was running across the open floor. "Altmeyer! Are you okay? Answer me."

The voice said, "Yeah. Fine," and Altmeyer appeared at

the end of the cargo container, his arms held out to embrace Rachel.

Bucky didn't hear what they were saying to each other. He began to walk toward them, then realized that there was something else that was bothering him. He turned and walked back to the doorway, bent down, and grabbed the ankles of the man in the suit. He hauled the body inside, then pulled the door shut.

Bucky walked back to the cargo container, where Altmeyer was saying to Rachel, "See? All of the bales we marked with the crimper are still here. They didn't even bother to open one or two to see if we'd cheated them."

Bucky said, "God, what a mess. What happened?" He looked down at the body of a man with blood coming out of the back of his head.

"Them?" said Altmeyer. "A complete screw-up. The one over there just opened up on me. Once it started it couldn't be helped."

"I suppose not," Bucky said without conviction. He looked around him. "Let's get out of here."

"We've got some time," said Altmeyer. "Everything they'd planned to do tonight seems to be done, and we've got to look around now or we'll never know."

Altmeyer pointed at the mound of cotton and cloth a few yards away. "See? They brought the container in here, opened a couple of bales of cotton, and drove a truck out of here. But they weren't interested in the ones we packed with guns."

"Fine," said Bucky. "Neither am I. Let's go home."

Rachel ignored him, and walked toward the container. "What do you think it was? Drugs?"

"It's possible, but I doubt it," said Altmeyer, staring up at the bales in the open cargo container. "This wouldn't be such a bad way of shipping, but Japan's not as good a market as the United States."

Bucky walked after them. "What are you two talking about?"

111

Rachel turned to him, her eyes tired and angry. "They used us. They found a little fish that lives by swimming in and out of the net, and made sure he did it in the right place and the right time, so a big fish could swim through after him."

"Okay. I think I see it in spite of the damned fish," said Bucky. "They bought the guns from you because they wanted to smuggle something else in. They knew you must have a good way of doing it, so they just waited and packed their stuff in with yours."

Rachel sighed. "That's what it looks like. There were fifty bales, including the twenty with the guns in them. They may have wanted the guns, but not as much as whatever was in these three bales."

"But it would have to be worth more than the two million they were paying for the guns," Bucky said.

"Maybe much more. Even if they were never planning to pay us, they still cared about it more than the guns."

Altmeyer was now staring at the cotton on the floor, examining the torn burlap wrappings and the steel bands.

Bucky continued. "And it was packed in three thousand-pound bales, so it might have weighed a lot."

"Right," said Rachel. "If they could have used one, they probably would have. If they packed it the way we packed the guns, it would be three hundred pounds, but it could be nearly ten times that."

Bucky surveyed the warehouse. "What a disaster," he said. "It looks like a war. I can't help wishing—"

They both noticed Altmeyer at the same time. He was sitting on the floor on the far side of the mound of cotton. Beside him was a toolbox. On the floor were the long-handled shears the men had used to cut the steel bands, three knives for opening the bales, and he was taking something out of a larger box on the floor.

He spoke quietly, barely above a whisper. "Oh damn. Oh damn." He was holding it in his lap now, a small metal rectangle with dials and knobs and a long cord. He seemed to

112

forget himself, rocking forward and back slightly without being conscious of it as he stared down at the small yellow box.

"What is it?" called Rachel. "A tape recorder?"

When Altmeyer raised his eyes to her they seemed to be all whites, wide open and empty as though they were looking at something much closer to him than she was. "It's a Geiger counter."

BUCKY FELT A PRESSURE in his ears, a sound like marbles rolling and clicking together in a jar. He gulped and opened his jaw wide, and the sound seemed to grow louder. His eyes were on Altmeyer, who sat gazing up at Rachel. The two didn't seem to move for a long time. At one moment he had the impression that they were diminishing into the distance, and then he noticed that he had been stepping backward away from them. He turned to keep from falling, then sometime later was aware that he was still walking, wandering aimlessly in the cavernous empty space of the warehouse. When he passed by the door he rediscovered the man in the dark suit lying face down on the floor. Bucky stood over the inert form, staring down at it.

He tried to exert some control over his feelings and make them into thoughts, but the only one he could identify was an impulse to roll the body over and look at the face. With the urge, he remembered firing twice at the head, so there could be nothing there except some palpable horror that would stay with him into the future if he let himself look. He walked on, crossing the broad, empty floor several times. Suddenly he identified another vague longing, like an appetite. He didn't want to be alone anymore.

"Jesus," said Bucky. He sat down heavily on the floor beside Altmeyer. He stared at his pistol as though he were surprised to see it in his hand, then set it down beside him and rubbed his face with both hands. "I can't believe it. I mean, there isn't any other reason to have a Geiger counter?"

113

Altmeyer looked at Rachel. "Can you think of one?"

"But that doesn't mean—"

Altmeyer stood up. "Right now I don't want to think about that." He was already walking toward the dead man in the middle of the floor, still talking. "Look for the one with the keys to that car out there." As he bent over the body, patting the pockets, he added, "While you're at it, take wallets, papers, everything."

Bucky crawled forward and pushed off the floor to his knees, then staggered to his feet and walked toward the man in green who lay beside the mound of cotton. Bucky was sweating, but he didn't feel exertion, only occasional waves of heat that seemed to wash up his spine to his neck and along the sides of his face to his hairline.

As he knelt beside the body, he wondered why he wasn't asking Altmeyer questions. He patted the chest and sides, then rolled the body over and extracted the wallet and put it in his coat pocket, then walked deliberately toward the next body. It didn't matter, he decided. That was why he wasn't asking: he didn't exactly care about knowing. This was what was happening, the search for keys and wallets. Another time something else would be happening. Then he noticed that he wasn't afraid. He thought about it as he worked on the next body. This is the lowest, he thought, but his mind didn't have the energy to qualify the thought. This is the lowest. He unzipped the neck of the next set of coveralls far enough to see that there was no shirt underneath, only the hairless chest.

"This is probably it," Altmeyer called from the doorway.

Bucky acknowledged it in his mind. Of course. The ones who had been running toward the car would have the keys.

"I'll bring the car around to the side," Altmeyer said. "Rachel, you see if you can get that garage door open. I think the control box is to the right of it somewhere." Then he went outside, and Bucky saw Rachel move toward the garage door.

He heard the door open, and heard the motor of the black car as it coasted into the warehouse, but he didn't watch.

"Come on, Bucky," called Altmeyer. "Lend a hand."

114

Bucky walked to the cargo container, where Altmeyer was standing with the toolbox. Altmeyer picked up the long metal shears and said, "There's no reason to be neat or careful about this. We just clip them open, tear our way to the guns, and leave everything where it falls. Let those bastards worry about cleaning up if it bothers them."

He snipped a metal band, cut through the cloth wrapping, then dug into the cotton to the box containing the guns. "Okay, Bucky. Help me pull it out." The two men hauled the heavy box out of its place in the cotton bale and set it on the floor. Altmeyer examined the next bale, running his fingers along the metal clasp on the band to feel for the mark of the altered crimper, then picked up the long-handled metal cutters. The tightly clasped bands gave an audible pop when they broke and sprung open with a twang. Bucky dug through the cotton quickly, and then the two men tugged the box out and lifted it to the floor. After they'd opened five bales, Altmeyer stepped back. "How's it going, Rachel?"

Bucky turned to see that the first two boxes had been opened. From somewhere in the distance he heard Rachel call, "I'm running out of ideas. Can you come here for a second? Bring a box."

Bucky and Altmeyer lifted a box together and carried it around the cargo container and across the floor to the other side of the warehouse, where Rachel waited. She was standing on a crate with her shoes off, peering down at the place where the paneling that covered the lower parts of the wall ended. The two men set the box down and Altmeyer climbed up beside her.

Altmeyer looked along the top edge of the line of panels. "It'll work for some, maybe four or five boxes. We'll just drop them along the top, and the insulation ought to stop them about halfway down. Bucky, open the box."

Bucky tore open the box, dug through the plastic padding, and handed Altmeyer a pistol, still wrapped in cloth. Altmeyer reached to the space between the panel and the wall, dropped the pistol, and listened. "It only fell a couple of feet," he said. "Perfect. We'll get a couple more boxes over here, and you can get started." He jumped to the floor, walked a few paces, then seemed to remember Bucky.

"Come on," said Altmeyer. When Bucky caught up with him, Altmeyer gently patted him on the back and said, "I know this doesn't make any sense right now."

Bucky shrugged. "It doesn't matter if it does or not."

Altmeyer watched him as they walked toward the cargo container. "Have you ever been in shock before, Bucky?"

Bucky glanced at him and heard himself laugh. "Not before I met you." Then he added, "I'll be okay."

Altmeyer patted his shoulder. "Sure you will. We all will. It's going to be a long night, though."

"Okay," said Bucky, without interest.

They faced each other as they prepared to lift the next box. Altmeyer said, "We'll only be able to hide about six or seven boxes around here, and take about three with us in the car to bury somewhere. The rest, I'm afraid, we'll have to dump in the harbor under the pier."

They walked toward the other side of the warehouse, where Rachel was dropping pistols, one by one, between the outer wall and the siding that covered it. Bucky said, "It doesn't matter. It's all a disaster."

Altmeyer's voice was calm and quiet. "Hold out. All we've got is the rest of the night to do whatever we're going to do here. After that we might never get the chance again. We're not doing this because it's such a great thing to do. We're doing it because at the moment it's all there is to do."

"What does it accomplish?"

"Here," said Altmeyer, and they lowered the box. He tore it open and began pulling out guns. "Probably not a hell of a lot. We stash a few here and there, so we know where they are and nobody else does. That gives us a little edge. We destroy the ones we can't hide—the salt water will turn them into little lumps of rust in a few months—and that takes a little of the edge away from this bunch of deadbeats."

Bucky looked around at the corpses sprawled on the floor. "Deadbeats."

Altmeyer kicked the box aside and started back for the next one. "You run into them sometimes in any business. Sometimes all you can do is repossess."

RACHEL AWOKE and stared up at the ceiling. It seemed to be evening, but beyond the thick double curtains there might be searing afternoon sunlight. She closed her eyes again, and the images came back to her. There was the clear, vast harbor, and all of that cotton, so much of it that she thought of it as measured in hours. They had torn into the bales, at first leaving them where they lay, until the sheer bulk of them had made it impossible to reach the next one, and Altmeyer had used the car to push them aside. There had been so many dead men— five or six, at least—like dolls thrown across a room to lie there, arms and legs limp and turned in unlikely directions. After that she remembered Altmeyer and Bucky dumping guns into the water at the end of the pier. Then there was the long ride in the dark, lying on the backseat of the car and watching the lights from other cars flashing across the upholstery on the roof.

Before dawn she had been awake twice more. Once Altmeyer and Bucky had been standing in a garden repairing a little dike so the water would run in again and cover the place where they had dug. The second time was when they'd had to walk to the railroad station at Fujisawa.

Now she was awake again. Beside her, Altmeyer breathed in deeply, and she waited for him to exhale. After a few seconds he gave two loud snorts, then the air wheezed out in a long, labored hiss.

Today, Rachel was almost sure. Maybe today was the day to tell him. If only there were doctors here. She smiled at the words. Of course there were doctors here, but she couldn't go to one, because of the rest of it. People were going to be

117

looking for them soon. The test took time—was it twenty-four hours or forty-eight hours? By then someone would have gone back to the warehouse on the pier.

She turned her head to look at Altmeyer. She wanted to see his peaceful, empty face on the pillow. She raised herself up on her elbow and looked down at him. His brow was furrowed and his jaw was clenched. As she watched, he ground his teeth, making a clicking sound.

He would wake himself up soon. He was thinking about the trouble already, and when he awoke he'd already be consumed by it, making plans and moving around too fast to listen. "You bastard," she thought. "Why couldn't we be like other people?" As she thought the words, the sadness she had been putting off seemed to overpower her resistance. It was too late to be like other people. Other people could wake up in a hotel room and know what day it was and when they were going home. Then Rachel thought, "I could leave."

She looked down at him and the tears came. The corners of her mouth stiffened involuntarily, and she began to weep. The thought of it was impossible. She felt ashamed, and angry at him, and drawn to him by an attraction so strong it obliterated everything else.

Once in awhile, when Rachel was driving a car, or buying something in a shop, or even making dinner, she saw herself from the vantage of the past. She would remember being a little girl, watching adults doing those things, and wanting to grow up and do them, too. As she performed the routine and simple actions, she would see herself doing them as the child Rachel would see, and she felt happy. Sometimes after making love, she would lie back and think about little Rachel, wishing that the little girl could have seen Altmeyer's hard, sinewy body, and known about the gentleness and the feeling of security, and known that she would be loved that way, that there was nothing to worry about. After the missed proms and the horror of the first dates when she could think of nothing to say to fill the tense silences, there would be Altmeyer.

For most of her life she had been waiting to test this feeling against the expectations of little Rachel. This was one of the things little Rachel had wanted most passionately, and wondered about, and worried about. Now she was almost sure, but she wasn't ready to let it be true officially. If she let it be said aloud and acknowledged, the moment would be forever what it was now. This wasn't the time.

Altmeyer's eyelids blinked, then stayed open. His face was already set in its expression, the eyes bright and alert. "Hi, baby," he said. "Get any sleep?"

"More than any girl needs." She leaned over and pressed her lips to his.

ALTMEYER SAT NAKED at the table, separating the Japanese bank notes from the licenses and identification cards. "It's a shame to have to throw away all this money."

"Why would you do that?" said Rachel. She stopped brushing her hair and looked at him.

"When we get to the airport the customs people will want to count our cash. You can't take more than a hundred thousand yen out of the country, and for all we know the serial numbers may be on somebody's list. We'll have enough to hide as it is."

"I thought we got rid of all the guns."

"We did. The ones we brought are buried with the others out on the farm. But we'll need to take all the licenses and things with us. They're the best way we have of figuring out what's going on. While I'm in the shower, will you run down to the gift shop and buy me a couple of decks of cards? Make sure they have cellophane wrappers."

"Okay," said Rachel. "Then you're going to tell me what's going on, aren't you?"

"Sure," said Altmeyer, staring at the kanji characters on a business card in the palm of his hand. "I'm going to open one of the decks, put this stuff inside, and reseal the wrapper

119

with a hot knife. The other one I'm going to bring with me on the plane to play gin with you and Bucky. The guy's a wreck, so we can probably beat him without much trouble."

"Care to tell me what plane?"

Altmeyer looked up. "You know we can't go home. They'd find us in a couple of days. Bucky wouldn't last a week."

"Where, then?"

His eyes lowered to the stack of documents, and he muttered, "Brussels."

"Any particular reason, or did you just wake up and think of Brussels?"

Altmeyer stood up and walked toward her, smiling. "I'm sorry. I know we should have talked about it, but you were asleep at the time, and there isn't much choice anyway. It has to be a place where the customs people don't look too closely, and a place where I know a few people—"

Rachel interrupted. "Those two always seem to go together, don't they?" She didn't wait for the answer, but walked out and closed the door behind her.

Altmeyer stared at the door for a moment, then walked toward the bathroom. He quickly washed himself in the shower and then stepped out into the deep Japanese bath, pondering Rachel. In a few hours they'd be on the Sabena 747 heading on the polar route for Zaventem airport. Maybe that would calm her nerves a little bit.

Rachel's problem was that she hadn't learned how to control her thinking. Right now it was time to consider what they could do to stay out of danger for the next few days. It wasn't time yet to think about the other problem. First you get out. That was always the rule. Bring in your merchandise, try to collect if you can, but in any case, get the hell out before either side thinks to stop you. The time to look back was when you'd crossed the border. Anybody who stopped to look before that was liable to find his ass turned to salt, like Lot's wife.

Altmeyer held his breath and sank down under the water. The main thing was to move a little faster than the other man, and the only way that could happen was if you concentrated on what you were going to do to him, not what you thought about it. When Altmeyer's chest began to feel tight, he exhaled a few bubbles of air, then raised his head above the surface for another breath and opened his eyes.

He climbed out of the sunken bath and reached for a towel, angry at himself. Just now, in the water, had been about the tenth time in the past eight hours he'd let himself see it. He'd closed his eyes, and in the darkness he'd let an image from a film he'd seen replay itself. In the film there was a blinding flash of light that made the whole screen white for several seconds, then receded into a glow at the center. Then there was a shape like the splash of a round object falling into water. It gave a single abrupt shudder and then, instead of falling, expanded upward and blossomed into a mushroom cloud.

BRUSSELS

"*C'est moi, Altmeyer. Oui.*" He listened, then said, "*Non. Ce n'est pas bon. J'aimerez cette fois quelquechose—*"

He paused again, then said, "*Oui. Rue de l'Étuve, vers le Manneken-Pis. Merci.*" Altmeyer hung the telephone in its cradle,

"Your friend only speaks French?" said Bucky.

"No, that was his brother, Bernard. I'm meeting Paul down the street from here in an hour. Paul isn't somebody you can reach directly."

"That's an endearing trait," Rachel said. "I don't remember hearing anything about Paul." She turned to Bucky. "Maybe he can't be talked about directly, either. I guess you have to talk about his brother, Bernard, and then wait an hour."

Altmeyer shook his head. "I haven't done business with him in the last couple of years. That's one reason he's the one I want to see right now. He may be able to help us without anyone making the connection."

"What sort of man is he?" asked Rachel. "Is he a friend? Do you trust him?"

Altmeyer put on his coat, then tugged at his shirt cuffs. "I trust him to hide us for awhile. He does that sort of thing

125

very well, and at the moment it's all we need. He can trust me to pay him for it."

Bucky said, "I don't think that's what she meant."

Altmeyer's face was expressionless. "I know what she meant. You two have been talking."

ALTMEYER CROSSED THE SQUARE, his eyes scanning the crowds of tourists surrounding the Manneken-Pis. The chubby little bronze cherub gazed intently downward, carefully aiming his perpetual urination into the basin of the fountain, oblivious to the dozens of cameras clicking around him.

The voice came from behind Altmeyer. "A tourist, Altmeyer?"

Altmeyer turned and walked in the other direction, and the tall, thin man fell into step with him. Altmeyer said, "He reminds me of a friend of mine. You'll get to meet him."

Paul Mazarin said, "Perhaps. It's surprisingly warm today, isn't it?"

"I want to drop out of sight. There will be three of us."

"Will there?"

"A thousand a day, American."

"Done." Mazarin glanced down at Altmeyer, then turned his eyes ahead. "Is there a price on you?"

Altmeyer smiled. "It wouldn't be worth your trouble, old friend. These people don't understand business."

Mazarin's long, thin hand touched Altmeyer's arm and held him while a battered green Citroën moved past. Then Mazarin gave the arm a pat, and they trotted across the Rue du Lombard. Altmeyer could see the gothic spire of the Hotel de Ville in the Grand' Place at the end of the street.

Mazarin walked on. "That's always the danger of trying to work in retail. Most of your customers are amateurs."

Altmeyer let his silence signal agreement.

"Are the others nearby?"

"Very near. They're in a cafe in the Grand' Place."

"How expensive do you want the arrangements to be?"

"Careful, but nothing too elaborate," said Altmeyer. "It's possible that they can figure out that we came to Brussels."

"I need to drive to Rotterdam two or three days from now. If you come along, it interrupts the trail a little bit. After that you can decide where you want to come to the surface. Anything else?" He held Altmeyer in the corner of his eye as they walked.

"We'll meet you in two hours in front of Notre Dame du Sablon."

"Why the delay?"

"I'd like to go to a bank now, before I go under."

Mazarin nodded, his eyes half closed. "Of course. Altmeyer never forgets the details. In two hours, then. That will give you time to decide what you want to tell me about your troubles. I assume your luggage is still at the airport?"

"Yes," said Altmeyer.

"I'll take the claim checks. That will give me something to do." He accepted them and started to walk away, then stopped. "Your bags—"

"No," said Altmeyer. "There's only clothes."

"Good," Mazarin said. "Then I can sell you something for once."

BUCKY STARED DOWN at the table and fingered the small silver spoon beside his cup. "You're sort of an odd pair, you and Altmeyer."

"Together, or each by ourselves?" Rachel managed a small smile, but Bucky didn't look up to see it.

"I'm sorry. For the last few days, everything I do, I feel as though the air around me has turned into Jell-O. I wanted to ask you how you met, but I guess what I really wondered is bigger than that."

"We were both at a party. It was a hot, sticky night, and the place was terribly crowded, but there was a little balcony and we both went out there to have a cigarette at the same time. Isn't that nice and dull?"

"And then he said, 'I'm a gunrunner. Come live with me and be my love?' Or did he give you the usual 'I'm a businessman, and you know that's too boring to talk about'?"

Rachel laughed. "If you must know, he was the businessman that night, and every night until I made him trust me. We were very cautious with each other, but we were in love in a way that's hard to describe. That first night I almost said out loud, 'So here you are.' " She frowned. "But at the same time, I took a good look at him and something told me not to cancel the lease on my apartment. I could see his nose had been broken at least once, and that's a bad sign in a potential husband unless you know for sure he was a linebacker for an Ivy League school. My mother told me that."

Bucky looked up from his cup. "She's a smart woman. But he charmed you into it, one step at a time, and here you are."

Rachel shook her head. "Of course not. Altmeyer isn't charming. I guess what you'd call him is magnetic. You know he's doing something, moving in some direction, and when he happens to go by you he doesn't even seem to slow down, but he takes you with him. Since then we've spent most of our time finding clever ways into Afghanistan and being in love. This scheme was supposed to be our Going Out of Business Sale. Instead—"

"Instead it's a Going Out of Existence Sale. I'd make a will, but there may not be anyone around to be left out of it."

"We don't know anything yet, and Altmeyer has been in trouble before."

"I guess that's what I was trying to ask you. It was about him. What is he thinking?"

"He's lived through some things—a lot of them before I knew him," she began, and hesitated. "They made him learn to think differently. He doesn't spend time describing things to himself in different ways so he'll understand them. He thinks about what he's going to do about them."

"Suppose he decides it's okay to let these people start

blowing up chunks of the world because there's no money in stopping them?"

"Then he'll give himself other reasons. He wouldn't like anyone to think he was risking his life for a cause. Right now someone is trying to kill his wife, and that makes him very angry."

"What if he gets over that?"

"Then," said Rachel brightly, "we can go home and forget that those people used to be alive."

ALTMEYER FOUND Bucky and Rachel at their table in the outdoor cafe in the Grand' Place. As he approached, they both started to stand up, but Altmeyer said, "If you see a waiter, order me an espresso. This will take a few minutes."

Rachel asked, "How did it go?"

Altmeyer sat down and opened the deck of cards from the Imperial Hotel. "Pretty well. He can keep us invisible for a few days in Rotterdam. After that, we can turn up practically anywhere." Altmeyer shook the pack of papers out into his palm, selected a few, and replaced the others.

When the waiter moved off with their order, Altmeyer took out a folded piece of paper and began to copy Japanese characters onto it.

Rachel watched him for a moment, then said, "It looks like you need help. You left off one of those cross-bars on the third one. It might mean something different."

"You're right," said Altmeyer, squinting at the paper. He handed it to Rachel. "From this card, copy this line here." He pointed his finger at it. "That's got to be the name of a company of some kind. Four of those guys had paper with that set of characters on them. And take the line under it, too. That must be an address or something."

"No," said Bucky. "Over here is one with numbers in it. That must be the address."

"Maybe. We'll find out. It's not his name. That's got to

be this line in the middle. We'll skip the names for now. I just wanted to know what these guys had in common."

Rachel looked up from her work. "You mean Paul got you a translator?"

Altmeyer shook his head. "We don't need him. About half a mile from here is Berlaymont, which is the headquarters of the European Economic Community. Brussels is full of diplomats and trade delegations and foreign businessmen. It shouldn't be too hard to find somebody who can read five or six lines of Japanese."

"Okay," said Rachel. "I'm finished." She pushed the paper and the card across the table to him.

Altmeyer compared the paper and the card. "Good. We've got less than two hours to take care of this. Give me any leftover Japanese yen you have."

ALTMEYER WALKED into the Banque Commercial Shikoku and scanned the faces of the employees in the tellers' windows. They were all Belgians. He moved across the polished marble floor toward the cubicles where the managers and accountants worked, and noticed a few Japanese faces. He stopped at a counter bristling with pens on gold chains, and counted his stack of Japanese bills. Finally one of the Japanese faces appeared at a teller's window. It was a young man with the look of a trainee. He was dressed a little better than the older men, with a crisp white collar and a dark blue suit that looked as though he'd had it tailored in a shop he couldn't afford.

Altmeyer stepped quickly to the window and said, *"Je voudrais echanger ces yen Japonnais, s'il vous plait."*

"Certainement," said the young man. As he consulted a computer terminal for the exchange rate, Altmeyer congratulated himself. The man's accent was so thick that it was possible he would mistake Altmeyer for a Belgian.

The young man counted the bills, then counted out a pile of Belgian francs beside it, smiled, and gave a perfunctory nod to indicate that the transaction was completed.

130

Altmeyer picked up the Belgian money and began to put it into his wallet, leaning away as though to start toward the door, but then looked back. *"Monsieur,"* he said. *"Ily à une autre chose. Peut-être, parceque vous êtes un Japonnais—"* He knitted his brows apologetically.

The young man leaned forward, eager to help. *"Oui?"*

"Si vous pouvez à lire ce papier pour moi—" He pulled out the sheet that Rachel had copied at the cafe, and studied the young man as he scrutinized it.

The young man's smile seemed to grow. *"Ce n'est qu'un fournisseur d'équipement électronique."*

"Et le nomme?"

"C'est 'Ashita.' C'est à dire 'demain.'"

"Merci," said Altmeyer, and moved from the window to make way for a lady who had been waiting. As he left the bank, he wondered. The young man had said, *fournisseur,* or dealer, not manufacturer. Did the distinction matter to him, or was it only lost in the confusion of languages?

Altmeyer glanced at his watch. It had taken only five minutes. As he walked on, he saw Bucky and Rachel coming down the street toward him. They were easy to pick out at a distance. Bucky's chubby body moved from side to side as the thick, short legs pumped along with the feet pointed outward a little. Rachel, an inch or two taller, seemed to stride along without effort, her head up and her steps steady and even. It was as though they were moving at different speeds. Altmeyer held up his hand, and they stopped to wait for him.

"Did you get us the American money for Mazarin?" asked Altmeyer.

"Of course," Rachel said. "They don't call him Buck-meister Carmichael in these parts for nothing. How did you do?"

Altmeyer started to walk. "We're ahead of schedule. We can see the inside of the church if we get there soon enough."

Bucky asked Rachel, "Is he being mysterious, or is it bad news?"

Altmeyer answered, "I don't know much, but what I know

131

sounds terrible. The deadbeats worked for a Japanese electronics company called 'Ashita.' At least they were carrying paper that said they did."

They were all silent for a dozen paces. When they came around the corner Bucky said quietly, "It fits, doesn't it? What government in the world is least likely to want an atomic bomb? Japan. So that leaves the field completely open for private enterprise, with no unfair competition. The technology is about forty years old. I suppose a company that makes electronic stuff now must be up to that. I just wonder what they plan to do with it."

Altmeyer shrugged. "What does anybody else do with them? Scare the shit out of people."

"Altmeyer," said Rachel. "I think it's time for you to formulate a plan."

"A plan? A plan for what?"

Bucky answered. "We're wasting our time screwing around here in this outdoor museum. We have to assume that a big electronics company is capable of making a bomb. We can't let them do that, so we'll need a plan."

Altmeyer snorted. "What the hell are you talking about? Bucky, this isn't your field."

"No, but it's your field, and I'll do what I have to, if you'll figure out what that is. Suppose we did something to the head man—Mr. Ashita himself?"

"Ashita isn't somebody's name. It means 'tomorrow' in Japanese."

They walked on, Altmeyer a half pace ahead, weaving at times to make way for other people approaching on the old, narrow sidewalk. Then Altmeyer stepped off the curb and waved his hand at a gray stone structure before them. "There it is, Notre Dame du Sablon. At least take a look at it while you're here." He threaded his way through a straggling queue of old men and women moving across the front of the church and speaking to one another in German, then sat down on the church steps.

132

Rachel followed and stood two steps below him, while Bucky stepped back and stared up at the facade.

"Have a seat," said Altmeyer.

Rachel shook her head. "We did a terrible thing, Altmeyer."

"It's by no means the first." He looked past her at the last of the German tourists, a plump lady wearing sandals that flapped against her heels when she lifted her feet.

"But this time—" she began, leaning toward him a little. Suddenly she was aware of someone standing beside her. She turned, and there was a tall, thin man with a bald head and a moustache. He nodded at her, a gesture that he carried out with a punctilious politeness, as though he were tipping his hat.

"On time," said Altmeyer. "Rachel, this is the gentleman I mentioned before, Paul Mazarin."

Mazarin turned to Rachel again and repeated his nod without changing the expression on his face. Then he said, "We can go through the church. The car is one street over."

Altmeyer stood up and beckoned to Bucky, who began to walk toward them. Mazarin studied Bucky for a moment, and said, "You're right. He is the Manneken-Pis."

They entered the dark, cool enclosure inside the door of the old church, and Rachel thought of the time her sixth-grade teacher had taken the class into the basement of the school to see the boiler room. They passed into the sanctuary, and her impression changed to space and light and impossibly high vaulted ceilings. Then they were in an alcove, and she passed rows of stone plaques she had no time to decipher, and in a few steps they were out in the sunshine again.

A brown Peugeot was just pulling up at the curb when they reached the sidewalk. The meeting was so smoothly executed that it looked to Rachel like a coincidence. The man at the wheel didn't appear to have looked in their direction, but then Paul Mazarin was opening the door for her, and immediately the car was moving again.

Mazarin leaned his shoulder against the seat to look at

133

them as he spoke. "I've decided not to take you to my flat in the city. It's too small for all of us, and a day or two in the country might be pleasant. I'm sorry Van Leuven, here, speaks only Flemish, but he'll take care of you."

Altmeyer said nothing.

Mazarin went on. "That is, if there's nothing about this Japanese business that you want to take care of while you're here."

"What gave you that idea?" said Rachel.

"The tags on your luggage," said Mazarin. "How unlike you not to think of that when you were checking your bags, Altmeyer. I took them off for you." He turned again to look out the windshield.

Rachel whispered in Altmeyer's ear. "There weren't any airport names on the tags, just numbers."

Altmeyer whispered, still lower. "They found something in the bags."

"They searched our things? Why?"

"It's business. He knows I'd have done the same."

They drove into the Brabant countryside, at first across green farmland, then almost immediately into a deep forest with tall, ancient trees. In the forest they passed several small inns, then a building that looked like a French chateau. Mazarin turned again and addressed Rachel. "This is the Bois de la Cambre."

"It's beautiful," she said. "Is this where we'll stay?"

Mazarin laughed. "It's not a good idea. Some of the best restaurants in the country are on this road, and the finest hotels. It's just the sort of place to look for Altmeyer."

Rachel smiled, but the muscles of her face felt stiff and tight.

IT WAS NIGHT when Van Leuven turned off the highway and made his way up a rutted dirt road to an old fieldstone farmhouse. In the beam of the headlights Rachel could see that the last vehicle to come up the muddy road must have been a heavy truck with four wheels on its rear axle.

"Is this it?" asked Altmeyer.

Mazarin stretched his arms and yawned as the car stopped. "This is it. I'll help you get settled before I start back to the city."

They climbed out of the car and Van Leuven left the headlights on to light their way up the cobbled path to the stone slab steps of the farmhouse. When Rachel turned to watch him coming up the walk carrying two of the suitcases, he was caught for a moment in the glare of the light, and she could see the shape of a pistol under the fabric of his jacket.

The floors of the farmhouse were gleaming unfinished wood that someone must have scrubbed on her hands and knees with a brush every day for a lifetime. No, she thought, several generations of women must have done it in succession. Rachel tried to sense something about the women who had lived there, but nothing came. The place was male and empty now, like a barracks. Footsteps echoed from the plaster and whitewash and seemed to form little bubbles of sound in the corners of the rooms.

Van Leuven carried the suitcases through a large common room with a fireplace and a ten-foot-long rough wooden trestle table, and into one of four little bedrooms. When Rachel saw the bedroom, she felt better. There was a wooden bed with a high headboard and slats along the sides that made it look like a cradle. The bed was covered with a thick down quilt with an embroidered rose in the center.

Rachel followed him out to the large room again, and saw Altmeyer and Mazarin sitting at the long table. "Very cozy," she said. "I'd like to clean up and go to bed, so please tell me there's plumbing."

"There are two bathrooms," said Mazarin. "That one is the better of the two, because I had it installed myself." He pointed to a door next to the bedroom. Rachel smiled politely and disappeared.

135

Altmeyer reached into his coat and took out a sheaf of money, and tossed it onto the table between him and Mazarin.

The long, thin hand slowly moved to scoop it up, then gave it a single shake as though Mazarin were judging its weight. Then he slipped it into his pocket. "Have you decided to tell me what you want?"

"No more than I told you," said Altmeyer. He stopped to light a cigarette, then looked back at Mazarin. "I want to be invisible for a few days. This place will do."

"You hardly need me for that. You've done it without help before. What does your Japanese business have to do with me?"

Altmeyer blew a puff of smoke into the air and watched it float toward the fireplace. "I'm not sure how serious these people are about finding me. They have the resources, and they might think it's worth the trouble."

"I haven't seen you in years."

Altmeyer studied him. "I've lost touch with the market in this part of the world, let a lot of my contacts slip."

Mazarin's head turned slightly to the side, as though he were having difficulty hearing. "You want to do business."

Altmeyer shook his head. "You work Africa and the Middle East. You might have heard something, that's all. I came to you for gossip."

"About you? Nothing yet."

Altmeyer said, "That's good. Keep listening. But I wondered about the market. I'd be especially interested in somebody new, probably dealing in premium handguns, things like Browning nine-millimeter automatics. And maybe promising bigger stuff."

"There are always new people. You know that. They make two shipments and maybe they lose their nerve, maybe they die. Maybe," he added with a trace of a smile, "they sell something to the wrong person and have to drop out of sight. There's always a brisk trade in name-brand small arms, but

136

there are still only a few people who can deal in volume. You know who they are as well as I do. Nothing changes."

Altmeyer sighed. "Nothing changes. You haven't heard of anybody with anything exotic to offer?"

"Now and then things become available. A year ago there was an Algerian in Paris who had nerve gas—I don't know how much. This year it's land mines and rocket launchers, all Russian, but nobody knows where they came from. If I were to guess, I'd say they crossed the Adriatic from Yugoslavia to Italy. Other people say they came out of Lebanon."

Altmeyer laughed. "No American tanks this year? No nuclear weapons?"

Mazarin gave him a sly glance. "For a modest commission I can get you a German Leopard tank." Then he added, "But you'd have to transport it yourself. No nuclear weapons. If you should ever get one, of course, I can find you a buyer. The Libyans were making incredible offers for months, and then gave up. There simply aren't any, and probably never will be. A group of very wealthy South Africans have been making discreet inquiries for five years. There are lots of buyers, but they might as well ask for pieces of the moon."

"I don't suppose any of these people stopped asking because they found what they wanted?"

Mazarin chuckled. "I haven't heard an explosion, have you?"

"Not yet," said Altmeyer. "Some day the price will be high enough. That much doesn't change."

Mazarin glanced at his watch and frowned. "I'm sorry, Altmeyer, but it's time for me to return to the city. I'll be back in two days to take you to Rotterdam. In the meantime, rest and enjoy yourself. Go out in the pasture tomorrow and watch Van Leuven talk to the cows."

"By the way," said Altmeyer, "this afternoon you offered to sell me some guns. Did you bring them?"

Mazarin was already moving toward the door. "Oh, we don't need guns here." He stopped and looked down at Altmeyer, his face contorted with suppressed amusement. "Always so careful, Altmeyer. You'll evade your enemies so long you'll get bored one day and shoot yourself."

RACHEL AWOKE to the roar of an airplane passing over. She waited for the sound to move off, and when it did she could hear the distant sound of the cows lowing. She sat up in the deep, soft bed, and carefully arranged the covers around Altmeyer before she stepped to the floor and went to pull a corner of the curtain aside to peer out at the pasture.

She pushed the curtain aside a few inches, but behind it was only the plain whitewashed wall. She lifted the curtain and saw that the window was only a single pane of glass a foot above her head. A cow gave another moo, and Rachel began to dress. She quickly pulled on a blue Dodgers sweat shirt and a pair of blue jeans, then slipped out into the large central room, carrying her comfortable shoes. As she pushed the door closed, she heard Bucky say, "Good morning."

"Hi there, Farmer Bucky," she said. He was sitting alone at the big table with a plate of scrambled eggs in front of him. She moved to the table and pulled out a chair. "You're up pretty early for a tycoon."

"I prefer to think of myself as a *macher*," he said. "A catalyst and deal-maker, not merely a crass acquirer, and that means getting up earlier than the competition."

"You mean you couldn't sleep."

"First it was birds. That was before sunup. Later it was cows. I've got a window in my room you couldn't throw a football through, and it must be seven feet up. I couldn't see, but I'm sure every cow in Europe must have passed by under that window."

Rachel looked around her. "There's no telling how old this building is, and when they built it they probably didn't want to lose a lot of heat. I heard cows, too, and tried to look outside." She looked at Bucky's plate. "Did Van Leuven make you breakfast?"

"Not exactly. He's a pointer. When I got up, he pointed at the eggs and pointed at the skillet. I'll share these with you and we can make some more when Altmeyer gets up."

"It's a deal," said Rachel, scraping some of Bucky's scrambled eggs onto an empty plate. "Where is he now?"

"Out with the cows." Bucky glanced at his watch. "He's been out there in the pasture milking for about four hours."

"Can't be," said Rachel, and started to eat.

"What do you mean? The guy is a master of pantomime. If there were a market in Hollywood for milking invisible cows, I could make him a rich man."

Rachel grinned. "Obviously none of your clients are cows. You don't milk them in the pasture. If he herded them past your window he was finished milking. That you do in the barn. He was trying to tell you where he'd been, not where he was going."

"What do you do in the barn?" Altmeyer was standing at the bedroom door, already dressed.

"Milk cows," said Rachel. "I wanted to know where Van Leuven was."

"Oh. Any more eggs?"

Bucky stood up and moved toward the kitchen. "More eggs are on the way. It's okay. I'm used to doing all the work and getting ten percent of the proceeds."

A few minutes later Bucky returned, carrying two more plates. Rachel kept her eyes on Altmeyer, her chin resting on her hands.

Altmeyer stared at his plate as though he weren't aware that the others were both watching him now. Then he said abruptly, "Don't start up. I still don't know what we can do except stay invisible until they lose interest."

Rachel stood up. "I'm going out to walk around a little. I feel as though I've never lived anywhere but hotels, and this place is built like a prison."

"Mind if I join you?" asked Bucky.

"Come on, old Buckaroo. I'll tell you about cows."

They all walked through the kitchen, stopping to leave

139

the plates in the sink. Altmeyer stared at the door. "It's an odd layout, isn't it? One door, and just those tiny windows."

"It's an ancient place," said Rachel. "Maybe it's cold in the winter."

They walked outside, and Altmeyer stopped again. "What did you mean about cows before?"

"It's nothing. Bucky heard Van Leuven herding the cows out to pasture this morning, that's all."

They walked past the small unpainted barn that sat at a slight angle on its stone foundation so that it leaned toward a distant stand of old trees clustered along the dirt road. There was a wide, muddy path that led from the barn to a green field, where five black-and-white steers stood behind a meandering stone fence to study them with placid brown eyes.

Bucky looked confused. He stared at the steers, then turned and shaded his eyes from the sun and scanned the surrounding fields.

Rachel smiled. "Lose something, old Buckskin? Maybe a few hundred head?"

Bucky said, "Wait. This isn't funny. What happened to the rest of them? It took a half hour for them to parade past my window. I heard them."

Rachel shook her head. "Here they are, and the house is way over there. Why would he herd them past your window? The sound must have carried from the pasture."

Bucky shrugged and walked toward the house, with Rachel and Altmeyer trailing behind. They walked a few paces, and then Rachel frowned. "Have you noticed? There aren't any cows."

"It stands to reason. There's no bull either."

"No," said Rachel, "but they could borrow one. When there are a lot of little farms like this, somebody buys a bull and runs a dating service. At least that's what they do everywhere else."

"So what's bothering you?"

"There are no cows at all. Not even one heifer." She

waited, then said, "Don't you see? Bucky said Van Leuven went out early this morning to milk the cows. But those are all steers."

"You forget Mazarin's not in the cattle business. They're all just props."

"But Van Leuven made signs to Bucky this morning to say he'd been milking the cows. And where is he, anyway? That was four hours ago. And what Bucky heard wasn't just those five steers, so what was it?"

Altmeyer walked a little faster to catch up with Bucky, who was kneeling beside the house under one of the small, high windows and squinting at the ground. Bucky looked up. "I guess the sound of the cows over there must have been amplified by the stone walls or something. I don't see any cow tracks."

"You wouldn't," said Altmeyer. "Get up. If he happens to be watching, he may figure out what the problem is."

Bucky stood up and the three walked on around the house toward the next field. "Just so I know, what problem do you mean?"

"There it is," said Altmeyer, nodding his head at a cubical cinderblock structure the size of a small room fifty yards away. It sat at an angle from the main house, and its foundation seemed to be half buried in earth. A small concrete trough stuck out on the side, and a slow trickle of clear water ran down it into a rock-lined ditch that led toward the pasture. Altmeyer kept walking.

"What is it, some kind of septic tank?" said Bucky.

"It's a springhouse," Rachel said. "It's from the old days. You built a little house on top of a spring, and you could keep your milk cool."

Bucky looked at it again. "If it's from the old days, why doesn't it look old? Everything else is stone, even the foundation of the barn."

"Because it's not from the old days," said Altmeyer. "It may have started out as a springhouse, but now it's something

141

else. Take a look at it. Cinderblocks and concrete, a big mound of dirt packed around it, just far enough away from everything else. It's Mazarin's magazine."

"His what?"

"The place where he stores his guns and ammunition. I'm afraid we're in trouble again. Did either of you see a car anywhere? Mazarin took the Peugeot."

"No," said Rachel. "There are big, deep ruts on the drive that had to have been made by a truck, but it can't be hidden anywhere."

Bucky said, "Wait. Take a second and tell me."

Altmeyer stared out into the fields as he spoke. "Last night Mazarin told me he didn't have any guns here. Then this morning Van Leuven gave you the idea he had been milking cows, but there aren't any. What you heard was somebody moving guns in or out of the springhouse."

Bucky closed his eyes and stopped. "It was something heavy, a noise like clopping sounds, I heard some moos, so I thought it was the cows. But the noises all went this way." He pointed at the springhouse. "Maybe on the way there they made noise, and on the way back they didn't have anything to carry anymore."

"I hope so," said Altmeyer. "They must have parked the truck away from the house or we'd have heard it. I guess we'll need whatever edge they left us in the springhouse."

"What about Van Leuven?" Rachel asked. "Last night I could see he had a gun under his coat."

"We'll have to keep him out of the way for a half hour or so. First we have to let him find us. Let's go back and do the dishes."

They walked back to the kitchen door and went inside. Altmeyer filled the sink and started to scrub the plates and silverware while Rachel made coffee in an old, scorched pot on the stove and Bucky searched the open shelves for cups.

Before Altmeyer had finished, they heard the sound of Van Leuven scraping his feet on the stone slab steps outside,

142

then kicking his heels against the edge to knock the mud off his boots. Then the door swung open, and he stepped into the kitchen in his woolen socks. When he saw the clean kitchen he smiled and said, "Yah," three times.

He swept back an unruly tuft of sandy hair with his plump, calloused hand and padded into the large open room, where Bucky and Rachel were drinking coffee. Rachel poured him a cup, and he clasped his hands in a gesture of thanks and bowed to her.

"You're right," said Rachel, as though she were speaking to Van Leuven. "The man is a master of the unspoken word."

Altmeyer spoke from the kitchen. "See if you can get him to tell you a long story while I'm gone."

Van Leuven sipped his coffee, and didn't appear to hear when the kitchen door opened and closed. Rachel said to him, "Have you eaten?" and moved an imaginary fork from an imaginary plate to her mouth, but Van Leuven held up his hands and shook his head.

Bucky told her, "He ate a long time ago." To Van Leuven he said, "I wonder if you play gin or something."

Rachel said, "It's worth a try. I'll get the cards out of the suitcase."

She moved toward the bedroom, and Van Leuven watched her with curiosity. When she returned with one of the decks from the Imperial Hotel, he began to move coffee cups away from the center of the table. Suddenly, a look of puzzlement appeared on his face, and he said to Bucky, "Altmeyer?"

Rachel said, "I guess we reminded him. There aren't many games you play three-handed."

Van Leuven stood up and walked to the kitchen. "Altmeyer?" he said. Then he went to the door and opened it. He appeared again at the table, pointing at his stocking feet and then shaking his head in consternation.

Rachel spoke through a smile that was intended to seem uncomprehending. "Altmeyer must have taken his boots."

Bucky raised two fingers to the sides of his head to indicate horns, and said, "Moo."

Van Leuven looked still more puzzled, and Bucky said, "I guess Belgian cows don't say 'moo.' " He pretended to milk a cow, then made horns on his head again, and Van Leuven sat down to watch him. Bucky said, "Altmeyer . . ." then walked his fingers on the table, "went for a walk in the pasture."

A look of recognition crossed Van Leuven's face, and he nodded, then watched Rachel pour more coffee into his cup.

Bucky said, "I, too, am a master of the mimetic arts. Not everybody says 'moo,' but everybody walks." He began to shuffle the cards.

Rachel said, "What game do you think he plays?"

Bucky smiled. "Leave it to me." He stared into Van Leuven's empty blue eyes. "I judge this to be a man of the world—not a sophisticate, necessarily—that's a different issue. Across the known universe, we men of the world—any world—know how to play blackjack." He placed a king and an ace face up on the table, and looked at Van Leuven. Slowly, Van Leuven's lips curled up at the corners.

ALTMEYER STUDIED THE SPRINGHOUSE. The door was a thick wooden rectangle so small a man would have to crouch to enter, but there was no lock. He examined the ground carefully before each step, then ran his fingers under the door to feel for a raised spot. It would be like Mazarin to rig an old-fashioned spring gun using a trip wire or an air hose the way moonshiners did. He felt nothing, so he slowly pushed the little door open and bent down to enter.

Inside there were long, narrow wooden boxes neatly stacked along the back wall, and to his right were rows of rectangular steel ammunition cans, all hastily sprayed with black paint where the stenciled labels had been. It took him a few moments to select one box and one can, and drag them around to the back of the springhouse.

He opened the box and took out the first of the heavy

black rifles, then removed the thick, boxlike clip, loaded it with bullets from the ammunition can, and clicked it back into the frame. He worked quickly until all five rifles were out of the box. Then he carried the ammunition can back to the springhouse and returned it to its place, and then the rifle box. It cost him thirty seconds to arrange the others so the empty one would be at the bottom, but he had to count on Rachel and Bucky for the time.

Altmeyer closed the door behind him, slung the five heavy rifles over his shoulders, and trotted toward the house. Near the corner of the house he laid three of them muzzle-to-butt along the foundation. Then he moved to the pasture.

He climbed over the low stone fence and laid the two rifles in the grass behind it. He looked across the open space to the house. It was too far. Three people running hard, even in the darkness, might make it half the distance. He leaned his back against the stone wall and watched an inquisitive steer with a black patch across its face plod toward him. It stopped a few feet away and stared at him, chewing methodically.

Altmeyer closed his eyes. He had to get them inside the house. Could he come in through the kitchen without Van Leuven seeing? It was nearly impossible. Altmeyer picked up the rifles and climbed back over the wall, and ran to the house to stand beneath the small, high window of the bedroom he shared with Rachel.

Altmeyer took off his belt and threaded it through the trigger guards of the rifles, then through the belt buckle, and lifted them so they dangled upside down. Then he reached up and carefully wedged the end of the belt under the edge of the screen on the window, and pushed it inward until it held. He gave the rifles a tentative tug, and then a harder one, but the belt didn't come loose.

Altmeyer walked around to the kitchen steps and sat down to clean the mud from Van Leuven's boots. As he slipped off the second boot he heard the door behind him swing open, and he turned to see Van Leuven standing at the threshold, the broad face staring down at him, the little blue eyes squinting against the sunlight. When he realized that Altmeyer was cleaning the boots, he smiled with exaggerated pleasure and bobbed his head.

Altmeyer held his hand up in deprecation, and said, "The pleasure is all mine, sport. Thanks for the loan of the boots."

Altmeyer entered the kitchen and watched while Van Leuven sat down on the steps to put on the boots. Altmeyer said, "It's a great day for a walk," and slowly closed the kitchen door, then ran to the bedroom. He pulled a chair to the window and stood on it. As he slid the window open, Rachel appeared beside him.

"What's going on?"

"Not much time." He grabbed her hand and pulled it up to the window sill. "Take the end of the belt and hold on to it tight. I've got to get the screen open."

Rachel took the end of the belt in both hands, and Altmeyer pushed the latch and popped the screen outward, then took the belt from her. Slowly and carefully he lifted the rifles to the window and maneuvered them inside. "Hold these," he said. Rachel cradled them in her arms as he replaced the screen, closed the window, and jumped to the floor.

From the kitchen Bucky called, "He's heading for the pasture."

Altmeyer took the rifles from Rachel. "Bucky, come in here, quick."

Bucky appeared in the doorway. "How did you get those past him?"

"Through the window. I expected the usual Belgian FALs, but Mazarin seems to have expanded his inventory. These are Heckler and Koch G-Threes. He must have found a way to tap into the German military supply system. Anyway, they're good. They work just like an M-16, see?" He turned one on its side and handed it to Bucky. "Just flick the selector forward with your right thumb. Two clicks and it's on automatic. Now hide it in your room."

Bucky left, and Altmeyer slipped the second rifle under

the mattress of the bed, then walked to the kitchen and looked out the window. When Bucky and Rachel joined him, he said, "There are three more in the shrubbery along this end of the house, if we need them. How long was I gone?"

Rachel looked at her watch. "A little over fifteen minutes. He seemed a little nervous, especially when he saw you'd taken his galoshes."

Altmeyer was still craning his neck to keep his eyes on Van Leuven. "I couldn't have him following me, and I didn't want to leave any unfamiliar tracks. By the way, those ammo clips hold thirty rounds. That's not much if you're blasting away on automatic, so curb your enthusiasm. The Mazarins want to come for us before we expect them to, and it's easiest to do this sort of thing at night, so tonight has got to be it. We might want to take turns sleeping during the day."

In the distance Van Leuven walked toward the spring-house. Altmeyer muttered, "You're getting warm." Van Leuven seemed to see nothing there that disturbed him, so he moved on toward the pasture. "Cooler," said Altmeyer. Van Leuven walked along the stone fence, peering down at the weeds, then moved toward the barn. "Cold . . . colder . . . You're dead."

IT WAS THREE IN THE MORNING, and it had been two hours since Van Leuven had noisily closed his bedroom door for the night. Altmeyer slipped out of the bedroom, and Rachel locked it from the inside. There was no light, but Altmeyer could feel the dimensions of the big room. When he neared the long table and chairs clustered around it, his imagination created the noise he would make if he tripped over them. He navigated as far from them as he could, made his way across the room to the fireplace, and sat down on the floor beside it.

By now Rachel was crouching in the closet where they wouldn't be able to hit her if they got far enough to fire on the empty bed. Where the hell was Bucky? All day they'd studied the house, paced the distances every time Van Leuven

147

had gone into the kitchen or the bathroom. It was three o'clock, and Bucky should be out of his bedroom and making his way along the wall to the corner ten paces to Altmeyer's left. He couldn't have fallen asleep. It was impossible.

Altmeyer stared into the darkness twenty degrees to the right of the corner of the room, and sensed a shape, just a difference in the shadows that hadn't been discernible when he'd looked straight at it. Bucky wasn't asleep. He was already crouching in the corner.

Altmeyer shifted his weight occasionally without moving his feet. He held his breath and listened for sounds from Bucky's corner, but detected none. After a half hour he allowed himself to change his position slightly.

At first Altmeyer didn't acknowledge the sound of the engine. A car passing by on the highway might be loud enough in this stillness to sound as though it had made the turn up the drive toward the farmhouse. When it grew louder, he began to listen to it, to try to measure it. He began to count the seconds. When he reached ten, the engine stopped. It didn't fade into the distance, just cut off abruptly. Altmeyer imagined it: the car would be about halfway up the drive, hidden from the highway by the trees.

He swallowed to clear his ears, and waited. There was a slight rustling inside Van Leuven's room. Altmeyer concentrated on regulating his breathing. He thought it through again. Had anything happened differently from the way he'd expected? No, it was the same. The only reason to stop the car that far from the house was to keep from waking Altmeyer, Rachel, and Bucky. There would be at least two men, but no more than four, or they'd be in danger of shooting each other in a space this small. They'd take positions in front of the two bedroom doors, and then Van Leuven would switch on the light. It had to be that way. If they hadn't been positive the three victims were trapped in their rooms, unarmed and probably asleep, they might do something else. Tonight they would turn on the light.

Altmeyer heard a creak of an old floorboard somewhere near Van Leuven's bedroom, then a long silence. Van Leuven was standing there now, listening for a signal that the creak had awakened someone. After a few deep breaths, Altmeyer sensed that he had begun to move again. There was a faint whisper of cloth on the other side of the room, and then nothing until Van Leuven passed through the doorway to the kitchen, where his body acquired a dark shape for an instant, and then was gone.

Altmeyer flicked the selector lever on his rifle forward with his thumb, then pushed it harder to be sure it had moved as far as it would go. He heard the kitchen door open, and there was a sound of movement, almost like a wind, that could have been breathing or the swishing of clothing, or stocking feet on the wooden floor. One by one the shadows passed across the doorway into the main room. Altmeyer counted four, and then the fifth startled him, until he remembered it would be Van Leuven waiting to turn on the light.

They moved along the wall, then stopped in front of the two bedroom doors. He heard a voice whisper, *"Allons,"* a hiss that carried no emotion or urgency.

The click of the light switch sounded to Altmeyer's ears like a piece of wood snapping. The room seemed impossibly bright and yellow. One man already had a foot raised to kick in the door of Bucky's room, but Altmeyer saw him through the high ring sight behind the muzzle of the rifle, and he fired a short, deafening burst that swept the man into the wall and jerked his raised foot to the side before it could straighten. The burst caught the second man in the side of the chest and turned him around before he arched backward. Altmeyer swung the rifle around in time to aim another burst into two men who were already falling, that seemed to punch their limp bodies upward before they crumpled. It was only then that he remembered the roar from Bucky's corner.

He stared at the bodies down the barrel of the rifle as Bucky stepped forward. Van Leuven's body had its back

149

against the wall and its legs extended, as though it had just sat down hard. Bucky pushed it over with his foot, so it lay on its side. "I know that's stupid," he muttered. "I just don't want to look at—"

"It's okay," said Altmeyer. "He doesn't give a shit." He stepped quickly to the kitchen door, then knelt and opened it a crack to peer out. "I don't see a truck. You'd better get Rachel."

Bucky knocked once on Rachel's door and said, "It's okay. Come on out," but the door was already swinging away from his knuckles.

Rachel looked around the room, her face tense and stony, then picked up the two suitcases and stepped past the body of Van Leuven. "You'd better get your luggage," she said. "You seem to have killed all the bellboys."

Altmeyer was beside one of the bodies. He stood up with a set of keys in his hand, and moved back to the kitchen door.

Rachel walked into the kitchen. "What's wrong?"

"I can't see the truck."

Bucky was already behind Rachel. "What truck is that?" He set his suitcase on the floor.

"There were four besides Van Leuven: Paul and Bernard Mazarin and two I've seen in Brussels on other trips. They sold us to Ashita, but how do they prove they got us?" He took one of the suitcases from Rachel. "I'll go first, then Rachel. Run around to the corner of the house as fast as you can, and then we'll move again." Altmeyer slipped into the darkness, and they could hear the sound of his feet beating the ground hard for a dozen paces, and then silence.

Rachel looked through the open doorway, took a deep breath, cradled her suitcase in her arms, and ran. The first step off the stone slab at the door seemed to give her momentum that carried her nearly to the corner of the house, and then she felt Altmeyer's arm pulling her around it. His other hand took the suitcase from her, and then Altmeyer held her still until he heard Bucky trotting toward them.

150

When Bucky came around the corner, Altmeyer knelt beside the house and picked a rifle out of the shrubbery. "Everybody gets a fresh one. It'll help balance your suitcase, if nothing else. Now let's get to the car before the truck gets here."

They set off down the drive, and Bucky said, "Why are you so sure about the truck?"

Altmeyer seemed to increase his speed as he spoke, almost trotting, his words coming in terse little increments. "There weren't any strangers to see us die." Then he said, "They'd want proof."

"Then why a truck?"

Altmeyer reached the Peugeot first, opened the trunk, and started loading suitcases. "Because if they weren't here to see it happen, they'd want some neutral party to identify us. The easiest thing to do is let the police find us and put it in the papers. Mazarin had a truck, and that's what he'd use to dump us someplace far away from here." He slammed the trunk, then took up his rifle again and moved toward the driver's side of the car.

Rachel ran to the other side and reached for the door handle, but then she stopped. She seemed to be looking up into the sky. "Wait," she said.

Bucky heard it. There was a high engine whine that seemed to deepen as it moved along the highway. Then he could hear it change pitch as the driver disengaged the clutch to coast into the turn. "Too late," he said.

Altmeyer called, "Come on," and ran around the car to take Rachel's arm. He pulled her with him as he ran into the grove of trees beside the road. Altmeyer seemed to judge the distance by the sound of the engine. He ran until the truck driver took his foot off the gas pedal somewhere far from the spot where the Peugeot was parked, and then he said, "Now, get down."

The three lay down on the ground. Bucky could feel cold water beginning to soak up through the spongy layer of fallen

151

leaves beneath him. He started to crawl forward, but Altmeyer whispered, "Keep your face down. It'll show up in the lights."

As though he'd ordered lights, they appeared, first a single beam bobbing up and down crazily as the truck bounced slowly up the rutted drive, then brightening into two headlights when the truck came around the curve and stopped behind the Peugeot.

Bucky spoke with his face pressed into the wet leaves. "They blocked the road. We can't get the car out."

"It looks like they're blocked too," Altmeyer whispered. "I guess Mazarin was planning to move the car up to the yard by now. Maybe they can get around it."

The truck's lights went out and Rachel said, "No such luck. They know something's happened."

"They need to move the car, and we need to move the truck," said Altmeyer. "It's too bad we can't talk it over."

There was the hollow, metallic slam of the truck's cab door, then another slam, then a loud creak as the rear door opened. Altmeyer said, "We'll have to spread out and do this the ugly way. As soon as they're all in the clear, away from the truck, open up." He crawled to his right, then reached a thicket and stood up.

Rachel followed him through the trees to the edge of the road, then raised the heavy rifle to her shoulder. "Where are they?" she whispered. "I don't see them."

Altmeyer leaned closer to her. "Take the car keys and stay here, where you can control the road. Remember, the car is the only thing that matters now." He leaned away again.

"Where are you going?"

"I guess they're too smart to stroll down the open driveway. They must be moving up through the trees on the other side. I've got to cover the house from the cow pasture. When they get that far they'll know as much as we do."

"Please be—"

"Careful?" She could hear a kind of amusement in his voice.

152

"I guess I mean be lucky." She knew he was too far away to hear her. Rachel steadied her rifle against a tree trunk and stared out at the empty road.

BUCKY LAY STILL, watching the truck. Altmeyer and Rachel had been gone for a long time. Was it as long as it seemed? Where were the men from the truck? He slowly counted to a hundred, imagining that at each number a man could take a step. Then he counted again, more slowly.

He studied the truck. It looked like the sort of truck people rented to move furniture. Bucky crawled forward a few feet, then counted to a hundred again. He crawled closer until he could see beneath the bed of the truck. He could pick out the shapes of the drive shaft and the rear axle and the wheels, but there were no legs standing on the far side. They must have moved down the other side of the road toward the house. He found himself thinking, "I have the truck." He wondered if he could push it aside somehow. Once, years ago, he'd seen two men move a railroad car on a siding by jamming long crowbars behind the wheels and prying upward. Maybe he could move it a few feet, just far enough to get the car around it.

Bucky stood up and walked slowly to the rear of the truck, then stopped to listen. He looked into the dark cargo box, but it was empty except for a few canvas tarpaulins in a pile near the front end. He moved farther and stared down the long side. He sucked in a breath of air and had to hold it to keep from letting out a gasp. There was room enough to get the truck past on that side. He was sure of it. They hadn't stopped here because the road was blocked, but because they knew something was wrong at the house. They'd closed the road themselves.

Bucky thought quickly. The men weren't going to get Mazarin to move his car out of the way. They were in the woods hunting Altmeyer and Rachel. He moved along the

153

truck toward the cab, but suddenly something silvery caught his eye. It was the big rearview mirror jutting out from the side of the cab. As he watched, something seemed to flicker across it, like a moving shadow. Bucky stopped and dropped to his knees. If the mirror were adjusted to give a driver a view along the side of the truck, then it must be aimed at the driver's face. What Bucky had seen had to be a man in the driver's seat, moving his head.

Bucky stayed low, stepping quietly forward, watching the mirror to be sure it reflected the edge of the cab's roof against the sky. When he was directly behind the door he stopped again. He heard the spring in the seat creak slightly as the man shifted his weight to look at something in the open space in front of the windshield.

ALTMEYER WAS IN THE PASTURE crouching behind the stone fence when he saw the movement in the woods across the dirt road. The first man came out into the clearing at a trot. Altmeyer aimed the rifle and moved it to follow him, but the other man was invisible, waiting for Altmeyer to fire. When the first man reached the corner of the house and took up a firing position, the second man dashed across to join him, then past him toward the kitchen door.

Altmeyer waited as the man's strides brought him closer. Altmeyer's mind searched for a solution that would keep the runner out of the house without revealing Altmeyer's position to the other man. The runner's speed increased as he reached the cobbled sidewalk, and Altmeyer chose.

He swung his rifle to the side and fired a burst at the corner of the house, then ducked behind the wall. Altmeyer moved as quickly as he could, scrambling frantically as the air above him exploded with chips of flying rock. He knew he had to come up while the man at the corner was still firing, the flashes of his own rifle blinding him, the recoils kicking the muzzle upward so that he'd have to fight his own rifle to change his aim.

Altmeyer balanced his weight on the balls of his feet, pressed his rifle tightly to his shoulder, bobbed up, and fired at the front door of the house. The runner was just reaching the steps, and Altmeyer saw him crouch and dive away from the door. Then Altmeyer was down again and crawling. Instead of moving back along the wall toward the car, he scrambled farther ahead toward the springhouse.

When Bucky heard the first shots, he took two steps away from the truck and fired three times into the window of the cab. He swung the door open and grabbed the man's belt. There was a soft, warm sensation on his knuckles as he hauled the body off the seat, and he knew it should make him feel something, but his thoughts now were coming only as steps in a task. He stepped over the body and climbed up into the driver's seat, then started the engine.

Bucky shifted to first gear and let the clutch out too quickly, so the truck jerked forward and stalled. He stomped down on the clutch again, started the engine, and eased the clutch out. Bucky steered around the Peugeot, his left wheel slipping into a deep rut that tilted the truck, then pressed hard on the gas pedal to bounce over the next one into the weeds. Then he cranked the wheel back, and the momentum returned him to the dirt road.

The truck was between the Peugeot and the house now, so he shifted to neutral and reached for the key. As he leaned down, a pattern of muzzle flashes sputtered at the far end of the drive. There was a gun at the corner of the house firing across the yard at the pasture wall. As he watched, the gun stopped, and a man ran behind the house. Then someone was firing from farther back, near the springhouse.

Bucky shifted again and rolled the truck forward. The engine whined and strained as Bucky fought for speed. He shifted to second gear, but then he became aware that there was a smell in the cab, as though something were burning. The cab was beginning to fill up with smoke. He glanced down at the seat, then remembered—the emergency brake was engaged. He leaned down and freed the hand brake, and the truck accelerated as though it had lost a heavy load. He reached the yard as the second man made his way to the spring-house.

Bucky made a wide turn in the yard so the truck was heading outward, and yelled out the open window, "Altmeyer! Jump in if you're out there!"

He inhaled to shout again, when a sudden burst of rifle fire roared behind him. He could hear bullets pounding into the back of the truck from the springhouse. At the same time, he saw the Peugeot moving up the dirt road toward him. He shouted, "No, Rachel. Get the hell out of here," but the next burst came, and he couldn't hear his own voice.

Bucky shifted into reverse and stared into the mirror beside him. At first the truck moved slowly, but as it crossed the flats near the house it gained speed. He watched the red image of the springhouse in the rearview mirror, but then it disintegrated into a shower of glass slivers. Bucky threw him-self down on the seat just before the truck crashed into the springhouse.

From behind the pasture wall where Altmeyer crouched, the truck seemed to slice the springhouse in half. The tailgate of the truck hit it in the middle, and the top half moved back two yards before it crumbled and fell. The bottom half was jammed under the body of the truck. Everything was quiet.

Bucky jumped from the high cab and staggered a few steps away, then cupped his hands around his mouth and shouted, "Altmeyer!"

Altmeyer vaulted the stone wall and walked to the car. When Bucky saw him, he trotted to catch up, and climbed into the backseat.

Rachel drove the car down the long, winding dirt road, then stopped at the place where it met the highway. She sat with the engine idling and stared forward. A set of headlights appeared, flashed past, and disappeared, but Rachel didn't move. "I don't know where to go."

Altmeyer lifted the rifle he'd been holding between his knees and pushed it out the window. "Any others?"

"I left mine someplace," said Bucky.

Altmeyer turned to Rachel. "I don't know where to go either."

Bucky cleared his throat. "Head for the airport. If I'm going to die, I'd like the pleasure of watching my clients die with me."

LOS ANGELES

"You agreed to come back here," said Rachel. "The time to complain was in the Brussels airport, not after we're home. We'd have gone anywhere you wanted." She turned away from Altmeyer and nudged Bucky's arm so the bottle of Scotch he was pouring moved past the third glass and dribbled a shining rivulet across the empty surface of his desk. "Wouldn't we?"

Bucky wiped the desk with his sleeve. "No, we wouldn't have." He handed Rachel a glass.

Altmeyer stared at Bucky's bookshelf. "Bucky, for Christ's sake. These are telephone books. Your ex-wife again?"

"I told you the woman was a mental. She had them bound in Morocco leather when she redid the room." He lifted the other two glasses and clinked them together, then handed one to Altmeyer. "Cheers."

Altmeyer sipped his drink. "They're not going to forget about us."

"I suppose not," said Bucky. "That makes us even, because we're not going to forget about them either. And we have the advantage, because they don't know who I am."

"I'm not sure I know either," said Altmeyer. "Isn't Bucky getting a little peculiar?"

"He's been through a lot," Rachel said as she placed her untasted glass of Scotch on the desk beside her. "We all have. It's good to be home—even if it's your home."

Bucky leaned back in his chair and said, "It's time to figure out what we're going to need to know, so we can get busy."

Altmeyer scowled. "Well, let's see. What don't we know? We don't know who *they* are, really. We don't know whether they already have a bomb in Japan or are just collecting materials. We don't know what the bomb will look like or how big it will be. In fact, we don't know much except that they're trying awfully hard to kill us."

"We'll have to start with the little we do know," said Bucky. "They're connected to this Ashita company, so we'd better find out about it. Do you know a lot about nuclear weapons?"

Altmeyer shook his head. "That's a gap in my education."

"Then we'll have to get in touch with an expert."

"I'm not sure if I know one, and if I did I'd be crazy to try to reach him. These people have been developing connections in the arms trade. They knew enough to get in touch with me, and then it took one day for them to make a deal with Mazarin to get rid of us. Maybe he was the one they'd picked to find them a market, but I doubt it. It's more likely they just put out the word that they wanted us."

"Don't worry. Arthur can get us an expert."

"Arthur?" said Altmeyer. "You mean that old drunk you lied to us about at the party?"

"I wasn't lying about Arthur," said Bucky. "I don't have enough imagination to think of a lie about Arthur. He has power. When you have a name like his, you can use it as a blunt instrument. If a restaurant doesn't have a table for him, they'll pay somebody else to leave early. And he hates that." He lifted the telephone receiver and rapidly punched the buttons. "Stephanie, this is Bucky Carmichael. Is he in?"

There was a pause, then Bucky said, "Today? What's the address? I just might stop by and remind him that hundred-degree heat isn't good for old men."

Bucky opened a desk drawer and produced a piece of paper and a pencil. As he wrote, he crooned, "Uh-hmmmmmm." Then he said, "Yeah, I know exactly where that is. I'll be in that neighborhood anyway. Maybe I'll pick up my ten percent of his sunstroke. Oh, and Stephanie, tell Leonard I've got something hot for him. If he calls me this week I'll share it, but he has to do me a favor first."

Bucky chuckled. "Stephanie, this has nothing to do with horses. Only Arthur has enough to throw it away."

He hooted. "Or women either. You'd be my only love, and Leonard's too, if you didn't cheat on us with your husband. No, this is for Leonard in his capacity as business manager of Paston Enterprises."

Bucky smiled into the telephone. "He is? Tell him I'll consider talking to him, but only if he's quick about it. I've got the Queen of England on another line begging to get in on this."

Bucky spun his chair slowly, pushing off with his short legs and whirling clockwise a full turn as the telephone cord wrapped around him, then whirling counterclockwise to free himself. "Leonard? Of course it's me. I was in Japan all week. You should try it. They say travel broadens you, and if anybody could use it—"

Bucky grinned. "All right. While I was in Japan I picked up a tip you might want to check out. It's a company called Ashita, A-S-H-I-T-A, that makes electronic stuff. I don't know much about it, but the source was impeccable."

"No, Ashita doesn't mean 'sucker.' It means 'tomorrow.' Hey—it's nothing to me. You jump in with Arthur's kind of money and your profits are worth something, like maybe Nebraska. All I can get out of this is a paltry Rolls-Royce. Hell, I'm a hero."

Bucky listened. "How do I know if it's a public corporation? I know it's no mom-and-pop grocery store. After you check it out, you'll be able to tell me."

Bucky spun his chair around, then spun it back. "You're welcome. Just don't forget to keep in touch. I don't know how

163

long we've got to get in on this. Oh, and Leonard? I know that if this is good there's no hope of keeping it to ourselves, but let's try to limit it to friends, relatives, and casual acquaintances, okay? I don't want to wake up tomorrow and read that some little shit who owns a computer company up north bought Ashita. And try to keep your hands off Stephanie—" Bucky spun his chair around and hung up the telephone, then glanced at his watch. "That ought to cover it. By tomorrow Leonard will probably know more about Ashita than the chairman of the board."

Rachel looked at the ceiling. "We have faith in you, Bucky, but that call didn't sound serious."

Bucky stood up and walked toward the door. "Come on. You don't have to worry. Leonard isn't some greedy investor. He's an amateur in the true sense of the word—he plays the game because he loves it. For him it's like playing poker with his grandmother's money. He's made millions for Arthur every year. If he never does another thing, Arthur will pay him a big salary until he dies, and probably pay his kids after that. It's a feudal relationship. Now forget that part of it. The man has spent his life feasting on tips. He won't pass one up now."

"Where are you going?" said Rachel.

"We're going to see Arthur. He's shooting today."

BUCKY LET THE MERCEDES glide into the center lane as a canary-yellow pickup truck with two upright motorcycles in its bed flashed by, and then he accelerated into the left turn. As he drove down Radford Avenue past the CBS buildings, Bucky said, "The place still makes me sweat."

Rachel patted his shoulder. "Nobody saw you that night."

Bucky pointed his finger out the window as he drove. "Those trees saw me, and that fire hydrant over there. I thought it would be different in the daylight, but it just feels like somebody turned on the lights and caught me." He turned left again onto a quiet residential street lined with low stucco houses and tall oak trees, then stopped.

There were long white tractor-trailer trucks parked along the right curb, and a vehicle that looked like a mobile home on a flatbed. Crowds of people were walking in the road, as others scurried back and forth carrying metal cases and coils of insulated cable, while still others sat on lawns reading newspapers or drinking coffee. A policeman in high riding boots strolled listlessly into the street and waved an arm at Bucky.

"The circus has come to town," said Rachel.

Bucky backed the car around the corner. "We'll have to park on Radford and walk."

"What are you going to tell him?" Altmeyer asked as he opened the car door for Rachel.

Bucky walked around the car to join them on the sidewalk. "Arthur is too complicated for a classical lie. It'll have to be one of my jazz lies, where I start out with a theme and improvise."

"But what's the theme?" said Rachel. "And what are we supposed to be doing here?"

"What you have to do with Arthur is appeal to what's left of his mind. He's been so big for so many years that he's lost all human feeling—no greed, no fear, no jealousy. You might say he's a diminished man. There's not much left except curiosity. He's interested in everything."

"So what are you going to do, tell him a riddle?" Altmeyer stopped walking and waited.

"Come on, trust me," said Bucky. "This is what pays all the alimony checks, and I've got more wives to support than the king of the Zulus. Today I'm playing packager. I'm bringing Arthur an idea for a movie. The idea is going to stink, so Arthur won't touch it. But he'll do whatever he can to help, which is a hell of a lot."

"Why?"

Bucky shrugged. "A rare form of senility. The last one

who had it was Good King Wenceslas. He can make somebody's career with a phone call, and the part of his brain that's
supposed to say, 'Why should I?' died of old age maybe thirty
or forty years ago."

They walked down the center of the street, and now Altmeyer could see there were fire trucks stopped down the block,
and beyond them a pair of police cars, an ambulance, and a
tanker truck. As they moved closer, they could see a movie
camera on a cart. A fat man with a beard sat on a tractor seat
behind it, while three young men pushed the cart slowly forward three or four feet on a track of wooden planks. A woman
with a shock of gray hair stepped into the street beside it. She
was wearing a red T-shirt and Marine jungle fatigue trousers,
and carrying a clipboard.

"That was wonderful," she shouted. "You were all wonderful. Let's do it again, only not so fast."

A man in his early thirties wearing a Cleveland Indians
baseball cap and a bright yellow Hawaiian shirt stepped forward and called in an officious tone, "This is a picture. Quiet,
please. This is a picture. Very quiet."

The woman shouted, "Rolling, we're rolling, okay. Ac-
tion."

The fire trucks pulled out, a beautiful woman with plati-
num blond hair appeared from somewhere in a police uniform
and got into one of the squad cars, and it too moved off. At
the same time, a tall, thin man in a tuxedo dashed across the
street and wailed, "Gretchen!" then tore off his jacket, crumpled it, and threw it on the ground.

"Cut!" the woman in fatigues shrieked. Then her voice
changed again and she was a teacher calling to her class. "Very
good. This time, keep your foot off the brake, dear." The
police cars backed up the street to their places, and the fire
engines drove around the block. The woman in the police
uniform reached into the window of the squad car, pulled out
a large oriental fan, and fluttered it back and forth in front of
her face as she waited.

A woman carrying a fishing tackle box wandered around

in the street dabbing at people's faces with the powder puff she wielded in her free hand. Another young woman came forward to hand the tall, thin man another tuxedo coat.

Four men in blue jeans who had rolls of tape dangling from their belts sauntered across the street and sat down on the front steps of the nearest house, and another man climbed out of the tanker truck to spray water on the pavement with a hose.

"There he is," said Bucky, pointing at a group of people sitting in a row of lawn chairs in the shade of a tall tree. "Whatever I say, don't look surprised. You're the ones who have the lousy idea I'm peddling."

They started to weave among the technicians and extras toward the tree when the man with the Hawaiian shirt announced, "Hot lunch, watch your back, please. Watch your back," in the same stentorious voice. They stopped, and a panel truck backed slowly through the crowd into the center of the street.

Arthur Paston was sitting on a canvas chair, peering through spectacles with half-lenses at a bound script. As they approached, he didn't look up, but said, "Hello, Bucky. I didn't think you'd show up on a day like this."

Bucky took two steps forward and patted Paston's arm. "When you skin wild boar for a living, sometimes you have to go to the woods. How are they doing?"

Paston shrugged. "Two days ahead and sixty thousand under budget. Ethel is no fool, but there are rough seas waiting for her in about three days, when Gunther has to start saying some complete sentences."

Bucky smiled. "You always said it's a visual medium. Here, let me introduce some people."

Paston looked up, then slowly rose to his feet, staring at Rachel. "I know you," he said. "There's something silvery and mercurial about you that sticks in my memory." He thought for a moment. "Martinis."

"That's right," Rachel said. "We met the night you were making martinis at Bucky's house. They were very good."

167

He bowed, then turned to Altmeyer. "And you're the importer. Very pleased to see you both again. Please, make yourselves comfortable. We've got dozens of chairs here."

Bucky dragged a folding chair close to Paston's. "Arthur, today he's not an importer. He's come to rescue you from your boredom." He glanced out past the fire trucks and police cars at a group of men who were setting up metal stands with reflective aluminum sheets on them. "I'm going to try to package something really interesting, and I'm bringing it to you first. This isn't enough to keep you busy."

Paston smiled. "Of course. What do you have?"

"It makes this stuff look like child's play—little toy fire engines and police cars. We're thinking grown-up, Arthur." He lowered his voice and leaned closer. "I'm talking nuclear war." His eyes widened. "There is nothing—nothing—that fills a screen like nuclear war."

"I'm listening."

"It's not Fail-Safe, and it's not Dr. Strangelove. I'm talking about something that's never been done. This is a motion picture that's going to be important. It's something that has been making the authorities wake up in a cold sweat for twenty years, but nobody in the business has seen the beauty of it. And nobody can do this one right except you, Arthur. This one is about what happens when private companies start making and selling nuclear weapons to whoever has the cash. We should have a treatment ready soon."

Paston closed his eyes, and Bucky smirked at Altmeyer, then continued. "There's this nice young couple, see. They live in Los Angeles, maybe right here on this street."

Paston held up his hand. "I'll do it."

Bucky's face went slack. "What?"

"I said I'll do it. You're right that I'm bored. Ethel's a professional, and having me sitting here in geriatric splendor while she wraps this one up isn't going to help her any." He turned to Altmeyer. "What do you need to produce a treatment?"

Altmeyer said, "There are a few minor things that we haven't been able to work out yet." He stared at Bucky.

Bucky spoke quickly, his face now bright with hope. "We need a consultant who knows all about nuclear weapons. We've got this great idea, but we don't know anything about it."

Paston pursed his lips. "No matter. We'll dig one up for you."

Across the street a voice crackled through a radio, "Are you ready, Audrey?" and a man's voice shouted, "Ready." There was a pause, then, "Wait. Somebody get that cat off the car. Get it off."

BUCKY STOPPED THE CAR with its nose to the closed door of the four-car garage and the rear wheels at the edge of the street.

"You mean he just called up the government and got them to send him a consultant on nuclear weapons, just like that?" Rachel watched him with only the corner of her eye.

"Not exactly," said Bucky. "He talked to somebody at the Gray Corporation in Pasadena. It's not exactly the government, but it's not exactly not the government, either. All they do is study things the government wants somebody to think about. Maybe they want to diversify—you know, get a second customer."

Altmeyer stood at the back of Bucky's Mercedes. "You're going to lose a foot of your car if somebody comes around the curve in a hurry."

Bucky sighed. "That's the chance you take when you visit Arthur at the beach. Arthur likes Malibu, which is why he owns so much of it. Every year he loses a car to the traffic and an acre of land to the ocean. In a thousand years he'll be a pauper."

They walked along the front of the windowless brick

house to the broad hardwood door. Before they could knock, Arthur Paston opened the door. "You're early," he muttered. "You're always early."

"You were waiting for us," said Bucky.

Paston turned and walked away from the door into a huge carpeted space that was interrupted by an iron railing. Thirty or forty feet beyond the railing, a glass wall stretched from somewhere above to somewhere below; it was made of tiers of glass sheets, each of which looked to Rachel at least eight feet high. She walked to the railing and looked down to the lower level, where there were leather couches and armchairs grouped around a big fireplace. From the edge of the balcony she could see the white, rolling line of the surf in the blackness of the windows. To the left of the window there were several tall, slender coconut palms in a stone enclosure on a patio. "It's beautiful," she said.

"Terrific," said Bucky. "Just like living in the Astrodome." He joined Rachel at the railing. "Hey, you've got different trees in here."

Rachel looked back to the left side of the living room below, and realized that what she'd seen in the window was only a reflection. The patio and palm trees were inside the house.

Paston grumbled, "I had to. The damned things dropped leaves all over the floor. At least you don't have to rake palm fronds."

Bucky said, "Tell us about this guy before he gets here."

"I've never met him. He's supposed to be an expert on the proliferation of nuclear weapons. He's on some kind of permanent leave from Cal Tech. They still list him as a professor of physics. His name is Robert Cord."

"How did you get him to agree to talk to us?"

Paston looked surprised. "I invited him. How would you do it? Promise to make him a star?"

There was the sound of a car in the driveway. "Here he is." Paston walked back to the door and opened it, then called, "The door is over here. That's right." In a moment a man appeared in the doorway. He was wearing a well-tailored dark blue suit, and glasses with a faint gray tint that hid part of his deeply tanned face so that it was difficult to be certain of his age.

Paston said, "I'm pleased to meet you, Mr. Cord. These are the Altmeyers, who are working with me on this, and that one is our agent, Bucky Carmichael. Don't let him talk or he'll become an expensive fixture in your life."

Cord's mouth twitched to display his teeth, then uttered three times, "Pleasure," as he stiffly shook each hand.

"Watch your step," said Paston as they followed him down the curved stairway to the living room. "I don't want anybody falling on me."

At the bottom of the stairs, Cord glanced up once at the tall palm trees, then sat down in the nearest armchair.

Paston moved into the space beneath the balcony, where there was a long bar with a marble surface. "I will construct drinks, but it will be strictly a buffet-style distribution system. I'll make anything, but I've recently completed intensive training in the martini." He started pouring gin into a large shaker on the bar.

"I'll vouch for him," said Rachel, and the three men joined her at the bar.

As Cord took his drink, he said, "Tell me about your movie."

Bucky answered, "Realistic. Chilling. No, make that terrifying. We see it as a motion picture that's going to get people thinking. We want them to start talking to each other about the spectre of nuclear proliferation."

Cord smiled. "What made you think of that? Did you run out of mechanical sharks?"

"We want this motion picture to be something more than that. This town is full of people who have done sharks, piranhas, frogs, rats, plants, maniacs, bears, bugs, even worms. We're after something that's going to scare the audience because it's real. We need you to tell us what it is."

Cord sipped the martini and said to Arthur, "This is very

171

good, Mr. Paston. I wondered why I didn't see any servants. I guess you do everything better yourself."

"No, I don't," said Paston. "The only thing I do better than they do is make pictures, which is why I don't need them now."

Cord set his drink on the bar. "I don't think much of your movie. Everything that can be done on the subject legally has been done a couple of times already. My best advice is to scrap it."

Bucky frowned. "That's not one of the options. We're committed to doing this—dedicated to it. This motion picture will make us legends." He glanced at Arthur. "At least those of us who aren't legends already—you, me, them. All we need is a little specific information we can use to punch it up. This could be the last disaster film—the Big Bang."

Cord leaned against the bar. "As soon as you get started on this, you'll find that everything you want to know is classified. You're going to need a lawyer more than a director. If all you want is a big bang, you can get one without the headaches."

"How?" said Rachel. Her expression was sincere curiosity, but the hand she held behind her back fluttered at the others.

Cord smiled. "It's one of the oddities of the planet that a lot of things explode under the right conditions: gasoline, certain chemicals, flour, fertilizer, sawdust. In 1919 a tank of molasses blew up and killed twenty-one people in Boston." His eyes narrowed. "Now that's a script. When a device that a thousand intelligent people designed to explode works, what's the big deal? It's like watching bread pop out of a toaster."

"But you only feel that way because you know so much." Rachel picked up the cocktail shaker and refilled his glass. "What if hardly anybody had a toaster? They'd watch it twenty times in a row, and toast whole loaves of bread just to marvel at it. That would be a good script too—people getting used to their new toasters."

Cord grinned. "You know, when I was a kid I did that

172

once. I'd forgotten about it. I toasted about twenty slices of bread, one after another, watching to see how it worked. My mother came in a little while later, and didn't think much of it." His eyes seemed to focus on something in the distance.

"Because of the bread?"

He gave his head a little shake and looked back at her. "Because when I ran out of bread I had to face the fact that the only way to understand it was to take it apart."

"I guess that's why scientists have laboratories," said Rachel. "So your mothers can't see what you're doing."

Cord nodded. "Tell me more about the movie."

"Well, it's still pretty vague. We know that we want some terrorist group to make its own bomb."

Cord shook his head. "You've already made a big mistake. You're right that pretty soon we're going to have to face that problem, but that's not how it'll come about. Terrorists aren't in the business of making weapons. They're in the business of raising money to buy them from companies that know how to do it right. The thing to worry about is terrorists who get too good at making after-dinner speeches."

"So they'd get rich enough to bribe some government?"

"No," said Cord. "Governments only deal with other governments on those terms. Regardless of how they feel about each other, governments all depend absolutely on stability. As a rule they don't have a lot of imagination, but they can think of enough reasons not to overequip anybody whose primary interest isn't collecting next year's taxes."

"Who, then?" said Rachel. "You said terrorists wouldn't make their own."

Cord looked around at the others until he was satisfied that he had their attention. "You're not really thinking this through. In the first place, governments don't make nuclear weapons these days, at least not in the West. They order them from private companies, just the way they order combat boots or ballpoint pens, and that should suggest something to you."

"To go to another planet," said Rachel.

Cord ignored her. "When it's done, it will be a small- to

173

medium-sized company in a high-technology field, probably a multinational operating in Western Europe or the United States. It will probably be a company formed no more than ten years ago, and won't have a direct connection with the arms industry."

"How do you know all that?" said Rachel.

"We don't, but it's a profile we've developed. That version is pretty crude, and most of it is obvious. It won't be a giant corporation that would be risking its existence to raise its annual take by four-tenths of a percent. It won't be somebody who already has lots of government contracts, both because that's a form of long-term security and because they're too closely watched. It'll be a company that decides to move into a high-profit area at some risk."

Rachel's eyes flickered to Altmeyer's, then back. "So a company will figure out how to make a bomb, then sell it to terrorists, and make a big profit. Then what? The terrorists blow up their own country and take over the rubble?"

Cord shook his head. "One of the things you have to do is look at history. Nobody has ever made one nuclear weapon. The smallest number was two, and that's the exception because it was the first try, and they were in a hurry. You need one as a demonstration that you're not just pretending. The second is the one you use for extortion once you've established your sincerity. So the customer will buy at least two or three, and set off only one."

"What about the company? Once they have the secret, are they going to just keep rolling those big H-bombs off the assembly line?"

"It won't be hydrogen bombs, and they won't be big. Making a nuclear weapon isn't really a question of discovering a secret. The fundamental principles have been known for over a hundred years. It's a matter of solving dozens of engineering problems as you meet them, and most can be solved in a number of ways. But hydrogen bombs involve some very difficult and expensive problems, and the profile company wouldn't even consider facing them."

174

"You're sure of that?" said Bucky, but Rachel waved the hand behind her back at him without appearing to move.

"I'm not going to discuss this in detail. If it were possible for the company, it wouldn't be cost effective. Very few companies—or governments, for that matter—are in a position to build what you see on the news sticking out of a missile silo. And the ones that can are already doing it." Cord lifted his glass so that Rachel could pour another martini into it. "If you're set on doing this at all, think smaller—something like the first-generation atom bombs, only modernized and miniaturized. If you start thinking clearly about that, the list of companies grows and grows."

Rachel appeared to be shocked. "You mean lots of companies fit the profile?" She wondered if she'd gone too far. If she seemed too stupid, he'd stop talking.

Cord nodded. "A company that can make a computer, or a good digital watch, or a first-rate line of dental equipment, is doing something that's harder than making a no-frills atomic bomb. It doesn't take a whole lot to fire one piece of uranium down a shaft into another one to reach a critical mass. It's a damned good thing the materials are hard to come by."

"But if they did—if they could—what would it look like on film?"

Cord stared into the distance. "We have some you can fire like artillery shells in an eight-inch gun. Figure that as a convenient minimum size. You can do things smaller if you're really trying, but I'd say in a movie anything smaller than a suitcase is asking too much of the audience."

"That opens up a lot of plot possibilities," said Bucky. "It's something the actors can carry around. A lot can be done with that." He stared at Altmeyer, who avoided his eyes and poured himself another drink. "Great, isn't it?"

"I was wondering whether Mr. Cord could give us some help on the part where they transport the bomb," said Altmeyer.

"You might be able to make something out of that. They'd move it in pieces and assemble it just before they wanted to

175

use it. I suppose it might make an interesting scene if it weren't too long."

"But what should it look like?" said Altmeyer. "We have to make it look ominous."

Cord walked toward the enclosure where the palm trees stood in windless stillness. "Do what you feel like doing. If you think you need a rat's nest of wires and a ticking clock, fine. The real thing wouldn't have to be bigger than a football, and the electronics—well, when they made the first hydrogen bomb in 1952, the circuits in your pocket calculator would have filled this house."

Bucky followed Cord to the little terrace at the edge of the stand of trees. "I say we go for realism, or we've compromised this motion picture at the start. Either we do it with some honesty or we don't do it." He turned toward the bar as though he were waiting for applause.

"Agreed," said Rachel. "The way I see it, one problem is how these people get the components from one place to another. We know they need some uranium or some plutonium or something, right?"

"We know how they'll get it, roughly," said Cord. "In the Western countries right now there are over two hundred nuclear reactors, about seventy-five in the United States alone. Each of them needs a supply of weapons-grade uranium. Over the years quite a few of them have been unable to account for some of it. Nobody knows if it was diverted, lost, or what."

"Wouldn't they have to ship it across at least one border?" said Rachel. "This company would want to be pretty sure they didn't have any local customers."

"The safest thing would be to ship it in tiny pieces," said Cord. "Each one could be sealed inside lead, or even gold. The way you make money in manufacturing is to make everything predictable and repeatable. This business won't be any different. Probably the only part that would make an interesting movie is the first part. You can't buy fissionable metals on the open market. One way or another, you'd have to steal them."

176

"I wonder if that's an angle we can use," Bucky said. "We should be writing this down."

"We'll remember," said Altmeyer.

Arthur Paston picked up the cocktail shaker and began pouring another bottle of gin into it. "We've got a lot to think about."

Cord set his glass on the bar. "I'm going to take that as a cue. I've got an appointment in Pasadena in less than an hour, so I'm afraid that's going to have to be it for me."

"Do you think you'll be willing to work with us?" said Rachel.

Arthur Paston interrupted. "Let's not press Mr. Cord tonight. We'll all have more to say when we've explored the idea a little." He followed Cord up the staircase. At the top of the stairs, Cord and Paston disappeared. There were sounds of quiet conversation, then the closing of a door. Paston reappeared at the railing of the balcony, looking down into the living room. He stood silent for a few seconds, both hands clutching the railing. Finally his deep voice rolled through the house. "Bucky," he said, "pour everyone another drink. Start with me. I have a feeling I'm going to want it while you talk."

"Good idea," said Bucky, walking toward the bar. "We were so busy filling Cord's glass I didn't have time to have one myself. Where do you want to start? Money or talent?"

"Start by telling me what's going on here. It's pretty obvious you're not talking about a film."

Bucky's face assumed a shrewd look. "Television? Maybe, but only if the price is right, and I mean up front."

"No, you jackass," Paston said in a soft, tired voice. "You've done your best to get me involved in something, and now you're going to tell me what it is. Stop this nonsense about motion pictures. You don't need to act out this elaborate farce to get help from me. I assumed you knew that."

Bucky said, "Okay, Arthur. So it's a lousy idea. There's no need to get—"

"Save it, Bucky," said Altmeyer. He was looking up at

177

Paston, and his face was expressionless. "Thank you for your time." He stood up and held his hand out to Rachel.

Paston called, "There's no need to leave. Very likely you'll get what you came for. Bucky is like a member of my family: they're all just as foolish and disappointing as he is, and I would never abandon any of them if they needed me." He turned to Bucky. "What is it? Are you in debt to these people?"

Bucky held his breath for a second. As he let it out, he said, "Yes."

"How much?"

Bucky hesitated, and Paston announced, "You're trying to think of a lie." He said to Altmeyer, "It's not just money, is it?"

Altmeyer's cold, dispassionate eyes settled on Paston. "You're too smart to be of any use to us. Anything we tell you will do you harm."

"Very well done," Paston laughed. "I know you now, Altmeyer. You're the Tempter. Well, you've got me on the hook. Does criminal conspiracy require a written application?"

Altmeyer sat down on the couch beside Rachel and lit a cigarette. "Tell him, Bucky."

Bucky's eyes snapped to Altmeyer, but he said nothing. Altmeyer watched the smoke from his cigarette rise in a straight line above his motionless hand for five feet, then curl and fold and spread. He said, "This is a serious man. He sees what his choice means, and he's made it."

"Altmeyer," Rachel said, "he just cares about Bucky, and wants to get him out of trouble."

Altmeyer looked at Paston. "What will you do if we walk now?"

"I'll find out what you're doing in any way I can, and I won't be under any obligation to keep it to myself. One way or another, I'm going to know everything."

"Tell him," Altmeyer said.

. . .

PASTON SAT BACK in his chair and closed his eyes. "A rational man my age would wish you hadn't told him. I can remember going to the hardware store with my father in a horse-drawn buggy. When I came to this town we used to stop what we were doing and look up if an airplane flew over."

"I know," said Bucky. "And when you did, a dinosaur ran over and bit you on the ass. A rational man wouldn't have looked up."

"Bucky," said Rachel.

Paston opened his eyes. "No, he's right. At a certain point your memory starts to get too sharp and it nags at you. Sometimes I remember things—sounds, smells, everything—but it's just some day fifty or sixty years ago. Nothing special at all." He shook his head, and his eyes brightened. "So you waste another day remembering it."

Rachel stood up and walked to the glass wall. "I'm sure we'll remember this one." She leaned close to the pane and stared out at the ocean. "If we're around."

Paston snapped, "What's that? Of course we'll be around. We've just got to do something about these people. If you think I'm just going to sit here like an idiot while they—"

"We can't go to the authorities with this," said Altmeyer. He glanced toward Rachel beside the glass wall. "Then again, in a year a private room in a place with no windows and nice stone walls five feet thick might be all the rage."

"Of course we can't call the police," said Paston. "After they'd arrested all of you for murder, I'd have to do everything by myself."

"I told you he was a compassionate man," Bucky said to Altmeyer. He walked to Paston's chair and tilted the cocktail shaker to refill the old man's glass. "Three years ago he gave Leonard a day off, and now this."

"Funny you should mention Leonard," said Paston. "That's the company he's researching, isn't it? Ashita."

Bucky nodded. "Of course. At the moment I wouldn't advise anybody to invest in anything. I just figured Leonard would find out whatever there was to know."

179

"He will." Paston turned to Altmeyer. "You know, it's very possible that Bucky will be our salvation. Think about it. He perceives the loyalty, the decency, the competence of a man like Leonard, and remembers it. When he needs it, he never hesitates."

PASTON LED THEM THROUGH the outer office to a room with a thick oak door, and knocked. A few seconds later the door swung open and a large middle-aged man in a white shirt stepped to the side and held it. "Hello, folks," he said. "Welcome."

"Leonard, these are the people I told you about. Mr. and Mrs. Altmeyer, Leonard Stahl."

Rachel scanned the room rapidly. There was a small computer terminal on a battered steel typewriter table beside the desk. The walls were covered with unframed photographs, posters, baseball pennants, newspaper clippings, and bits of paper all tacked up in no discernible order except that some must have been more recent because they obscured others. She sat on an old green couch near the desk and felt the right leg of her pantyhose catch on something behind the knee. When she surreptitiously ran a finger to the spot to free it, she recognized that it was the metal spiral binding of a notebook that had found its way under the cushion.

Leonard walked from place to place in the office picking computer printouts off chairs and dropping them on the floor. "Please make yourselves comfortable. Coffee, anybody?"

Rachel glanced at the coffee machine in the corner of the room, where four cracked white china cups sat before a Pyrex vessel filled with coal-black liquid. "No, thank you." The others seemed to share her thought: "Makes me nervous." "Not right now, thanks."

Paston said, "Have you found anything yet?"

Leonard sat behind his desk and started hunting through piles of papers and files and ledger sheets. "I don't know everything yet, but I know something. It's sort of a profile."

180

Altmeyer and Rachel glanced at each other.

Leonard continued. "Things have gotten tougher in the last few years. Any company smaller than General Motors feels like a pussycat in the jungle. They see a chance to grow a little, and whatever they do to get the capital might attract attention for an unfriendly takeover. If they go public they're liable to come to work next morning and find out somebody bought the place out from under them. So they hide in the tall grass as long as they can."

"Is that what Ashita is doing?" asked Altmeyer.

Leonard selected a file and opened it. "It sure looks that way. They're being secretive as hell. They used to deal through local distributors, but in the last couple of years they put their own in place in just about every market. I haven't got any figures, but the one here can't possibly handle the volume they got from the wholesalers two years ago."

"What does that mean to you?" said Paston.

Leonard didn't look up from the file. "What it might mean is that Bucky's right. They might have something going, and they're not planning to reveal what it is until they've got their own retail outlets set up and ready to sell it."

"So they've got a mystery product," said Rachel. "But how does anyone get in on it?"

Leonard shrugged. "It's hard to be sure of anything. A new product can mean new factories, retooling, lots of expenses. If it's really new, they'd have to face advertising costs. They haven't gone to any of the major banks in Japan or here. They haven't filed to go public on any of the exchanges."

"How do you know about the banks?" said Paston.

"Ashita is private, and the banks won't answer a straight question, but you can find out about big loans by doing a credit check. Anyway, if they're not selling stock and not borrowing money, it's possible they might be willing to talk about making a limited partnership available. There's no way of telling who they might be talking to about it already."

"It sounds as though we've got to move fast," said Paston. "What else have you got there?"

181

Leonard handed him a glossy booklet covered with model numbers and prices. "It's their catalog. If they have a mystery product, I don't imagine it's in there."

Bucky stood next to Paston. "Can we take it with us?"

"Sure. I don't know what it'll tell you."

"We're going to order a sampling of this stuff," Bucky said. "What's the sense in trying to invest if you find out later that everything they make is a piece of crap?"

"Look, Bucky. I don't know what these people are doing. I don't know if they'll let you in on it if you find out. But I'd say that you haven't got six weeks to wait for delivery from God knows where. If people are talking about it already, you've got to make up your minds."

Paston held the catalog at arm's length to examine it. "All right. I'll get back to you very soon." He moved toward the door. "In the meantime, please keep at it. Concentrate on finding out who actually owns it, who runs it, and how to get in touch with them. If we decide to make a move, I want to be able to talk to the man who's going to sign the papers."

"But Arthur," said Bucky. "We've got to—"

Altmeyer touched his sleeve. "Relax." He turned to Leonard. "Thanks very much for everything."

Rachel moved up between Bucky and Leonard, smiling. "Yes, thank you so much. Arthur said you were the best, and now we know what that means." She sensed the door opening behind her and knew Altmeyer would be guiding Bucky out, so she backed up to cover their retreat. "It was so nice to meet you."

As they walked to Bucky's car, Rachel moved up beside Paston. "Arthur, what did you notice? Was it something in the catalog?"

"One thing is that Leonard was more right than he knew, and we don't have six weeks to wait for delivery. The other is that we don't have to. They list a wholesale outlet in Westwood." He handed Rachel the catalog as he eased himself into the backseat of the Mercedes.

Rachel studied the catalog, sliding her finger quickly down the columns, then turning the pages rapidly.

"The store locations are on the last page," said Paston.

"I saw it," said Rachel. "805 Westwood Boulevard." She frowned. "Altmeyer, take a look at this. 805 Westwood Boulevard." She pushed the catalog over the front seat.

"I heard you," said Bucky. "We'll be there in twenty minutes."

Altmeyer examined the catalog. "I'm sure we will," he said, then closed the booklet and left it on his lap. "It should be interesting to see."

"What do you mean?" Paston asked.

"Think about where that is," said Rachel. "It's right on the edge of the UCLA campus."

Bucky said, "Whatever else these people are, they're not stupid. Who do you think buys all the electronic equipment? If I were selling stereos and tapedecks and all that stuff, I'd—"

Altmeyer interrupted. "Rachel's right. I'd show you the merchandise list if I didn't think you'd drive us into a tree. I don't see anything kids would buy. They've got fifty kinds of wires and cables. They've got temperature control systems for office buildings and swimming pools. They even have a humidity machine for greenhouses. The only business they could be doing is a wholesale trade to contractors. So the location doesn't fit."

"Think about it," said Rachel. "It's right between Brentwood and Beverly Hills, on some of the most expensive real estate in the world. But why? Contractors aren't going to be impressed with a chic location, and I can't think of another advantage. It's at least twenty miles from the harbor."

Altmeyer nodded, and added, "Besides, think about the traffic around there. Most of the streets are too narrow to take a truck bigger than two and a half tons. It's practically impossible to park, and every day twenty-five or thirty thousand cars clog every street just to get to the campus. Then there's the Veterans Administration hospital complex, and—"

183

"I know," said Bucky. "And Century City and Fox Studios on the other side. I spend half my life in that part of town, and Arthur probably holds the second mortgage on it. We already know these people aren't just selling electronic pool-warmers, so what's the startling hypothesis?"

Rachel shook her head. "I don't have one, do you?"

Altmeyer studied the catalog again. "No. I can see why they had to take risks to ship their uranium to Japan. Apparently you have to take it when it's available and use whatever is handy to move it. I can't see why they'd do anything peculiar with their regular business. I wonder if there's anything odd about their other locations."

"I'll ask Leonard to check that out," said Paston. "It's a reasonable question if you're thinking of investing, isn't it?"

"Sure," said Bucky. "We don't want our stores in run-down locations trying to sell our bombs to people who can't afford them." He stopped at Wilshire Boulevard, where he tried to turn right to join the westbound traffic, but it wasn't moving.

When the light turned green, Arthur said, "Go straight, and then get us back to my house."

"Don't tell me you're going to give me a lecture on traffic patterns, too."

"No, I just think we'd better go to the Ashita store at another time of the day. Altmeyer probably knows when would be best."

Altmeyer answered without hesitation. "About ten, after the second showing starts at the movie theaters around that part of town. We want to be finished shopping about the same time the movies end." He leaned back in the seat and closed his eyes.

MOST OF THE PEOPLE on the street seemed to be in their twenties or thirties, and they were in pairs or groups of pairs, as though somewhere nearby there must be an old-fashioned dance, and partners had strolled outside to take the air.

184

Altmeyer glanced around him. "We should be on track. It's in this block, and the movies will be starting in ten or fifteen minutes." He cradled the shopping bag under his arm.

Rachel veered away from the store windows toward the curb, and leaned her head to the side to look ahead. "You're not going to believe it."

"Probably not," said Bucky, "but I'm getting used to that."

"It's the bookstore. They must have bought the lease and closed down the bookstore. What a shame."

Altmeyer said quietly, "I guess it won't be hard to find our way around, will it?"

"I could do it with my eyes closed," said Rachel. "I used to spend hours in there. A couple of times, I remember people coming up and asking me for some book or other, because they thought I worked there."

"They were trying to pick you up," said Altmeyer.

Rachel frowned. "No, it wasn't that at all."

Paston chuckled. "Yes, I'll bet it was. That used to be my favorite ploy a lot of years ago. I found the perfect bookstore in New York. It specialized in symbolist poetry, and—"

"Arthur, this is a sordid aspect of your character I never suspected," said Bucky. "You've never told me."

"You've never been interested in women who could read," said Paston. He surveyed the front window of the store. The glass had recently been reinforced with wrought-iron grillwork. The display consisted of a few plastic boxes that could have been components of any kind of electronic system. "Not very inviting, is it?"

"We'll get in," said Altmeyer. "The bars are a good sign. It means they probably don't have an alarm system. They don't want anybody getting far enough to trip it and bring the police. Let's go around to the back."

Behind the Ashita store there was still a sign on the steel double door that said BOOKSTORE PARKING ONLY. Altmeyer set his shopping bag on the concrete platform and studied the doors.

Bucky sighed. "I was hoping for a sign that said BUR-GLARS' ENTRANCE. Are you going to pick the lock?"

Altmeyer grinned, and reached into the shopping bag.

"This, ladies and gentlemen, is called a crowbar." He slipped it under the edge of the door. "It's not pretty. It's not complicated." He moved it along the crack beneath the door until he reached the center, directly under the doorknob. He wrenched downward on it, and there was a tearing sound. Then he set it aside and pulled out a metal strip that had been screwed to the floor. "It doesn't require that you know any mathematics, or even that you can read directions. You just have to be persistent."

He pushed the crowbar under the door again, this time a little farther, sliding it from side to side, feeling for something. Finally, he found what he was looking for, and set the flat fork of the crowbar against it. He turned to the others. "This door has a vertical rod that goes into a hole in the floor. The rod is a half-inch of steel, but the floor isn't." He leaned on the crowbar, and there was a cracking of wood. He shifted the bar again, and slowly pushed down. As he did, he reached up to the doorknob and pulled the door open an inch with his left hand.

"Very convincing," said Bucky.

"Yes," said Altmeyer. "I like to think of the crowbar as the tool of the analytical person. Given enough time and patience, you can divide just about anything into its basic parts." He faced the door and slipped his hand inside, pushing his palm against the rod and raising it. The door swung open.

Bucky hesitated. "Lately I seem to spend a lot of time stumbling around in dark places."

"Don't worry," said Rachel, slipping past him into the darkness. "When you shop with me, you get all the conveniences. Come in and close the door. I've got my hand on the light switch."

There was a faint scraping noise and then a clank, as Altmeyer pulled the door shut. The lights came on to reveal a large room filled with cardboard cartons and a doorway that led to the front of the store. "Are you sure the lights aren't a mistake?" said Paston.

"Pretty sure," Altmeyer said. "When this was a bookstore the front door was glass. Now it's wood. You used to be able to see past the window display into the store. Now the cases in the back are closed like cabinets. That's a lot to do for no reason."

"They probably cut expenses by shooting the carpenters." Rachel walked along a row of boxes. "Arthur, here's the product list. You can check off each item as you find it, and Bucky and Altmeyer will open the boxes and see what's inside." She moved away through the doorway to the front of the building.

"Where's she going?" asked Bucky.

"To do some browsing. Okay, Arthur. What's first?"

"Let's start over here with these big ones. It says they're Model R1X-5937, which is a Happyboy Humidfier. I've never heard anything so sinister in my life."

Altmeyer tore open a carton and pulled out a large black box with a louver in front, stared at it, then pried off the back panel with his crowbar. Two small screws popped and spun over his shoulder, then bounced somewhere behind him. He tore out the workings and tossed them into the carton, one by one. A little silver fan missed the carton, but Altmeyer ignored it.

"Eager shoppers, aren't we?" Bucky said.

"They'll know we were here anyway," said Altmeyer. "What's next?"

Paston tilted his head to read the label on another box. "NIR-2130, the Receptaphone."

Bucky wrenched open a carton and announced, "Sounds like a musical instrument, but it's only an answering machine. Here, Altmeyer. You can analyze this with your crowbar while I get the next one."

RACHEL WALKED QUIETLY into the front of the store. The long aisles of bookcases now held plastic packets containing

187

coils of wire, plugs and clips, circuit boards, and other para-
phernalia that seemed to go with the various kinds of plastic
boxes displayed beneath them. As she walked the aisles, she
could hear the hushed voices of Altmeyer and the others, and
occasionally a sharp crack as they broke something open.

She turned toward the stairway that went up to the second
floor. A couple of months ago, that had been the part of the
store she'd liked the best, where the books had ripened past
the stage where they were displayed sideways like pictures.
Upstairs had looked like a library, with books shelved in neat
rows. She remembered that there had been a little office upstairs, where the manager did the paperwork. It opened into
a shallow alcove lined with expensive reference books. She'd
wondered whether the manager had chosen those books for
the spot because few customers looked at them, or because
they lent dignity to his little office. Now those shelves would
hold more of the rectangular electronic boxes, some with lights
on them or digital displays or dials, but all of them ugly and
threatening as rat traps.

Rachel made her way up the stairs and paused at the top,
feeling a mild dizziness. She stood there as her heartbeat
slowed. "Not now," she thought. "It's too important. Later I'll
make up for it."

The upper floor had been remodeled. The shelves were
gone, and the alcove was now open. Four large wooden desks
with computer terminals shared the space with a row of black
filing cabinets. Without hesitating, she moved to the nearest
desk and began to shuffle through the papers. She worked with
a methodical calm, forcing herself to study each sheet on the
desk, then opening each drawer and reaching in to be sure
nothing was taped above it.

When she had finished the first desk, she moved to the
second. As she opened the third drawer, she could feel that
the muscles in her legs were tense, urging her to jump up and
hurry downstairs to summon the others. Rachel crossed her
ankles tightly and kept on with her work. After this, there
would still be the filing cabinets.

．　．　．

IN THE STOREROOM, Bucky watched Altmeyer demolish a Cozy Paradise Industrial Thermostat. "Is that one a possibility?" he asked. "It's pretty well sealed."

Altmeyer moved to another box. "I doubt it. There's not much to it. If Cord is right, then whatever they're using has to be heavy enough to allow them to replace the guts of it with lead-plated uranium." He examined the carton. "We've done these, haven't we, Arthur?"

Paston tilted his glasses on his nose and squinted at the list in his hand. "Is that the smoke detector?"

"No, it's the water purifier."

"Then you've already wrecked one." He ran his pen down the list and then back up to the top. "I'd say we've seen everything except the G-96 High Voltage Safety Cable and the battery-operated smoke detector."

"I don't see anything like that back here. Let's check out the front part of the store. If they don't have a stock of them, they'll at least have one on display."

They filed through the doorway, and Bucky strolled along the first row of shelves. "Wires and cables are over here. What was the number again?"

"G-96."

Bucky held up a clear package containing a red coil. "Here you go. Should I wrap it up, or would you like to wear it home?"

Altmeyer opened the package and peeled a strip of plastic insulation off the end of the cable. "I don't think this is it either. They'd need something a little heavier gauge, so they could fit a hollow jacket into the center." He dropped it and moved to the next row of shelves.

Bucky wandered to the front counter and called, "Hey, they've got a really good catalog up here, with pictures and everything." He picked up the catalog and rapidly flipped the pages. "Here it is. The Sleeping-Tite Smoke Sentinel. It's sort of ivory colored, about the size and shape of a soup bowl, with a little red light in the middle. Do you see anything like that?"

After a pause, Paston said, "Not on this side. Everything over here is square." Altmeyer said, "There's nothing over here we haven't seen. Let me look at the picture."

Altmeyer and Bucky met at the counter, then moved closer to the stairway, where the light was brighter. Altmeyer studied the catalog, then handed it to Bucky. "See that? It says 'Temporarily available only in the United Kingdom.' "

"At least I found the catalog," said Bucky.

"Hold on to it. So far it's about the best thing we've got." He moved up the stairs to the lighted office, where Rachel was opening and closing file drawers.

"Find anything interesting?" he asked.

"A few things." Rachel's voice was soft and distant. She moved quickly to the next filing cabinet and opened another drawer.

"They don't seem to lock anything, do they?" Paston said as he reached the top of the stairs.

"There's not much reason to," Rachel muttered into the drawer. "There's practically nothing here. There are a few purchase orders, but there aren't any copies of invoices, not even bills of lading for the merchandise they have in stock. They probably delivered everything in one load, including the furniture. Take a good look at the computer terminals. They're not hooked up to anything."

Altmeyer surveyed the room. "There's not even an electrical outlet close enough to this one to plug it in."

Rachel closed the last drawer and stopped. "That's it. I guess I'm done. Maybe we should get out of here and talk about it."

"I'm not sure we're finished," said Altmeyer. "Can you give me a quick version?"

Rachel sat down behind the nearest desk and looked straight ahead, as though she were reciting from a dim memory. "That desk over there and most of the file drawers are empty. There's nothing here that looks like they're doing much actual business. I suppose the surprise is that they're doing any at all, but I guess they couldn't avoid it." She smiled, but her eyes rested on his face only for a second, then moved away. "Let's see. Everyone who works here is American. There's nothing that's not in English anywhere, not even scrawls on scrap paper."

"You're building up to something."

She nodded. "It's not helpful, just scary. I found five handguns in the office, and there's an Ingram MAC-10 in the bottom drawer of the second filing cabinet that's got a three-position selector lever. At the moment it's on full auto, which shows somebody is no genius."

Altmeyer touched her arm. "And the handguns?"

"At least they're not Brownings," she said.

"We can't supply everything for these deadbeats." He paused. "Is there something worse?"

"There was a sheet of paper in that desk that had our address on it."

He put his arm around Rachel. "Come on, baby. Let's get out of here."

Bucky spoke. "Wait a minute." They turned to see him climbing up on a desk. He got to his feet unsteadily and stared up at the ceiling, where there was a disk-shaped object about nine inches in diameter with a glowing red dot in the center. He pointed at it. "Look," he said. "I can't read it from here, but it sure looks like a battery-operated Sleeping-Tite Smoke Sentinel to me."

Altmeyer climbed onto the desk beside him and pulled the chair up after him. "Hold the chair steady," he said, and stepped onto the seat. He reached up and touched the disk, turned it, than tugged at it. "You're right, old Buckeye."

Rachel said, "There must be more of them downstairs. There's no reason to break your neck."

Bucky didn't take his eyes off Altmeyer. "They don't sell them here. Only England."

"They may not sell much of anything," said Rachel, "but they sure ordered a bunch of those. The requisition is over here

191

someplace." She stepped to the row of filing cabinets and opened two drawers before she found the one she wanted, then extracted a folder.

Altmeyer climbed down to the desk and stood beside Bucky, holding the smoke alarm. Bucky said, "I want you to know before you set it off that my nerves are already shot."

Altmeyer squeezed a notch on the side and pulled off the cover. He stared inside for a moment, then handed the alarm to Bucky and pointed at the words etched deeply into the shiny metal box beside the battery.

Bucky read aloud, "Caution. No user-serviceable components. Contains radioactive material."

Rachel looked up from the file as though she hadn't heard. "They ordered two thousand of them from Japan last month, but the delivery date is over a year away."

"Thank God for that," said Paston.

"But it means they're already planning," said Rachel. "They think that someday they'll want to build a bomb here."

"Time to go," said Altmeyer. "I left my shopping bag and crowbar downstairs. Anybody else leave anything?"

"We didn't bring anything," said Rachel. "If we want to make it look like a burglary, shouldn't we steal something?"

"I'll take the MAC-10 and a couple of clips," said Altmeyer. "Somebody else take the handguns."

Arthur Paston steadied himself on the railing as he started down the steps. "It's very clever of these people to ship radioactive material clearly labeled. I suppose if we weigh that part of the smoke detector and multiply it by two thousand, someone would be able to tell us the size of the bombs, wouldn't they? Maybe Mr. Cord could do that."

Bucky took a handgun from Rachel and followed her toward the stairs. "I'm not sure we need to know that, Arthur."

Paston was at the foot of the stairs. In the dim light he looked very tall and straight. "You're right, of course. Very early in my life I learned that all intelligent, serious people are obsessed with the specific, with seeing the details clearly. But this is different, isn't it?"

192

"No," said Rachel. "It isn't. We just have to put off some of the thinking for now."

Altmeyer examined the little submachine gun. "I'll put this in the bag. If anybody has an impulse to destroy anything, please feel free, if it's not noisy."

"No thanks," said Bucky. "I couldn't spoil such a beautiful evening." Rachel walked toward the front door, and Bucky called, "You're not really going to break—"

Rachel spoke over her shoulder. "Don't be silly. I'm just going to see if the time is right for leaving the scene of the crime."

Altmeyer returned from the storeroom with his shopping bag. "How does it look?"

"Just a second. Oh, here it is." She leaned over and peered through the tiny fish-eye lens set in the door. "The street looks good. There are lots of people out there, moving in both directions."

"The theaters must be letting them out about now. Bucky and Rachel go first, and we'll follow. Bucky, do what Rachel does. You go out, and turn right into the crowd. Don't look anybody in the eye, and keep moving, like everybody else."

"We're not going to sneak out the back?"

"It's a waste of time and it's dangerous. What kind of person comes out of an alley at night?"

"The kind who goes shopping with a crowbar."

RACHEL STEPPED OUT ONTO THE SIDEWALK and Bucky followed her. Altmeyer had his hand on the door handle and his eye at the peephole, watching the reactions of the people he could see on the street until Rachel and Bucky had taken ten paces and disappeared from his vision. Then he swung the door open and pulled Arthur outside and closed the door. He held the shopping bag in the crook of his left arm as he walked.

Paston said quietly, "We seem to have made it."

Altmeyer shrugged. "All we really found in there was more to worry about."

"We had to find out what we could."

They turned the corner, and now they could see that Rachel and Bucky were nearly to the car. Altmeyer said, "How much do you have to find out before you figure it's time to dump us and go to the authorities?"

Paston slowed down to stay out of the others' hearing. "My experience with the authorities is that they're slow. When they're dealing with outlandish accusations against a legitimate company they'll be slower."

Altmeyer stopped walking and waited.

Paston spoke with impatience, as though he were reciting. "I know we can't afford to wait for months while the police of several countries are inventing procedures to keep from stepping on each other's toes. Thousands of people might be dead by that time."

"What will it take to get you to make the call?"

Paston scowled. "We don't need to talk about this. Bucky said it. Once you know, there's no way out but forward. If I thought the police would be able to stop this after they had locked us up, I wouldn't need to call them."

Altmeyer studied Paston. "What are you talking about?"

Paston leaned closer. "It pleases you to say you're in this to get your money, but you know there probably never was any money of the sort you could walk away with. You say you can't stop because these people are trying to kill you, but you know that once their weapons are delivered they have nothing to fear from you. If it's time for the police I won't need to call them, because you'll do it."

"You forget who I am. This is what I do for a living."

Paston watched Rachel climbing into Bucky's car. "I don't forget anything."

A TELEPHONE RANG somewhere in the distance, and Rachel listened, trying to find it. The sound seemed to be coming from some other part of the house, past the tall palm trees.

Paston opened a box on the table beside him and lifted a

receiver out of it. "Yes. Oh, hello, Leonard. Bucky and the Altmeyers are here now. All the partners ought to hear this, so I'll switch you to the intercom."

Leonard's amplified voice swept into the room from a speaker somewhere near the bar. "Don't do it yet. Look, I've been checking this deal out from all angles, and none of it looks right. This Altmeyer—"

"I didn't ask you to do any checking there, Leonard," said Paston.

"When you go into a partnership, you'd better know who your partner is. Now don't say anything, just grunt or something if I'm getting through to you. Altmeyer is solvent. He's got a big house in Laurel Canyon that's worth a couple million. He's got a very solid credit rating, the kind that goes with somebody who owns a bank instead of cashing paychecks there. But I can't find any sign of where it all comes from. He and his wife supposedly own this crappy little import-export business."

"That may be better than it looks. Let's not worry—"

"Trust me on this, Arthur. I don't have any proof, but this guy isn't what you think he is. He doesn't need a partner for a deal like this any more than you do. He's got to be using you to front the deal for him. Most likely he's a drug smuggler up to his ass in hundred-dollar bills he has to convert."

"It's probably just inherited."

"Careful, or he'll figure out what we're talking about. I know you said Bucky was with you, but I've got a feeling this guy can cause problems an agent can't get you out of. I knew that sooner or later Bucky's generosity with cocaine was going to turn up some snakes, and this is one of them. This is not a man who inherited anything."

"Not him?"

"Her? I doubt it. I know the last girl who altered your pulse was Marie Dressler, but take a look anyway, and it may stir a dim memory. Women who look like that get rich only after puberty, and most of them do it by marrying men like him. The first time I saw him I knew he was trouble. Look at his eyes, for Christ's sake. When you brought him in I thought you'd finally hired a bodyguard."

"Ashita."

"Are you even listening? Arthur, if nothing worse happens, some day the IRS is going to stumble on this guy and declare a national holiday. I picked a bank just because they have a branch near his house, and asked if he could cover a movie development deal for half a million, and they didn't have to put me on hold. When they get him, you're going to be on the seven o'clock news."

"I understand. Now I'm going to put you on the intercom." He pushed a button twice, and Leonard's voice changed.

His tone was friendly and informal. "Hello, everyone."

Bucky and Rachel sang, "Hi, Leonard."

"I've got a little more information on Ashita Electronics. First—well, I guess I'd better dispel the suspense. My advice is to forget it. They have a source of capital. They're busy setting up headquarters in six or seven countries. If I were to guess, I'd say somebody already bought a controlling interest."

Altmeyer's voice was low and respectful. "Why, exactly, Leonard?"

"Because there's a change in management style. For years they've built things in Japan and sold them to wholesalers in other countries. All of a sudden they started quietly setting up their own stores in foreign markets. They don't seem to be doing any more business, but they're getting ready for something. It's got to be big, because they're going to a lot of trouble to find prime locations. All the stores are near universities. By the way, you were the one who gave me that lead, and it's a big one."

"It was the UCLA store that made us wonder," said Rachel.

Leonard spoke thoughtfully. "That alone tells you a lot. They've got a mystery product for retail marketing. They're obviously planning to sell it to university students, and hope it turns into a fad. It's such an old pattern that I can hardly believe I didn't catch it."

196

"Don't feel bad," Rachel said. "We just wondered about the locations, but we didn't have a theory. But it looks good, doesn't it?"

"No," said Leonard. "It means everything is wrong. They're investing a lot of money in stores that won't make anything unless the mystery product is a winner. We don't know whether it's going to be the best thing since the Frisbee or a complete failure. What we know is that they already have a partner with risk capital."

"Can you figure out when they plan to introduce this product?" asked Paston. "Maybe we can get in after the first splash while they're wondering if they've made a mistake."

"I doubt it," Leonard said. "Honestly, Arthur. You know I have other reservations about this as it fits into your total financial picture. But this is a separate issue. Whoever is paying the bills has set things up to take a loss for a long time just to have all the licenses and stores ready in advance. They'll introduce the product in one place, then let it hit the magazines. If they can get the hype they want, then it will suddenly appear in the other stores that are set up to sell it."

"Why?" said Rachel. "They're obviously preparing well enough to do it everywhere at once."

"That's no marketing strategy for a small corporation," Leonard said patiently. "People in Minneapolis and Düsseldorf buy things that somebody convinces them are fashionable in London and Paris. If the product flies in their showcase market, they'll release it in the other places, and probably bump up the price."

"What do you think is the showcase market where they'll introduce this product?" asked Paston.

"All I can do is guess, and my guess is London. It's the first foreign store they opened, which means it's the one they wanted most. London is the place where some of the biggest trends have started over the years, and they even seem to have set up their London outlet as a test market for some of the boring products they sell now."

"What do you mean?" Rachel asked.

"This year's catalog lists a smoke alarm that's available only in the United Kingdom. I'm not saying that proves anything, but it would be a lot easier to run your tests in your home country unless you've got something special in mind. I'm telling you, everything about this looks as though we're seeing phase twelve of a thirteen-phase plan, and not the sort of venture where they take a shot and then go out to look for capital."

"Thanks, Leonard," said Paston. "I'd like you to get Stephanie to set up a trip to London for us. We'll all be going, and I want it to look as innocuous as possible. Maybe the best idea is to set it up as a search for locations. I guess that means I'll bring some cameras, and maybe a tape recorder."

"Arthur, this is not a good idea."

"Thanks, Leonard. Keep in touch." Paston punched the button on the telephone and closed the box on it.

Altmeyer stood up and stretched. "Bucky, would you mind staying here with Arthur tonight and letting us go back to your house alone? We'll try to be here around noon, but don't panic unless you don't see us by ten or eleven at night."

Paston began, "I hope you weren't offended. Leonard is only—"

"Not at all," said Altmeyer, examining Bucky's key chain. "See you tomorrow."

Bucky followed them up the stairs to the door. "What are you going to do?"

Rachel said, "Check on the goats."

Altmeyer lifted the shopping bag at the door and looked inside. "We'll just take a couple of the handguns. Keep the rest of this stuff with you." He handed the bag to Bucky. "Remember to think ahead. If you hear a knock at the door, look for the guy outside the big window before you move." Without waiting for an answer, he followed Rachel outside.

Bucky whispered to the closed door, "Be safe." He turned and walked down the steps slowly, holding the heavy shopping bag at the bottom. When he reached Paston he said, "Do you want one of these?" He held out the bag.

"I hate the things, but I'd better get used to holding one without shooting myself." Paston gingerly lifted one of the pistols by the barrel and stared at it, then glanced at Bucky. "We'll all be here tomorrow night."

"What do you think they're doing?"

Paston shrugged, and studied the gun. "I suppose this thing is loaded."

Bucky reached for it, checked the magazine, then clicked it back into the handgrip. "Yes." He handed it back to Paston. "Do you think we're being fools?"

Paston said, "Altmeyer seems to know what he's doing." He paused for a moment, then added, "What Leonard said about Altmeyer wasn't wrong."

"Leonard doesn't know."

"But he isn't wrong. You have to be very unlucky to meet a worse man than Altmeyer. He's a predator."

"If you feel that way, why are you—"

Paston put the gun on his lap and clasped his hands over it. "People like him win wars."

ALTMEYER LET THE MERCEDES coast up the driveway, and the automatic garage door swung open to admit them. When the door closed, Altmeyer glanced at his watch. "Very good. We've got plenty of time to set ourselves up in the bushes behind the koi pond before old Calvin comes to work."

"They're not bushes, they're dwarf spruce trees."

"Whatever. Let's go change our clothes."

Rachel stepped out of the car. "I know, my late-night sneaking ensemble in olive drab. It's a good thing I know what to pack."

"Just be sure it's something that'll keep you warm and dry for a couple of hours."

She paused and studied him across the hood of the car. "That's the sort of thing I'm supposed to say. If we live another year, we'll be like those old couples who never have to talk at all."

"We'll talk to the kids."

She felt the skin of her face tighten, as though she weren't controlling the muscles anymore. There was a false smile there, protecting her from something, and she heard herself say, "Yes, and the adult goats too."

Altmeyer was already opening the door to Bucky's house for her, and she couldn't see his face. She swept past him, as though she could evade his next sentence by outstepping it. Then she was in the guest bedroom, and she could hear Altmeyer somewhere near Bucky's library. She wondered what he would have said next. He might still be thinking about it, alone in the other room. He might have been trying to tell her something important. It might not have been just another empty remark. Rachel sat on the bed staring at her suitcase, listening for his footsteps. Finally, as her eyes traced the metal strip along the top and settled for the fourth time on the little dent at the corner, she let the moment go.

She opened the suitcase and pulled out a sweat shirt and running shoes, then tied her hair back in a loose braid. As she dressed, she heard Altmeyer walking down the hallway again. "I guess I'm ready to go," she said. "There's not much point in overdressing for these occasions."

As they walked along the edge of Bucky's patio and stepped on the mosaic near the swimming pool, Rachel thought about the party. That night it had been easier to take the short-cut along the hillside because the flood lamps above the eaves of Bucky's house had lit the path for half the distance. She followed Altmeyer along the hedges and into the weeds. She started watching the ground for the little stone ridge fifty feet before it came. In the 1920s there had been another house farther down the hill, and the little ridge was the remnant of the rock border of a terraced garden. Rachel had always thought of it as an old-fashioned garden of flower bushes that people didn't grow anymore, pink bleeding hearts and white primroses and purple lilacs.

Then they crossed into the thick stand of old eucalyptus trees that must have been planted to mark the edge of the original yard, and onto what Rachel thought of as their land. Even though Altmeyer had paid money to somebody to get a deed that said the boundary line was around the middle of the old garden they'd just passed, it had always seemed to Rachel that the real line was where the trees began. Fifteen feet into the grove, the tall chain-link fence that protected the goats meandered among the tall trunks.

Altmeyer was leaning down to work the combination lock on the little gate when she caught up with him. "Can you see well enough?" she whispered.

He nodded, and slowly swung the gate open so she could pass inside. She noticed that he left the lock unclasped on the gate behind them, and it reminded her that they weren't really going home. They might have to run for the gate, and hope that nobody had noticed it there in the trees.

They were careful now not to step on the eucalyptus twigs that stuck out here and there in the litter of fallen leaves. A few more paces, and Rachel set her feet on grass. They moved quickly around the edge of the lawn to the little collection of dwarf spruces she'd planted to shield the koi pond from the hot afternoon sunshine, then huddled together among the thick, dark shapes. Rachel stared across the lawn at the house, and felt cold and lost. It seemed deserted, as though everyone had moved away and died.

The moonlight reflected on the still, flat surface of the koi pond, and staring at it made her feel even colder. As she looked, there was a quick flicker of motion and a brief glimpse of a shining, round shape that rolled on the surface and then disappeared again, leaving only an expanding series of rings that faded before they reached the land. The koi were alive. She closed her eyes and tried to see the image of the fish again. It could have been Robert, the white one with the black splotches. There hadn't been any color, but the gold ones would be pale in this light, too. At least they were alive, and that meant that Calvin had been here every day, and—no, it didn't. Fish could live in the pond for months without anybody feeding them. "Maybe even if everybody did die, and nobody

201

ever came here again," she began, but then she identified what she had really been thinking and remembered that it wasn't like that. The pond would turn to steam in a thousandth of a second, and the fish in it would be vaporized.

Altmeyer touched her sleeve and pointed at the house. A light swept across the kitchen, and she could see a shadow moving about. Then the light seemed to go dim before it went out. At first she decided it was a flashlight, but then she realized it was something else. It was the light in the refrigerator. They were opening the door of her refrigerator to find their way around her kitchen in the darkness.

Altmeyer didn't move or speak, so Rachel waited. Every few minutes she began to lose the familiar outline of the house, and it would begin to look like a flat pattern hanging before her at an indeterminate distance. Then she would close her eyes to erase it, and then try to look at Altmeyer. His face didn't move, and no light fell on it. The only way she could see it at all was to look to the side of it and let a faint image form in the corner of her eye that could have been half imagination.

She turned to the house again, then back to Altmeyer, but he was moving this time. She watched him stand and walk around the koi pond and across the lawn. He never stopped until he was standing beneath the kitchen window. His dark shape stood out against the white siding so that he looked like a crude drawing done with five strokes. His left arm crooked and moved up near his face, then straightened again at his side, and she realized he'd been looking at his watch. He slipped around the corner of the house, and Rachel was alone.

Time went slowly now. Each minute that passed seemed to have a shape and proportions like a room Rachel moved through in a museum. She heard the back door of the house slam, then heard the footsteps of two or three men on the driveway. She pulled the heavy gun out of her jacket and lifted herself to her knees. The sounds slowly faded into the distance. She stepped forward, listening for the sharp noise of whatever Altmeyer was going to do to them. She crossed the lawn to the house and crouched at the corner. Then she heard the starter of a car, and a cold engine giving its hollow growl as the driver stepped too hard on the gas pedal to warm it. In a moment that sound too faded away.

Rachel slipped the big automatic back into her jacket and warmed her hands in the side pockets. She sat down and leaned her back against the house, staring out at the trees where she and Altmeyer had hidden, and noticed that she could see better now. The sun was about to rise, and where was Altmeyer?

She heard the heavy steps coming up the drive, so she stood up and cautiously moved her eye to the corner of the house, then stepped out. "Calvin."

He was a thin man in his fifties who wore a stiff, white straw cowboy hat and blue jeans pulled down over the tops of low-heeled black boots. He squinted at her and said, "Did you have a nice trip?"

Rachel felt an impulse to say something that was true. "It's not over yet. We just came by to see if everything was okay before we go off again. Is it?"

"The goats took my truck downtown the other day and went to fourteen Chinese restaurants. They ordered everything on the menu à la carte and charged it to you. Other than that, we're getting along fine."

He walked past her toward the little goat barn at the other end of the yard. When he got there he gave a shrill whistle, and two of the goats trotted out and followed him to the feed trough under the overhanging roof, then nudged him as he tore open a feed sack and hoisted it to his shoulder to pour it.

Rachel joined him, and three more goats came out of the barn to gather around her. "Hello, girls," she said. "Calvin, they look great."

"They look like goats," he said.

A young nanny dashed into the herd and nipped at the rump of one of the bigger goats to clear a path to the trough. "Betty!" said Rachel. "Wait your turn."

Altmeyer's voice came from the back steps. "Morning, Calvin."

Calvin glanced over his shoulder. "Sure is."

Altmeyer took a handful of feed and held it while one of the goats nibbled at it. "Did Rachel tell you we have to go off again for a few days?"

"No problem. Me and the goats are always here."

"Thanks, Calvin. I guess we'd better get moving if we're going to make it to the airport." He and Rachel started to walk toward the driveway, but Altmeyer stopped and came back.

"By the way, you haven't seen any signs of prowlers or anything, have you?"

"Not yet, but I'm not in the habit of looking for them, either."

"Well, don't start now. If you see anything, remind yourself that there's nothing in that house that's worth getting shot over."

Calvin smiled. "My mother didn't raise any fools."

Altmeyer and Rachel walked down the driveway, then cut back along the fence to the gate in the eucalyptus grove. As Altmeyer locked the gate behind them, Rachel said, "It's horrible."

"Oh, I don't know," he said. "I was thinking things were looking up a little."

Rachel turned her head to glance at him, and nearly stumbled on the outcropping of the old stone terrace. "What can be good about it? There are people waiting in our house to murder us."

Altmeyer patted her shoulder and then held it. "We already knew that they were doing their best. Now we know what their best is. They figure when we come home it'll be at night, so they sit in there every night waiting. During the day they have to give the place up to Calvin and the goats."

Rachel grumbled, "That doesn't sound comforting to me."

"Of course it is," said Altmeyer. "Calvin is safe, the goats are safe, the fish are safe. Come to think of it, our guests are

204

even protecting the house from burglars. If we want them, all we have to do is wait for the night shift to begin."

Rachel walked faster. "You know, you're beginning to sound like you're crazy."

"I've always felt that my optimism was part of my charm," Altmeyer said. "It's what made me go check the license number of the car, for instance. Lots of people who've seen everything they've done for months turn into a waste of time might not have bothered."

"You honestly think they drove a car that can be traced?"

"All cars can be traced, which is the only known benefit of living in the age of computers. It takes the cops half a minute to get an identification. For that reason alone these people won't be using stolen cars. They'd have to get a new one every night, and that's more dangerous than waiting for us. If it's rented, someone rented it. If it's not, someone owns it."

"When you don't know anything, imagining you know something certainly does cheer you up."

"It's the way of the optimist."

"Look, Dave." Altmeyer paced the length of Arthur Paston's bar twirling the telephone cord, then turned. "I've been buying insurance from you for a long time. You know I'm not some lunatic. I'm asking you to do what you'd do anyway, just a little faster. I'm leaving town in a day or so."

He listened, then said, "That's the spirit. The license number is 048 KPJ, and it's a maroon, late-model BMW. The damage isn't going to break me, but the guy did back into my truck, and I have a right to know who he is."

Altmeyer paused. "That's right. 048 KPJ. How long do you think it'll take?"

Altmeyer sighed. "I guess that's okay. Look, I'm out trying to make a sale. The number is 555-4012. Call when you can. Thanks."

Altmeyer hung up the telephone and rubbed his hands

together. "There. They can fool just about everybody, but nobody fools the California DMV and the Pyramid Insurance Company of Hartford, Connecticut."

Bucky leaned on the bar with his fist under his chin. "That may be an amusing pastime for you, but it has a certain air of futility. It's either a rental or it's owned by the Ashita Corporation."

Altmeyer watched Arthur Paston close one eye to pour a tiny splash of vermouth into the cocktail shaker. "You know, Arthur, it's barely noon."

Paston lifted his head to fix Altmeyer's image in his spectacles, which were near the end of his nose. "It takes a great deal of practice to be able to make a fine dry martini. Even in the best of times a man my age would have to hurry if he wanted to become an alcoholic, and I'm under extraordinary constraints."

Rachel frowned. "Has anybody thought seriously about that?"

"About what?" said Bucky.

"Extraordinary time constraints. Before we go, shouldn't we leave some kind of message for the authorities? I hate to be morbid, but—"

"You're right," said Paston, pouring careful measures into a long line of glasses. "Morbidity in beautiful women is tiresome. I ruined my adolescence by an early reading of Poe. Suddenly lots of girls I knew seemed to be dead or dying."

Bucky seemed agitated. "Of course Rachel is right. I was thinking the same thing. I guess it was the insurance company that reminded me. What are the odds that we're going to do anything conclusive? We're going to die."

"What could be more conclusive?" asked Altmeyer.

Bucky snatched up one of Arthur's glasses and drank it, then banged it down on the bar. "We've got to have a way of blowing the whistle on Ashita if we don't come back. We need insurance."

"Have it your way," said Altmeyer. "Just don't put it anyplace where I can't find it. Don't put it in your will or leave

206

it in your safe deposit box. When we come back, Rachel and I don't want something like that waiting for us."

"You're sweet," said Rachel. "But I'd feel better some-how if I could believe there was a back-up."

"It has to be Arthur," Bucky announced. "Even if he's dead, he's got more credibility than we have." He stared at Arthur, who was thoughtfully sipping the third glass in his row of martinis. "Especially if he's dead."

"To your health," said Paston, and lifted his glass.

"Will you do it, Arthur?" said Rachel.

"If you and Bucky type it up, I'll sign it. But we have to think of a suitable way to hide it. There are always the luggage lockers at Union Station. I used that in three films in the forties. Every detective always recognized the key at first glance. Of course in the next scene someone always hit him on the head and stole it."

"It may be a bit too elaborate," said Bucky, "but that's the general idea."

Paston stared into the distance. "There was an Amos and Andy episode where they found a valuable coin. Andy put it in a pay telephone, and the Kingfish called him a big dummy and went away. Andy just smiled and dialed the operator, so the coin came back. I've always admired that."

Altmeyer grinned. "Just mail it to yourself."

Paston looked disappointed. "That's not very clever."

"We all have keys to this house. Whoever comes back can walk in and pick it up. Nobody has the heart to read a dead man's mail for a few days, but if none of us came back, somebody would have to do it eventually."

The telephone rang and Altmeyer picked it up. "Hello. Oh, hi, Dave."

The others left the bar and moved out into the big room. Bucky walked off to another part of the house, and returned carrying a typewriter. He plugged it in and rolled a piece of paper into the carriage, then stepped back to let Rachel sit at the table.

She turned on the machine and typed in upper-case letters, "URGENT! IMPORTANT! URGENT!" and skipped two lines. "I am mailing this letter to myself, in case I am killed attempting to act on this information. Take this letter to the police."

Bucky read it over her shoulder. "To the police? That doesn't sound right. How about the FBI?"

At the bar, Altmeyer was speaking into the telephone. "Are you sure? 048 KPJ. A maroon BMW." He listened, then asked, "Did you check to see if it's stolen or anything?"

After a few seconds, he said, "I know you're not a moron, Dave. I'm sorry, but I was a little surprised. Maybe I'll claim whiplash and make a bundle." He chuckled. "I know. I know that's not funny to you." He wrote something on a paper napkin. "Can you repeat the name and address?" He corrected something he had written. "Thanks a lot, Dave. What? No, don't bother. I can see this is a waste of time. All right. Goodbye."

Bucky was saying, "Don't forget the farm in Belgium. That might help them figure out who's doing the distributing and who's buying."

Altmeyer walked to the table. "Arthur, if you can drag yourself away from your Warning from Beyond the Grave, I'd like to have you bother Leonard some more."

Paston followed him to the bar and traded his empty glass for a full one with a single sweep of the hand. "I'm always delighted to bother someone, but why Leonard?"

"The people waiting at our house were driving a car owned by a different corporation."

Arthur turned to Bucky and Rachel. "Hold the presses. We have yet another corporation to add to my posthumous memoirs."

Altmeyer handed Arthur the napkin, and Arthur read it aloud. "The Twenty-First Century Medical Group Clinic of Santa Barbara, California."

.   .   .

RACHEL SURVEYED THE EQUIPMENT CASES on the living room floor and sighed. "They're big, very metallic, very heavy. I'm afraid they'll never do for England."

Altmeyer opened the nearest packing case and ran his fingers slowly over the thick padding. Then he closed the silver lid, snapped the clasps, and lifted it by the handle, staring into the distance. He opened the other two cases and frowned. "Is this what you normally take on these trips?"

Paston glanced at the cases. "That looks about right. All that's necessary is a still photographer and an assistant to help carry his equipment. The rest of the group varies, depending on how many people the producer feels like sending to Europe and charging to his budget. At this stage we wouldn't be bringing much. We'd just be looking around, getting a feel for things we've read in a script."

Bucky sat down next to Altmeyer and studied the equipment. "What's wrong with this? It looks like it would hold an arsenal."

"It's too right," said Altmeyer. "This kind of smuggling is mostly optical illusions, like doing magic tricks. Everything depends on making the hiding place feel wrong. The rabbit doesn't belong in a hat, and the rabbit looks bigger than the hat, but most important, the hat doesn't remind you of rabbits. We'll never get into the United Kingdom without having these cases checked. Photographic equipment feels like guns."

Bucky shook his head. "What you brought to Japan would have made a good start for a war."

"England is different. They've been at war for a long time now, and the only people who think about it that way are the ones we have to fool—the customs inspectors, the people who work for airlines, people who handle baggage, policemen. Anything that looks like a suitcase might blow up in their faces or it might be guns for the Irish. Most are paid for and shipped by Americans."

Paston said, "I can have these sent by air freight to the Savoy in London tonight."

209

"You might as well get at it now," Altmeyer agreed. "We're not going to do anything with them."

Bucky said, "Altmeyer, this is depressing. You've done all kinds of things just to get rich. Can't we take some chances now? These people are going to kill us. Come to think of it, that's the minimum."

Rachel stood up and patted Bucky's shoulder. "We hardly ever take chances, old Buck. It's just a business, and we weren't making money for taking risks. You don't pay a steeplejack a lot because he's going to fall, and he's not cheating you if he comes down safely."

Altmeyer sipped his drink and said, "Your attitude needs some thought, old Buckingham. I hope you'll work it out before your eagerness to sacrifice yourself for the cause gets too strong."

"Bucky is doing penance by taking risks," said Rachel. "The problem is, the futility of our already futile cause would be complete if we got arrested at Heathrow Airport."

Bucky walked to the stairway and climbed to the second floor. They heard him step to the hallway leading to the row of bedrooms.

Paston poured another martini into Altmeyer's glass. "I'm surprised, Rachel," he said. "You make a very good cynic."

Rachel looked up at him. "You make a very good bartender. Maybe I'll break my diet and have one of those, too. Do you know how to make a small one?"

Altmeyer sipped his drink. "This isn't the time for Bucky to cleanse his soul for cheating on his income taxes. We need him."

Paston shrugged. "Bucky has killed people. He's committed murder."

Rachel's eyes filled with tears. "He hasn't got the right to feel guilty. He hasn't done enough to feel guilty. He was just a fat little man trying to stay alive."

Paston walked toward the bar. "He loves you, too."

LONDON

The tall, pale Englishman studied Bucky's passport photograph, then glowered at him.

Bucky smiled. "I know. They put the eagle in the seal on my head, so I look like Mercury."

The man turned the pages with one hand and held them down with his wrist as he searched for a blank space. He found one on page seven, and left the imprint of his stamp: "Given leave to enter the United Kingdom for six months. Immigration Officer 694 Heathrow (3)." His long, fleshy face didn't alter its expression. "Thank you, sir."

Bucky moved down the line and through the glass doors to where the others were waiting, and whispered to Altmeyer, "You were right. They went through everything."

"That's why they're more civilized than we are. They're thorough, and they're enthusiastic about finding things to tax or prohibit."

Paston muttered, "I suppose we're going to be up all night again. I can never get comfortable in those damned airline seats."

"I suppose so," said Altmeyer. "We might as well get to the hotel and sleep until evening."

Bucky brightened. "You mean we don't have to go through all that nonsense about outlasting jet lag like we did in Japan?"

"Not this time," said Rachel.

"Bless you," Paston said. "If I die after I'm rested, at least there'll be enough contrast so I know the difference."

They made their way to the outside of the building and spotted the line of black cabs waiting for customers. Bucky said to the first driver in line, "The Savoy, on the Strand."

"You don't have to tell a driver where anything is, sir," said the cab driver. "We've got The Knowledge. Nobody is allowed to drive a cab in London until he's been tested on The Knowledge."

"Sorry," Bucky said. "We're Americans. Nobody is allowed to be an American until he's been tested on The Chutzpah."

THEY SAT in the Grill Room of the Savoy Hotel. Solemn waiters passed each other in the dim light carrying silver vessels that implied a ceremony in which food was a symbol for something.

"I could stay here," said Bucky.

"We are staying here." Rachel watched one of the silent caretakers remove half the objects on the table and disappear.

"I mean stay right here without moving for a very long time. After a year or two I'd probably move to another hotel somewhere, and everybody in this hotel would know me. They'd have a going-away party for me, and maybe retire this table in my honor."

"They could present you with the bill and bury you in Westminster Abbey the same day." Altmeyer glanced at his watch. "It's time."

As they moved out of the Grill Room and into the lobby, Altmeyer said, "Let's go out the river entrance. I don't want Arthur to meet some admirer and get held up for half an hour." They went out through the tall glass doors and passed under the curving molded concrete awning that jutted into Savoy Place. The uniformed doorman gestured for a taxicab, but Altmeyer said, "No, thank you. We'd like to walk."

214

Bucky turned and looked back at the entrance. "I'd get rid of that wavy roof they have over the door. It's like putting a Chevrolet bumper on a Rolls-Royce."

They walked along the wide empty stretch of the Embankment, past ornate green benches. Rachel stared across the river, where the light was just beginning to take on a hazy, blueish color.

"Beautiful, isn't it?" said Paston. "It's dirty, but that just makes it seem like part of the antique. London still feels like the capital of the world, just the way it did fifty years ago."

Rachel turned away from the river. "I was thinking it's a good way to move something heavy that you don't want bumped around a lot. Water is gentle."

Altmeyer folded the map he'd been studying, and looked out at the water. "We turn north up here. Aldwych to Kingsway, then bear right on Theobalds Road. It's only a few blocks, and I promise we won't walk back."

They made their way up the street, looking at the people who seemed to be hurrying in various directions, their faces set in concentration as though they were thinking about their destinations. "We're right on the edge of the theater district," said Paston. "I'll bet that's where a lot of these people are going. Covent Garden is two blocks that way."

"We always seem to be shopping when other people are going to theaters," said Bucky. "Maybe it's because we sleep during the day."

They crossed High Holborn, and Bucky asked Paston, "What's over that way?"

Paston's eyes narrowed, and he said, "Let's see. One big thing is the British Museum. I used to spend hours and hours there. I once spent three days just looking at Egyptian mummies. Remember *War of the Pharaohs* with Walter Langston?"

"I saw it on television a few years ago."

Arthur chuckled. "That's the only place I've seen it in the last twenty-five years myself. Was it worth staying up that late for?"

Bucky walked on for a few paces, then said, "The mummies were terrific. You don't see mummies much anymore. They seem to have gone out with knights and circus movies."

"They'll be back," Paston said with assurance. "Anything that fills the screen with color and sheer strangeness the way Egypt does will be back. I'd like to remake *War of the Pharaohs* now. This time I'd get somebody who didn't act like he was embalmed in the first scene."

"Old Walter was a little stiff," Bucky conceded. "What else is in that direction?"

Arthur shrugged. "Some parks."

Altmeyer said, "London University."

They walked on in silence for a block, and at the end of it Rachel said to Altmeyer, "This is it. Lamb's Conduit Street."

Bucky laughed. "It sounds like something they'd eat here —boiled lamb's conduit."

The street was nearly empty, with only a few people on the sidewalks, most of them young and alone. A hundred yards up the block, Altmeyer stopped before a two-story brick building with darkened windows. "Here it is," he said quietly. "I wish we'd brought one of those cameras with us. It might come in handy." He examined the brass plate on the door that said ASHITA, LTD.

Paston said, "There's not enough light for a camera, and you can't see anything from out here anyway."

"Exactly," said Altmeyer. "Let's go around to the back."

"This one doesn't look as easy," said Bucky. "I don't suppose you brought your shopping crowbar?"

Paston said, "I didn't come all the way over here to file an inquiry with the American consul. We'll just have to find a way."

Altmeyer slipped into the narrow alley between the building and the one next to it. The space was so tight that Bucky had to turn his shoulder to the side to keep from brushing against the dusty bricks. The rear of the building was enclosed by a low stone wall with a wooden gate. Altmeyer reached over the gate and unlatched it from the inside, so they could enter the little yard. At the far end of the enclosure,

Rachel noticed a patch of carefully tilled ground with little wooden stakes on each end. It was getting too dark to identify the green shoots that had just pushed through the soil, but they seemed to be growing from the far wall to the little wooden shed near the gate in straight, even rows.

Altmeyer tugged at the rear door of the building. "It feels as though we should have brought a crowbar after all. I guess it will have to be one of the windows. Rachel, do you think you can fit through this cellar window?"

Rachel looked through the dusty, rectangular pane into the opaque blackness. "I suppose so." She hesitated. "I know I can." After another pause, she said, "There are rats in there, big ones with red eyes that have been in there breeding for two hundred years, waiting for me to break my leg."

"Sorry," said Altmeyer. "It was just a thought."

Rachel was suddenly cheerful. "There's a little garden over here, right next to the shed. It looks like they take good care of it."

"I noticed that," said Paston. "When you think about it, the idea is insane, but it's very British."

"You don't understand. I mean they must have tools, and the shed must be for something."

Altmeyer opened the shed and looked inside. When he returned, he was carrying a flat trowel and a long-handled spade. "Bucky, jam the spade under the door and pry it upward." He slipped the trowel beside the door handle and jiggled it, then pushed it hard. Then he pulled the door open and stepped inside.

Altmeyer flicked the light switch and said, "Come on. We ought to be getting good at trashing these stores now that we know the line of products so well."

BUCKY MOVED toward a stack of cardboard cartons along the wall. "It's exactly the same stuff, in about the same order." He tore open a carton and peered inside. "The Happyboy Humidifier—what are you doing in England?"

217

"Don't bother with that," said Rachel. "We know it's the Sleeping-Tite Smoke Sentinel. They wouldn't mislabel it, or they'd be taking an even bigger chance."

They walked past the stacks of boxes and down a narrow hallway. There were two doors along the hallway, and Altmeyer opened them as he passed, looked into the dim spaces beyond, then closed them. "It's an interesting layout," he said. "One goes upstairs, and the other goes down to the cellar."

"It's an old house," said Paston. "The stock room was probably the pantry and the kitchen and maybe a scullery maid's closet, and they knocked the walls out when they made it into a shop. That stairway was for servants. There will be another one up front somewhere, unless they took it out."

They moved to the end of the hall into the larger room at the front of the building. The room was bordered with glass display cases, and behind them, shelves that reached nearly to the ceiling but were empty.

Altmeyer stepped quickly along the line of display cases, and Rachel took a parallel course on the other side. "I suppose it's a clear sign," said Rachel. "We know this is the only place they can be, but they're not for sale."

Paston was already climbing the stairs to the floor above. "This isn't the original staircase," he said to Bucky. "It would have come down practically in the center of the foyer, opposite the front door. The people who owned the place would spend most of their time up here."

Bucky reached the top and looked down the long hallway. All the doors had been taken off their hinges. He and Arthur walked from room to room. Three of them had stone fireplaces, and one central room had shelves on the walls like those in the shop downstairs, but all were empty of everything except a thick layer of gritty dust. There was only one bathroom at the end of the long hall, and the bathtub had a long streak of rust below the faucet that might have been there for decades.

218

They went down the back stairs and returned to the shop. "No Sleeping-Tite Smoke Sentinels up there," said Bucky.

"There's nothing here either," Rachel said. "What's it like up there?"

"It looks like they gave the maid the day off in 1912 and she married an Australian and emigrated."

"They've had the place for over a year, according to Leonard," Paston said. "They don't seem to be in a hurry to get it renovated."

"It's got to be the cellar," said Altmeyer.

Rachel said, "I just hope there's a light."

Bucky held up his hand. "There's no point in everybody going. Why don't you and Arthur see if there's anything up here we missed?" He opened the wrong door, then found the one that led downstairs. Altmeyer followed him into the darkness.

At the bottom of the stairway, something thin and cold brushed across Bucky's face. "Ugh," he cried, and batted at it with his hand. "Horrible." As he touched it, he realized it was the chain on the light switch. He held his hands up until he felt it swing back, then caught it and tugged. The bare bulb above him lit, and a dim, yellowish glow illuminated the gray stone walls around him.

In one corner of the cellar was an old coal furnace that looked as though it hadn't been used for years. One of the air ducts had been disconnected, and hung downward like a broken tree limb.

"No rats, anyway," said Bucky. "But there doesn't seem to be anything else either."

Altmeyer walked to the furnace, swung the iron door open, and closed it again. Then he walked along the cellar walls, staring at the stone. Twice he stopped and ran a finger along the crumbling mortar, then went on. "I'm starting to get annoyed with these people," he muttered. "There's nothing here."

.   .   .

ARTHUR AND RACHEL stood at the front of the shop. "Think about this place," Rachel said. "It's exactly like the store in Los Angeles. It was an old building converted to a shop, and then these Ashita people took over. Look at it."

"They seem to have a formula they like," said Paston.

"No, you're not following. Think about the differences. Do you see a cash register? You said there was nothing upstairs, so there's no office. Arthur, there's not even a telephone."

"We know they're not doing a retail business."

"No, think for a minute. They must have a telephone. They're doing something dangerous and illegal. It would be stupid not to have a telephone. Besides, it's not natural."

"All right," said Paston. "Let's look for a telephone."

They moved around the store, looking at the woodwork for a disguised wire. Bucky and Altmeyer came up the stairs to see the pair crawling along the walls on their hands and knees. "What are you doing?" asked Bucky.

Rachel said, "Did you see a telephone?"

Altmeyer grinned. "Of course." He reached into his pocket, then slapped coins into Bucky's hand. "On the corner where we turned down this street there's a telephone booth. Call information. I think the number is 142, but they'll have it listed on the booth. Call Ashita Electronics, and keep ringing if it takes all night."

Bucky slipped out the back door, and the others waited. After a few minutes, they heard a muffled ring.

Altmeyer walked slowly to the center of the room and turned his body slowly. He said, "It's near the back."

They all moved toward the sound, and found themselves in the stock room. When the telephone rang this time, Rachel said, "No, I think we've gone past it." They moved into the hallway again, and the sound was louder.

Paston whispered, "A dumbwaiter," then said more loudly, "A dumbwaiter. This was the kitchen." He moved along the wall, tapping it. "The dining room would be upstairs. Somewhere along here would be the dumbwaiter."

220

Altmeyer moved up beside him and put his ear to the wall. "It still sounds farther back." He moved around the corner into the stock room and pushed aside three cartons at the top of a stack. There was a varnished wooden cabinet door with a brass handle. He swung it open and found a black telephone, its ringing suddenly louder. He picked up the receiver and said, "Hello, Bucky. Come on back."

"Okay," said Rachel. "We've found their telephone. I wonder what it's going to take to find the smoke detectors."

"Maybe not a whole lot," said Altmeyer. "It looks like we found their whole office." He reached to the back of the dumbwaiter, pulled out a revolver and a box of ammunition, and set them on a carton beside him.

"That's not much of an arsenal," said Rachel, "but I suppose it's plenty when the police don't have anything."

"What else is in there?" Paston snapped. "I can't see with you standing there."

Altmeyer handed Paston a thick sheaf of British twenty-pound notes. "I guess we'll tap the petty cash. Put it in your pocket." He turned away from the dumbwaiter, clutching some translucent onionskin sheets. As he read each one, he moved it to the bottom of the pile. Finally he stopped and handed one to Rachel.

Bucky slipped in through the back door to the storeroom and closed it behind him.

Paston nodded to him, but said nothing.

Rachel scowled and handed the paper to Paston. "They've shipped the smoke detectors already."

"That doesn't make sense," Bucky insisted. "This is the place. Everything says this is it. This is the most suspicious place since the Black Hole of Calcutta."

"It makes too much sense," said Rachel. "Look where they were shipped."

Paston passed the paper to Bucky, and he read it aloud. "Presold merchandise," he said. "Of course. 'Delivery: Physical Sciences Annex, London University, Malet Street, London WC 1.' " He leaned against the stack of boxes. "Oh," he said.

221

"London University. Oh." He didn't move his eyes from the paper. "Physical Sciences Annex. Oh shit."

"What is it?" asked Paston.

"It's the same thing they did in Los Angeles," said Rachel. "This is just a shipping address, like a post office box you take out in a false name. The company ships things to its own store, so nobody asks any questions. But when it gets here, it's pre-sold, so nobody asks any questions about why it's shipped out right away in the store's own delivery truck."

"But why this university annex? Why are all of the stores on the edges of campuses?"

"I recognize it," said Altmeyer. "It's camouflage. If your fake customer looks like a big enough operation, you can ship almost anything to him without raising any eyebrows. But you can't start a big factory or something just to cover a one-time shipment. The best thing to do is put yourself on the edge of a big operation and call yourself an annex. Universities are big and complicated, and are divided into colleges and departments and research institutes and whatever other divisions they've invented since I graduated. It takes years for them to notice if somebody takes something, so it might take decades for them to notice that something's been added—a building on the edge of the campus with an academic-sounding name on the door."

Bucky sighed. "It's perfect. They must need what amounts to a science lab to put the bombs together. So where do they hide it? Right next to a place that has hundreds of science labs."

THEY WALKED UP LAMB'S CONDUIT to Guilford Street and past the Square to Montague Place. Arthur pointed at the giant building to the left and said, "That's the back entrance of the British Museum."

Bucky glanced across the street at it, then looked down at the sidewalk. "If there's an afterlife, then right about now

222

your mummies are spinning in their cases like chickens on a rotisserie."

Rachel stared ahead. "If they were alive they'd be unwrapped and standing in line to bid for what Ashita is selling. Malet Street must be around here."

Altmeyer pointed ahead and to the right. "That's where the University starts, and the first street is the one we want."

Paston spoke again. "Look at all these people. There must be night classes or lectures or something. You know, we could ask someone for directions."

Altmeyer shook his head. "They all look smart enough to remember us."

They walked along the line of large, white buildings, reading the small signs above the doorways, until they seemed to have passed the university. There were still a few buildings that obviously had been built for some institutional purpose, but now there were also short rows of old townhouses, set close together, that had been converted to offices and flats. Near the end of one of these rows, Altmeyer stopped.

There was a single brown-brick facade with seven sets of steps leading up to seven pedimented entrances, each with a large, heavy wooden door. It was difficult in the dusk to tell where one house ended and the next began. Altmeyer walked up the steps of the house, one hand in his coat pocket. A small stenciled card over the mail slot read PHYSICAL SCIENCES ANNEX. Altmeyer said to the others, "I guess we've found it."

"It's not what I imagined," Bucky whispered.

"One of the buildings back there had a sign that said it was a Mathematics Institute," said Rachel. "They must be running short of space and spilling off campus. At UCLA all Ashita could do was get into the neighborhood of the university. Here they can edge up close, put an academic name on the door, and let the real university flow out around them."

Altmeyer pressed the button beside the door, and a loud buzz came from somewhere inside.

"What are you doing?" Bucky whispered.

223

"It says, 'Please ring for admittance.' I'm ringing for admittance."

"You want to go inside?"

"That's the first thing I want." He listened, but there was no sound inside. He pressed the button again and held it, then played it as though it were a telegraph key, sending a series of short buzzes into the building. He kept at it for over a minute, then said, "My finger is getting tired. Would you agree it's safe to say they aren't having night classes?"

"I suppose so," Paston conceded.

"Then go back to the hotel, all of you. From here on there's nothing I can't do alone."

Bucky folded his arms. "No. We want to see."

"Bucky, there's not going to be anything to see but a bunch of fake smoke detectors in a storeroom. Didn't you read the order sheet? They only shipped them here two days ago."

"Wonderful," Paston said. "I was a little nervous about what might be in there. Do we go around to the back of this building, too?"

Altmeyer sighed. "This lock probably belonged to Disraeli." He took out his wallet, selected his plastic Automobile Club card, slipped it between the door and the jamb, and opened the door.

"The lights are on," Rachel whispered. "Suppose there's a janitor?"

"Then he'll be able to tell us where the lecture is. If they let a janitor in, this isn't the place we're looking for," said Altmeyer.

"If there is a janitor," said Bucky, "his ears aren't much use to him. Maybe these people leave a few lights on in the hallway to keep from breaking their necks on the way to the laboratory. That's why the sun never sets."

They closed the door behind them and studied the place, listening for a sound. Slowly, Altmeyer moved forward, and the old wooden floor creaked under his feet. The others moved to both sides of him to avoid the spot that had made the noise.

"That looks like an office down at the end of the hall," said Paston.

"Then it's not what we need," said Rachel. "There's only one way this makes sense. They pay astronomical leases to have their stores near universities. If they just needed an office they could go anywhere. This is a physics building."

Altmeyer nodded. "Look for a way to the basement. The lab we want should be in the cellar."

"How do you know?" said Bucky.

"They all work by jamming together a bunch of uranium or plutonium or something with a plain old explosive, don't they?" He tried a door, then slipped his plastic card in beside the lock and opened it. "That part I know about. They'd want to store detonators and explosives below ground level." He frowned and closed the door, then moved to the next one. "And who knows what else they need? If it's water, power, heat, drainage, the lines and pipes are all down there."

Paston stared down the hallway. "It should be in the back, just like it was in the other building. They didn't deliver coal by bringing it in through the parlor."

"That's the spirit, Arthur," said Bucky. "It's an honor to be in the presence of a genuine antiquity."

"Antiquary."

Rachel was already turning the corner at the end of the hallway. "This has to be it." The sign in red on the door said HAZARDOUS APPARATUS. AUTHORISED PERSONS WITH THE PROPER PROTECTIVE APPAREL WILL BE ADMITTED WITH THE PRIOR APPROVAL OF THE UNIVERSITY PROVOST.

Altmeyer examined the lock. "They must have a better class of burglars than we do. Most of ours would have this lock open before they could read all that."

"This is a university, after all," said Bucky. "Or I guess it isn't, but it's in the neighborhood."

Altmeyer opened the door, and found a light switch. Before them was a steep stairway leading downward. "Wonderful. I'm beginning to feel that I know these people. We are about to see the world's only supply of genuine Ashita Sleeping-Tite Smoke Sentinels."

They reached the bottom of the stairs and found themselves in another narrow hallway, with a door on each side. The walls were white and plain, with no woodwork, and the floors were dark green linoleum. Both of the doors had the same HAZARDOUS APPARATUS sign on them, and beside each was a bracket with a red fire extinguisher.

Altmeyer opened the first door, and they all entered slowly. The room had four gleaming stainless steel tables. On them, in orderly rows, lay black metal boxes like suitcases, some of them long and narrow, and others not much larger than attaché cases.

"What do you think all that is?" asked Paston.

"I don't know," Altmeyer said. "Maybe it's portable electronic equipment of some kind. They sometimes box it up like that."

"Of course," said Bucky. "It's their traveling atomic bomb factory. They probably just shipped it in after the smoke detectors got here." He stepped to the table and flipped the latches on the nearest case, opened it, then moved quickly to the next one.

"What's wrong?" said Rachel.

"They're empty. There's nothing in them but foam rubber padding."

Altmeyer opened two more cases and said, "These are empty, too, but the spaces for whatever goes into them are all sort of chunky and square. They probably are for lab equipment of some kind. It doesn't matter. Let's—"

"Wait," said Rachel. She was standing beside the next table, where one of the long, narrow cases lay open. "This one is strange. The shape of the hollow part is different."

The others gathered around her and examined it. "That is odd," said Paston.

"It's like a fossil," said Bucky. "It looks like the imprint of a big fish. There's the tail, and it even has a dorsal fin."

Altmeyer's face seemed to harden. He turned and moved

226

across the hallway to the other door. He fumbled with his plastic card for a moment, then pushed the door open. As he turned on the light, the others heard him say, quietly, "Shit."

When Rachel reached him, he was walking around the room, staring closely at the clutter on the counters and tables. There were small silver screwdrivers and soldering irons and voltmeters with tangled red and black leads. Some of the counters had big black boxes with dials and meters on them. Rachel said, "It looks like a television repair shop. What a mess."

Altmeyer turned and looked at her. He pointed at one table, where there were four stainless steel cubes that seemed to be lined with circuitry on their inner surfaces. "These look like they fit into the small suitcases. You can't beat them for convenience." Then he walked to the other end of the shop. "These are the ones that ought to turn the profit, though. They're not for the peasant revolutionary with holes in his pants. You need to have a military airplane to deliver them."

There was a row of six long, thin, gleaming silver shapes lying on the table in padded wooden frames. Rachel moved closer. "They're sort of—beautiful, almost. Bucky was right. They're like big fish."

Altmeyer called, "Bucky, Arthur. Look everywhere for anything with writing on it, and put it in your pockets."

"What do I do?" asked Rachel. "We still haven't found the uranium. These are all empty shells."

"Get the fire extinguishers off the walls and set them in the corner, and after that, herd Bucky and Arthur out. Take them down to Russell Square." He opened a cabinet beneath the sink and began pulling out metal cans and reading the labels. "And you said this place was a mess. Look at all the nice petroleum products they have for keeping their equipment free of dust and corrosion."

Rachel returned with the two fire extinguishers from the hallway and said, "Is this the smartest thing we can do? I mean, you just reminded us that there will be high explosives and detonators, and what about radioactivity?"

227

Altmeyer shrugged. "If you hear a bunch of explosions, it was a lousy idea. I haven't found anything that looks like any explosive I ever saw, so I'm assuming they haven't gotten to the tricky parts yet. I'll try for enough delay to get out of here anyway."

"So what am I supposed to do if you're wrong?"

Altmeyer pushed a wooden desk up to the wall and began pouring clear liquid onto it, then piled the drawers beside it and doused them. The sharp smell reached Rachel, and it reminded her of lighter fluid. Finally, Altmeyer said, "I guess if you run out of ideas, the best thing to do is sell all our land. It just occurred to me that at the moment we are the only thing that's holding up a hell of a crash in the value of real estate. You might invest the money in Ashita."

She rushed to him and hugged him, hard. She pressed her face into his chest and said, "I'll go up to Oregon and marry Raymond and live in the woods. Every day we'll tell the livestock what a good sense of humor you had at the end."

"Thanks, baby," said Altmeyer. "I don't have any good last words, but I'll give you something that's worth more: Ray wears a moneybelt."

She stopped at the door. "Altmeyer, there's something I want you to know. I think we're going to—"

"Please get out," he said. "Those two won't know enough to leave unless you tell them."

ALTMEYER WORKED IN THE BASEMENT until he was sure he'd gathered everything that would burn. Then he ran up the stairs and found the room Arthur had called an office. There was a long oak counter, and behind it an old desk, and rows of books on shelves. He pushed the desk to the wall, moved four chairs around it, then threw armloads of books under them, above them, around them, and soaked the pile with the cleaning fluid he'd brought with him.

In the opposite corner of the room he found a row of filing cabinets and emptied three drawersful of papers around the oak counter, leaving the wooden drawers where they fell.

228

He rushed back into the hallway and up the stairs, then studied the place. The walls looked old enough to hide thick, ancient timbers that would catch in seconds, but he couldn't count on that. The basement laboratory looked as though it had been built by firemen. He moved from room to room opening doors until he found one that looked right. It was another office with a wooden desk, wooden cabinets, and a disorderly array of books and papers. He built another pile in the corner, then stopped for a moment to think. This room was at the back of the building. The first office was near the center, above the room in the basement. There had to be another near the front.

As he went down the hallway, he followed a vague, imaginary blueprint of the house to find the spot. It was an old-fashioned paneled sliding door that reminded him of his grandmother's dining room. When he slid the door open, he smiled. He could tell from the shelves that it had been a large linen closet at some time, and the row of brass hooks told him that it had probably been converted to a cloak room. Now it was filled with cardboard cartons someone had used to store books and papers.

Altmeyer lifted one of the boxes and dumped it on the floor. A cascade of magazines appeared at his feet: *Der Spiegel, Le Monde, Vogue.* As he looked down at them, he fought the urge to wonder about the person who owned them.

He closed his eyes and scanned his imaginary map of the house. It had to be done quickly. For all he knew, the place might have a storage tank for heating oil, or a laboratory full of ether. He began by setting a match to the pile of magazines. As the first layer blackened and curled, it sent a flame up the side of the cardboard carton above it.

Altmeyer ran to the room at the other end of the hallway and lit the pile of papers and furniture, then dashed to the stairs. The next one had to be the basement. When he reached the room, he tossed the match from about eight feet away, and the fumes of the fluid went up with a flash. He glanced inside to see flames licking the wall and spreading along the

229

floor to eat up a row of droplets he'd spilled when he'd tossed the first can onto the pile.

He turned and scrambled up the cellar stairs, taking three steps at a time. When he reached the office, he lit the pile of papers in the corner first, then tossed a burning file folder onto the long counter. The flames flickered along the stream of cleaning fluid on the counter top and engulfed the desk beyond it.

He turned and sprinted down the hall to the front door, then pulled it open with an easy and deliberate movement that kept his face turned downward. As he slipped out into the cool damp night, he heard a crackling sound somewhere behind him.

Altmeyer kept his hands in his coat pockets, his eyes toward the pavement, and his shoulders hunched forward slightly as he walked quickly down Malet Street. In seconds he was one of a hundred men walking along at about the same pace in the neighborhood, but as Altmeyer walked, he took deep breaths and counted his steps.

When he turned the corner of Montague Place, he glanced at his watch. It was only nine fifteen. He imagined the fires he'd set. By now the one on the ground floor would be going well enough to bring some of the interior walls into it. Had he left all of the doors in both hallways open? He'd remembered to do that so whatever draft could be gotten in a closed building would help it along. Now it was a kind of race. If enough of the building were in flames before the firemen got there, the most they could do was keep it under control and wreck the place doing it.

As he approached Russell Square, he met Rachel, Bucky, and Arthur. Bucky shook his hand and said quietly, "You didn't explode."

"Neither did you."

"I wasn't scheduled to. What do you want to do now?"

"The tube station is right over there," said Altmeyer. "Two stops on the Piccadilly Line and you're at Covent Garden. Fifteen minutes after that you can be asleep."

"Asleep?"

"Sure. If you don't explode."

"Stop being difficult," said Rachel. "You know none of us can just go off and pretend it's over. We have to know what happens, don't we?"

Altmeyer sighed. "It would take an orangutan about two seconds to figure out it's arson. I set fires everyplace but the water pipes. One of the things about arsonists is they hang around to watch."

Paston patted Altmeyer's shoulder. "They'll be looking for a solitary man. If we go together, you can watch them arresting a few."

"Look," said Altmeyer. "We don't know a lot about what's in that building, or what happens when it burns. This is my wife here, not Wing Commander Smathers of the Royal Airborne Horse Marines. All this bravery is starting to get on my nerves."

"You know we have to be there to see who else shows up," said Rachel. "It's easier with four people."

"It is unless you think you have to save the world alone," said Bucky.

Altmeyer snorted. "Save the world? Is that what you think? I'm just looking for some deadbeats. I was planning to hang around until I saw somebody get out of a cab and slip into the crowd without paying. If I thought we were saving the world, I'd get ruthless."

ALTMEYER TILTED HIS HEAD and stared across the Square, then turned it to the other side. "Listen," he said. At first the sound might have been a variation in the constant traffic two blocks away on Tottenham Court Road. Then the siren seemed to rise in intensity. It was a rhythmic, pulsing, high-pitched signal that seemed gradually to overwhelm all other noises as it approached. "That's a disappointment, but I suppose I should have expected it. If they weren't efficient, there wouldn't be so many old buildings."

231

"Is that what fire trucks sound like here?" said Bucky.

"That's it," said Paston. "During the war—"

Rachel interrupted. "Do you think there was enough time?"

"I couldn't tell," said Altmeyer. "There's a lot of old wood that's been varnished a hundred times, but there's a lot of brick."

Across the Square they could see people coming from the direction of the tube station. As each appeared on the sidewalk, he started to walk quickly, than slowed his pace and seemed to stare into the sky and listen. After a few had stopped, others gathered around them, and a small crowd began to collect behind. One of the first to stop, a man in a trenchcoat, sidestepped a few paces and stopped under a streetlamp. Rachel could see his bright green felt hat moving from side to side. Then he raised his arm and pointed. Rachel turned her head to follow the line of his arm. Above the top of the looming university building she could see a reddish glow that seemed to brighten and waver as she watched. "Look at the sky," she said. "You must have done an adequate job."

The man in the green hat began to walk toward the glow. Before he had taken three steps, a young couple passed under the streetlamp where he had been and trotted to catch up. Then others followed, and soon there was a steady stream of people moving toward the fire.

The sirens seemed louder and slower, and the tone fuller and deeper now, and Rachel decided the trucks must be off the larger thoroughfares and converging on Malet Street.

The front door of a building off to their left swung open and young people began pouring into the street, some clutching jackets, books, hats. Some came down the steps, then stopped to thrust their arms into their coat sleeves before drifting forward, while others strode with long, purposeful steps across the street. All held their faces to the sky, gazing up at the glow that drew them toward itself.

"Maybe we'd better go look for our boy," said Bucky. "There's going to be a hell of a crowd."

Altmeyer began to walk. "He probably won't be there right away. If I owned a bomb factory, I wouldn't spend much time in the neighborhood. Look for somebody who arrives in his own car and might be able to afford a serious investment."

As they walked, three young men ran past them. The one who came nearest to Paston muttered, "Pardon, sir. Lovely fire." The three men disappeared around the corner just as the first of the sirens stopped.

Just past the corner they met the first knot of people, a group who stood with their arms folded or leaned against the post box or the large tree beside it and exchanged observations on the nature of the fire. "Looks like chemicals to me. See that bright yellow? It's sulphur burning." Another said, "It's plain old paper and wood. I hope that's where the bursar's ledgers are stored." There was a girl's voice. "It's just a science building."

They made their way through the crowd, Altmeyer first, then Rachel, Paston, and Bucky. In the center of the street the firemen were running to haul hoses to a tall red fireplug. Bucky said, "We should have sabotaged that."

Altmeyer leaned close to him and said, "I didn't know what it was."

They reached the ring of people around the two fire trucks, where one harried policeman was trying to take control. "Stay back, please," he called. "Give these gentlemen a bit more of the street, please." He held his arms out in a sweeping motion to indicate an invisible police cordon moving toward them.

Rachel could see through the upper windows that the fire had engulfed the top floor. The flames filled the windows. But the glow in the sky seemed to be coming from farther back. Then there was a cracking sound, and she could see a flame flickering up into the air above the roof.

The bobby saw it too, and announced to the crowd, "Fires are unpredictable. Fires are best seen from a distance." Then he performed his part in the imaginary line of policemen again.

233

Rachel studied the people around her. They were all turned toward the flames, which illuminated their faces and glowed in their eyes. Whenever the solitary policeman urged them to move, they'd step backward a couple of paces without looking away from the fire, but within a few seconds they'd begin drifting inward again. Almost all of them seemed to have the young, smooth faces of students; only a few older people stood here and there.

Altmeyer skirted the circle and kept moving. "Come on," he said. "I think our friend will meet us down the street." They moved past the main herd of people and stood on the sidewalk two doors away, where the light of the flames didn't reach them. "He'll come by to see if it's burning, and just stay long enough to convince himself there's nothing he can do about it."

They watched as a pair of firemen broke the lock on the front door and stepped to the side. When they kicked the door inward, a bright light from within seemed to come out and float into the air. Then Rachel realized it was billowing clouds of thick smoke caught in the light of the fire. Three firemen crouched in the street like a team of gunners, clutched the long brass nozzle of a hose, and trained it into the doorway, blasting a thick stream of water inside. It seemed only to increase the outpouring of smoke.

There was a continuous crackling noise, then a terrible creak as one of the floors inside gave way, and a deafening crash as it came down on the one beneath it. Still more smoke poured out of the house, and the flames on the roof were higher now. Other firemen were trying to move a hose into position to reach it with an arc of water.

Arthur coughed and held his handkerchief to his mouth. "We must be downwind."

They started to back away, when another sound startled them from behind. It was a high-pitched, constant, electronic buzzing noise that came from deep inside the next house on the street.

"What's that?" said Bucky.

234

"I can't place it," said Paston.

Then the noise seemed to grow abruptly, as though the volume had doubled. They looked at the house, but there were no lights visible. Then the sound swelled again. In the time it took to realize it, the buzz grew four more times, and kept adding volume in sharp, rapid increments. In a few moments it was loud enough to compete with the engines of the fire trucks, and it was increasing. People began moving from the fire toward the novelty of the noise, and soon there were dozens of them standing there staring at the dark building, as others drifted to join the throng.

Suddenly the door burst open and three men dashed out of the building into the crowd. Rachel saw them clearly for a second as they ran down the steps. At first she thought they were wearing identical whitish pajamas, but then her mind rejected that, because they had little hats with goggles on them, and that meant they must be firemen in special gear. But the men all had their hands over their ears because of the horrible noise, and firemen never did things like that. She managed to get the shout into Altmeyer's ear just before the sound grew again. "Smoke detectors."

Altmeyer was already moving, cutting through the crowd at an angle behind the first man as he broke through in the middle of the street. Altmeyer dropped three paces behind, falling into step with the man.

In a quick, unexpected movement Bucky stepped out of the crowd, threw his arms around the man in white, and whirled him about to face Altmeyer.

Bucky held the man, who struggled to free his arms. The pinioned man seemed to be trying to say something, but it was impossible to hear him.

The noise grew still louder, and Bucky's lips moved. Altmeyer could see his throat straining to make his yells audible above the hundreds of shrieking smoke alarms. Altmeyer saw Bucky's lips form the words, "Kill him."

The man seemed to hear Bucky's shout, and he gave a wrenching twist that broke Bucky's grip and pushed him away.

235

Altmeyer's arm came up out of his pocket. He fired once into the man's forehead, and backed into the crowd.

In a moment he was almost abreast of another man in a white suit. The man never saw Altmeyer, but he seemed to sense something, because as the muzzle of the silencer came up behind his ear, his hand started to reach upward to brush it away. As he slumped to the ground, Altmeyer walked past at the same pace, then cut to the right toward a white hat bobbing above the crowd. The man who wore it seemed to be surrounded by people who were trying to hold him. When Altmeyer moved closer he saw that the man was coughing and gasping for breath. He was leaning on a woman, his arm over her shoulder.

Altmeyer moved into the group and saw that the woman was Rachel. Then beside him the crowd parted and Arthur Paston appeared, carrying a blanket. Paston threw the blanket over the man's shoulders, and he and Rachel ushered the staggering man out of the crowd and away from the smoke. Altmeyer followed, and noticed that the blanket had some kind of emblem on it and the words FIRE BRIGADE. When they reached the opposite curb, Paston turned to Altmeyer. His face was grave, and looked pale in the flickering light. As his eyes met Altmeyer's, Paston nodded.

The shot at the base of the man's skull puffed a wisp of his hair but left him standing. As the man's knees lost their tension, Rachel and Paston eased him to a sitting position and pulled the blanket up over his neck.

The three fanned out through the crowd, and met again on the other side. As they converged, Bucky joined them. None of them turned to look back. They walked quickly and without hesitation, stepping toward their own long, wavering shadows. Behind them the whole neighborhood was bright with the leaping flames of the ruined house, and the air was vibrating with the terrible, deafening shriek of two thousand Ashita Sleeping-Tite Smoke Alarms.

236

LOS ANGELES

R achel opened the sliding glass door and walked out onto the sun deck. Arthur sat back on his chaise longue, pulled the plaid blanket up over his chest, and stared out at the ocean.

"Leonard is on the phone for you, Arthur."

"Tell him I'll call him tomorrow. I'm feeling a little peaked today." He bent his long right leg under the blanket and tapped his foot against the frame of the chair.

"I'll tell him," said Altmeyer. He stood up and put on his shirt, then went inside and closed the glass door.

Rachel touched Paston's shoulder. "How about a martini, Arthur?"

"No," said Paston. "I think not."

"It's eighty degrees, and you look like you're on a ship in the North Atlantic. You need something to warm your innards." She waited for a few moments, then said, "Come on, talk to me."

Paston shrugged. "There's not much to say, is there? We were all present."

"We had to do it, Arthur," said Bucky.

"We were the only ones who were there, and knew, and could do it. Now we're here and I don't feel like having a martini." He gave a cold, tired half-smile. "People used to think I had a drinking problem. They didn't understand."

"What didn't they understand?"

"What it was like to be Arthur Paston. I had accomplished everything I ever wanted to do, and collected a great deal of money without spending much time thinking about it. And over all the years I had tremendous fun. What I was doing was celebrating."

Rachel sighed.

Paston looked up at her. "Things changed. Somehow while I was enjoying this long and interesting life, I didn't pay attention. Then that night it was like a film. There was an ancient, weak, greedy, twisted old creature that looked like the corpse of a pharaoh from the British Museum and he got out of his box. And he was walking the streets killing young men to protect his treasures. Or maybe it was to suck their blood so he'd live forever." His empty half-smile returned. "There are always a few bugs in the script, but already I can tell that the final shot isn't the pharaoh sipping a martini."

Bucky stood up so quickly his chair clattered to the deck behind him. "You're right, Arthur. A lot of things have changed, including us, and the change stinks out loud." He bent over to pick up the chair.

"Bucky," Rachel began.

Bucky held up his hand. "No, the pharaoh is right. It's possible to cross a line, to do something that ruins you forever. Think about those three scientists. They had crossed the line. They went to a hell of a lot of trouble to put themselves so far over the line that somebody else had to cross it to execute them. As long as they were alive there was a distinct possibility that ground zero would be the Beverly Hills Hotel."

Paston shook his head. "We murdered those people to save the Polo Lounge."

"Absolutely. I'd do it again, and be glad I had the chance. I've had an interesting life, too. I am late paying alimony at this minute to four of the most beautiful and stupid women in America. If killing scientists is what I have to do to keep

240

on making a fool of myself with beautiful women, okay. It's already put me over that line, and that's tough for me. I just have to live with it, because the other choice is to die."

ALTMEYER SAT AT THE BAR. He poured himself a glass of Scotch with one hand and held the telephone with the other.

"Sorry, Leonard. The old guy is exhausted from the trip, and he's asleep. If he's up to it later, I'll have him call you."

Leonard said, "I told him he was too old to go all over the place looking at investments. Besides, it's a waste. I'll bet you didn't learn anything, did you?"

"Not much. By the way, did you find out anything about the clinic in Santa Barbara?"

"Oh yeah. I found out what I could, which isn't much, of course."

"Why not much? It's a corporation, isn't it?"

Leonard chuckled. "A businessman like you should know better than to ask. I found out they're prosperous, which is not a shock. They own a lot of real estate around Santa Barbara, mostly rental property. The chief executive officer of the corporation is also the head doctor. His name is Bernard Felitan."

"What kind of clinic is it?"

"Gynecologists. That's the funny part. One of their investments is a place in Nevada called the Hummingbird Ranch Club. It's a legal brothel."

"Doctors own a whorehouse?"

"It's probably the least earthshaking news of the week. Doctors make a hell of a lot of money, and they invest it, and make more money. At least this is legal. When I had my brokerage, doctors used to come in all the time with big piles of cash they wanted put into something that would pay a quiet, modest return."

"And you think this Dr. Felitan is somebody who might do that?"

"Look, hiding money from the IRS is the national sport. You're probably a fair player yourself, so you don't have to

241

waste all this righteous indignation on me. If I were to guess about the biggest skimming operation in the country, I'd say it wasn't casinos. It's doctors by a mile."

"What about Felitan?"

"If he can hide money from the IRS, he can hide it from me. He's got what amounts to a hospital up there, and a list of associates that makes you wonder if you're reading some of the names twice, and about eight medium-sized businesses on the side."

"Is he big enough to buy Ashita?"

"I don't know. He might have a hard time if all he could use was the money he's showing, but I wouldn't rule it out. Besides, as you know, we're not sure anybody bought Ashita. You don't have to buy the whole thing to control its assets."

"But it's not out of the question?"

"I've got experience with doctors. I went partners on some land with a psychiatrist once. His credit was terrific, he had the down payment, and everything was rosy until the bank put a lien on the land. And even then, his credit was great. The man bought an airplane with a credit card. I'm telling you—"

"Thanks, Leonard. There's somebody at the door, and I don't want them to wake Arthur up."

"Right," said Leonard. "Tell him we'll talk tomorrow."

Altmeyer set his drink on the bar and turned up the sound on the television set. Then he stepped to the glass door and called, "The news is on again."

ALTMEYER RETURNED TO HIS STOOL at the bar and sipped his Scotch, gazing up at the television set.

"Today the British government has released more information on the three American scientists who were murdered during a fire two days ago in London. The three were identified as Paul Weston, thirty-seven, William Lister, forty-eight, and John Tedesk, twenty-nine. Tedesk and Lister were physicists on leave from the University of California at Santa Barbara, and Weston was a physician, also a resident of Santa Barbara."

"I'll bet I know where his office was," said Altmeyer to the television.

Anchorman David Harden looked up from the stack of papers in his hands and stared into the camera. "The three men had been in London preparing scientific equipment for an expedition, scheduled for next spring, to study drift ice off the Princess Ragnhild Coast of Antarctica. Although the project was first reported to be associated with London University, officials there were unaware of it. We have since been informed that it was a privately funded research expedition."

"Hard to believe, Dave," said Altmeyer. He sipped his drink.

David Harden's left eyebrow lifted sardonically. "The three men are survived by their wives and children." He moved a sheet of paper to the bottom of the pile and his face moved with precision into the delicately gauged expression of concern he reserved for international developments. "The British government spokesman said that five terrorist groups have claimed responsibility so far, but none has offered an explanation for the large quantity of weapons-grade uranium that was found in a second building near the university involved in the laboratory blaze."

Altmeyer smiled. "The next one will, if you keep talking."

"The British said it was too early to speculate on the possibility that this is the same uranium reported missing from a Canadian storage facility that serves four nuclear power reactors in Alberta."

"They'll work up to it."

ALTMEYER WALKED BACK OUT TO THE SUN DECK and sat down beside Paston. "It looks like they were going to set one off on the ice near Antarctica."

Bucky sat down. "Broiled penguins?"

Altmeyer stared at the ocean. "No. I mean that was the

243

menu, but it's like Mr. Cord said. You make a bunch of them and then set one off somewhere. Then everybody knows you've got something to sell. But Antarctica . . ."

Rachel said, "I get it. There aren't any people, just outposts of scientists from all over the world, and they've got all kinds of seismic equipment and thermometers and wind velocity meters and God knows what else. And they're from just about every country, so no government could hush it up."

"Very clever," said Paston. "So much for the Beverly Hills Hotel, Bucky."

"The penguins might not have come up with enough money to buy them off after the first demonstration," said Bucky. "The next one might have been right in the middle of your martini shaker. I know pharaohs don't care, but think about the rest of us."

Altmeyer studied Bucky for a moment. "I want two things from you people." He turned to Paston. "You bestir your ancient bones and get on the phone to Leonard. Tell him to submit an official offer for you to buy Ashita to their home office in Japan. We'll negotiate the price later."

Rachel said, "What's the other thing?"

"I need a volunteer for that one. The person must be brave, intelligent, observant." He paused for a moment. "And female."

"Am I going to hate this? Is it awful?"

Altmeyer sipped his drink. "Yes."

RACHEL WALKED DOWN THE COLD, EMPTY LITTLE HALLWAY past the row of curtained booths, trying to hold the white tunic closed. She slipped into the third one and started to dress. She felt dizzy and breathless and had to lean against the wall for a minute before she could step into her shoes without losing her balance.

As she straightened her skirt, she thought about Dr. Schumaker. She was sure he didn't know. He was too foolish and pleased with himself to be mixed up in something like

244

that. The examining room, with its little clock shaped like the steering wheel of a ship, and the fake porthole on the wall, seemed so childish. But most of all, it was the little leather pads on the stirrups that convinced her.

She listened at the curtain, then slipped down the empty corridor to the other door and through it into the main hallway. It would have to be big, and it would have to be far away from the main reception area. At the end of the hall, she saw a sign that said CONFERENCE ROOM, with an arrow. Conference rooms were where bosses called everybody in to sit around a table, so the room must be near there. She cautiously turned the corner, listening for the sound of approaching footsteps, and made her way along the wall.

ALTMEYER SAT IN THE BRIGHT SUNLIGHT staring up at the gnarled green hills that dominated the space beyond the low, glass-fronted building. When Rachel came through the glass doors, he started the engine of Bucky's Mercedes, then got out to open the door for her.

"How did it go?" he said.

"Awful, but not surprising. There's the blood test, then the pee test. Then there's the ladies-only special featuring pain, probing, humiliation, and a device that automatically turns up the air conditioning when anything touches the stirrups. I'll bet it's made by Ashita."

"What did you find out?"

She fished in her purse. "I'll draw you a little map."

Altmeyer put the car in gear and let it drift forward. "Draw it in the hotel room. I don't want to navigate using a bunch of jiggly lines on the back of an old shopping list."

She looked up at him. "Altmeyer, what exactly are you going to do?"

Altmeyer kept his eyes on the road ahead. "I told you that you were going to hate this. You will."

Rachel put her sunglasses on and closed her purse. "It doesn't feel as though you're hunting deadbeats anymore."

"I'm not in business anymore."

"Next week there might be another fifty men like this doctor who have a few million and an urge to speculate."

"Can you make a map to their offices?"

ALTMEYER KNOCKED ON THE DOOR at the side of the conference room that said PRIVATE.

A man's voice inside called, "I'm here."

Altmeyer tried the door, and it opened.

A man in a camel's-hair sportcoat and regimental striped necktie was sitting at a desk. He was about sixty years old, but trim and tanned, and his eyes were clear and alert. He looked confused for an instant, then smiled and said, "I'm Dr. Felitan. If you're lost, maybe I can help you find your way. This floor is for ladies."

Altmeyer said, "No thanks. I'm Dr. Altmeyer."

Felitan looked puzzled, then stood up and breathed, "You."

Altmeyer could see Felitan's hands were trembling. The fingertips were pressed to the desk, but the wrists fluttered.

"What do you want?" the doctor snapped. Then, as an afterthought, he added, "Get out."

Altmeyer pulled the pistol out of his coat and trained it on Felitan's forehead. The big silencer made the barrel a foot long.

Felitan said, "Say something."

"Pleased to meet you."

Altmeyer fired. The first shot jerked the head back, and the second punched through the center of the necktie. The office was quiet and strangely undisturbed as Altmeyer turned his back to the body and went through the conference room to the stairwell.

He'd expected to have to look hard, maybe tear through files and desk drawers for scraps of paper. But he'd seen it at once, behind the glass ashtray. It was a book of matches with a black two-headed eagle and the words "Prince Andrei Hotel."

246

He only hoped Felitan had picked him at the trade conference for some reason. He hoped Altmeyer hadn't just been the first name on some alphabetical list.

ALTMEYER LAY BESIDE THE KOI POND and tossed crumbs of bread onto the surface of the water. Four big, bright, speckled fish rose up from darkness and made their mouths into little circles to nibble the crumbs, then flicked their tails to dart toward the next disturbance on the surface.

He looked up to see Rachel walking slowly across the lawn, reading something. Two nanny goats followed, stopping every few feet to nudge each other away from her. When she was ten feet from Altmeyer, she looked up from the paper and said to the goats, "Girls." Then she looked at Altmeyer. "I got a bill from the clinic in Santa Barbara."

"It's safe to pay it. Hundreds of women go to that clinic every week."

"Altmeyer, I've been thinking. There's a pretty serious possibility that they'll accept Arthur's offer to buy Ashita, isn't there?"

Altmeyer lay flat on the lawn and closed his eyes, letting the sun warm his face. "It's possible. A lot of executors want to convert assets to cash, and don't know the real value of what they've got."

"What is the value?"

"It depends on what you are. If you're an electronics manufacturer, it's probably worth very little. There's one factory and warehouse, and a few stores with high overhead. Arthur is a movie producer."

"And what are you these days?" Her eyes slowly filled with tears. "Are you going after the people who worked in the stores, and the ones who worked in the factory, and at the hospital, and—"

"I have a theory," Altmeyer said quietly. "Felitan could only have let the very few people he needed know much. Nobody's left who could put the pieces together now if they did.

247

I might be wrong, but then again something else might kill us off before this becomes a problem again."

"You didn't really answer my question."

Altmeyer lifted himself on his elbow and looked up at her. "I've been thinking about it. I guess you'd have to say I'm a retired businessman and assistant goatherd."

"The report from the clinic says you're going to be a daddy."

Altmeyer grinned and eased himself back on the thick, fragrant grass, then closed his eyes. "That, too. Seems like enough."